Pigeon River Blues
A Sam Jenkins Mystery

Wayne Zurl

Published by
Melange Books, LLC
White Bear Lake, MN 55110
www.melange-books.com

Cover Art by Lynsee Lauritsen

For Bazzie,
A story of an adventure in the "forbidden city."

Prologue

An oddball named Mack Collinson sat in his mother's office discussing the upcoming auction of farmland straddling the border of Prospect and neighboring Seymour, Tennessee.

Jeremy Goins, part-time real estate salesman at the Collinson agency, defrocked federal park ranger and now full-time maintenance man in The Great Smoky Mountains National Park, walked into the room and tossed a newspaper on Mack's lap.

Collinson, a short, dark man in his late-forties, had close-cropped, almost black hair, a single bushy eyebrow spanning his forehead and a thick beard that covered his face from just below his eyes and disappeared into the collar of his sport shirt.

"You seen this article in the *Blount County Voice*?" Goins asked.

Mack shrugged. His mother neither commented nor gestured.

Goins sighed and continued, seemingly unimpressed with his male colleague. "'Bout how Dolly's havin' a benefit show and that lezzy bitch—'cuse me, Ma—C.J. Profitt's comin' back home fer a week a'forehand."

People showing deference to her age referred to Collinson's mother as Miss Elnora. Those who knew her more intimately called her Ma.

"Lemme see that," Elnora snarled, screwing up her wide face, one surrounded by layers of gray, arranged in a style the locals called *big hair*.

"Yes, ma'am." Anxious to please his employer, Jeremy snatched the newspaper from Mack and handed it to Mrs. Collinson.

The Collinson Realty and Auction Company occupied an old and not very well maintained building on McTeer's Station Pike just below the center of Prospect. Sixty-five-year-old Elnora Collinson had been a realtor for more than forty years, first with her late husband and now with her son. In either case, Ma represented the brains of the operation.

After allowing the woman a few moments to read the article, Jeremy Goins continued the conversation.

"I hated that bitch back in hi-skoo," he said. "And I hate her even more now that I know what she is and what her kind means ta the rest o' us."

Goins was a stocky, rugged-looking man, approaching fifty, with a liberal mix of gray in his dark brown hair. The gray hair was the only liberal thing about Jeremy Goins.

"I s'pose she's fixin' to stay around here and mebbe bring some o' her pur-verted women friends with her," Mack said. "This world's goin' ta hell when ya got ta be subjected ta the likes o' her on the same streets good Christian folk walk on."

"Amen ta that," Jeremy said.

When Ma finished reading, she snorted something unintelligible, rolled up the paper and threw it at a wastepaper basket, missing by a foot.

"Boys, this is shameful." She took a long moment to shake her head in disgust. "Downright shameful."

Both men nodded in agreement.

"When that girl went ta Nashville an' become a singer I thought Prospect was rid o' her and her kind once't and fer all. Lord have mercy, but we're doomed ta see her painted face on our streets ag'in."

"Momma, we ain't gotta take this," Mack said.

He spent a moment shaking his head, too. Then he decided to speak for the rest of the population.

"Don't nobody here want her back. Mebbe we should send'er a message if the elected leaders o' this city won't. We kin let her know."

"You're rot, son. Ain't no reason why that foul-mouthed, lesbian should feel welcome here." Ma Collinson, who resembled a grumpy female gnome, sat forward in her swivel chair and with some difficulty, pulled herself closer to the desk. "Jeremy, git me that li'l typewriter from the closet. I'll write her a note sayin' as much."

Goins nodded and moved quickly.

"And Jeremy, afore yew git ta work at park headquarters, mail this in Gatlinburg so as ta not have a Prospect postmark on it."

Goins stepped to a spot where he could read over her shoulder and said, "Yes, ma'am, I'll do it."

After inserting a sheet of white bond paper under the roller, Elnora Collinson began to type:

> *Colleen Profitt, we know you. We know what you are. All the money you made don't make no difference about what you have became. You are a shame to your family and the city of Prospect. Do not come back here. We do not want you. God does not want you.*

SIGNED
The Coalition for American Family Values

That was the first of six messages sent to country and western star C.J. Profitt. The last letter, typed almost two weeks later, said:

> *CJ Profitt, you have not called off your visit to our city. We repeat. You and your lesbian friends are violating God's Law. You must not come here. If you do, you will regret it. The people of this city will not suffer because of you. Your ways are the ways of Sin. Your life is a life of SIN. If you come here, YOU WILL suffer and then burn in Hell. Do not show your painted face here again. If you do, you better make your peace*

*with GOD. You will face HIM soon
enough. Sooner than you think.*

*The Coalition for American Family
Values*

* * * *

On Friday morning February 2nd, Mack Collinson slammed the front door to the real estate agency, shrugged off his brown canvas Carhartt jacket and tossed it on an old swivel chair. He spent a moment blowing his nose in a week-old handkerchief and stormed into his mother's office.

"Well, she's here," he said, putting his hands on his hips. "She never done took your warnin's serious-like."

Ma Collinson looked at her son over the top of reading glasses she recently purchased at the Wal-Mart Vision Center.

"This mornin' Luretta and the kids was watchin' that Knoxville mornin' show," he said. "And there she was—film o' her at the airport 'long with some others goin' ta perform at Dolly's benefit thing. She never listened ta ya, Ma. Now she's here."

At five after nine, a cuckoo clock in Elnora's office struck eight.

Mrs. Collinson pulled off her glasses and tossed them onto the desk. She wrinkled her brow and puckered her mouth in disgust. Elnora did not look happy.

"She'll be talkin' 'bout her ideas and her ways like she always does," Mack said. "It's *un*-natural is what it is. Against God's way. Why does God let people like her live, Ma? Makes me jest so gat-dag mad. Makes me think we ought ta kill her. Kill her our own selves."

Chapter One

I'd been Police Chief in the City of Prospect, a small town tucked into the foothills of the Great Smoky Mountains, for a little over six months. With its thirteen sworn members, Prospect PD was a far cry from the department of three thousand cops where I had worked for twenty years on Long Island, a crowded place just fifteen miles from the five boroughs that made up the infamous 'Big Apple'.

I sat in my office on Friday February 2, 2007 trying to plan a memorable Groundhog Day. The wall behind my oak desk was two-tone, beige over light brown. To my right, the evidence locker took up half the wall and built-in cabinets the rest. A mini-fridge and Mr. Coffee sat on the counter above the cabinets. To the left, a row of three file cabinets and a bookcase that would make a lawyer jealous. A half wall and wide row of picture windows separated me from the lobby and desk officer's command post. I picked up yesterday's Knoxville News-Sentinel and tossed it into the trashcan.

No one else at the department seemed enthused about the holiday but me. From the importance of my current endeavor, one might infer that winter months in the Smokies can be boring. They can be—extremely so. Even the weather that year wasn't very exciting.

Having precious little else to do, I left my office and sat in an armchair next to my attractive blonde desk sergeant, Bettye Lambert.

"Hey, Betts, has anyone asked us to provide security and traffic control for the Groundhog Day parade?"

She dropped a pair of reading glasses on the desktop. The hint of pale eye shadow she wore complemented the green turtleneck under her khaki uniform shirt.

"And what parade might that be?"

She waited. I shrugged.

"I'm glad you've got nothing to do, Sammy."

I shrugged again and began to feel like a bad little boy.

"And I guess you're looking for some trouble to get into?" she said.

I didn't get an opportunity to answer before the phone rang, and Bettye spoke into the receiver. "Yes sir, I'll tell him. Okey dokey. He'll be right there. And a good day to you too, sir."

"What did you just okey dokey me into now, woman?" I asked.

"That was the mayor. He'd like you to come up right away."

"The mayor himself?"

She nodded, and her ponytail jiggled.

I continued, not trying to hide my surprise. "He called directly? That wasn't his secretary and official mouthpiece, Trudy Connor, daughter of darkness?"

"Darlin', you can be so hateful. Why do you call Trudy that?"

"She doesn't like me."

"You don't know that. Trudy is nice. And she probably likes you. She just acts very...professional."

"She treats me like I'm the cause of all Ronnie's problems." I shook my head. "No way. I'm the first real cop Prospect has had as a chief in...probably ever."

"That's true—about you bein' a real cop. But you are a bit different than other department heads in the city. I guess you're an... uh... an acquired taste." She giggled—cute and feminine, but un-sergeant-like.

"Et tu, Portia?"

She only smiled and blinked a few times and didn't answer. Probably doesn't speak Latin.

"What's Ronnie want?"

"He didn't say."

"Remind me to talk to you about how to screen calls."

"Okey dokey."

"It's a good thing I like you."

"Bye, Sammy." She fluttered the lashes above her hazel eyes and made *bye* sound like something a sheep says.

I grabbed my Harris Tweed sport jacket from the back of my office door, left the PD and walked across the main lobby, climbed the glistening marble staircase of the municipal building, and approached the mayor's office on the second floor. I pushed open one of the two wide glass doors that led to his reception room.

"Morning, Trudy." I said. "That's a snazzy suit you're wearing. It's new, isn't it?"

"Why thank you, sir. Yes, it is new. I bought myself a present at the big sale in Belk's last weekend."

Trudy Connor was in her early fifties and every bit the proper Southern lady.

"Very nice," I said. "It looks good on you."

She smiled. I could smell nicotine on her new clothes and always thought of her surreptitiously sneaking a smoke in the ladies room whenever she could abandon her post.

Ms. Connor isn't as bad as I may have implied. But she's overprotective of her boss and can be a mild pain in the ass when I need to see him without what she considers *proper notice*.

"He wants to see me?" I knew the answer.

"Yes, sir, he surely does. Y'all go right in." She smiled again.

I nodded and added a diplomatic grin of my own.

The only office I've ever seen to rival Ronnie Shield's sportsman's hideaway was Teddy Roosevelt's library and gun room at Sagamore Hill—the former president's Long Island home, now maintained by the National Park Service. On the walls of the mayor's room hung a deer head with big antlers, some sort of long and mean-looking fish, a bunch of wildlife prints, a fly rod and reel, an old Winchester rifle and other things a woodsy person would collect. Ronnie never spoke about a passion for the outdoor life, but he certainly played the part.

Behind the raised panel oak door to his inner office, I found Ronnie standing between his desk and picture window, talking to a blonde woman sitting in one of the green leather chairs he reserves for guests. My entrance caused Ronnie to look toward me. The blonde turned her head and looked in my direction, too.

7

Over the last forty years, I've known very little about the movers and shakers of popular music, but I immediately recognized her as C.J. Profitt, an East Tennessee girl who had made it big in country music. And C.J. was famous for more than the numerous hits she had on the Nashville charts. She usually portrayed an "in your face" kind of person who minced no words in telling the world about her sexual preferences, alternative lifestyle and lack of patience for the rest of humanity.

I once heard her sing a non-country song and thought she had a great voice. I also thought that without a short, spiky haircut, a pound and a half of makeup, and clothing I'd describe as Nashville slut, she'd be a knockout.

C.J. was Ronnie's age, about forty-five. They had graduated from Heritage High School together and remained friendly over the years. I thought her tight, low-cut blouse had been inspired by the modern cowboy shirts guys wear; the ones with pearl snaps instead of buttons. Her short leather skirt showed off some really fine leg, and her foot gear looked like a cross between go-go boots and knee-high western ropers.

"Good mornin', Sam!" Ronnie spoke loudly for some reason. "Come on in here. There's someone I want y'all to meet."

Our mayor can be an enthusiastic guy, but his greeting this morning went over the top.

As I approached his desk, he stuck out a hand, gave me a huge smile and pumped my arm like he was priming the old well. "Good to see you, Sam. You doin' aw right today?"

His dirty-blond hair shined from lacquer spray. His smile could have been packaged and sold at political conventions the world over while he treated me like a long lost buddy. Funny, we had seen each other yesterday afternoon.

"Howdy, Mr. Mayor." I say down-home things like that to make him think I'm assimilating into the local culture. I nodded in C.J. Profitt's direction and offered her the irresistible smile I practice in front of a mirror. "Hello."

She chose to remain silent, but nodded to acknowledge my existence. I glanced over C.J.'s head at a pretty young woman sitting on Ronnie's burgundy leather couch. She wore her dark hair pulled tightly against her head in a ponytail and large eyeglasses that reminded me of the 1980s.

"Hello," I said again.

She smiled and said a barely audible, "Hi."

"Sam," Ronnie said, "I'm sure she needs no introduction, but I'd like y'all to meet my good friend, Miss C.J. Profitt. C.J., this is Sam Jenkins, our Police Chief. Sam's kinda famous himself."

"Ms. Proffitt, it's nice to meet you." I started to extend my hand, but pulled back in time to keep from feeling ridiculous. C.J. gave me a curt nod and crossed her arms across her chest. I felt crushed. My smile and warmth usually gets great results from the ladies.

C.J. Proffitt, on the other hand, only mumbled, "Mr. Jenkins," and decided she needed to stare out of Ronnie's big picture window into the town square.

Maybe I should have started a new adage—great legs, lousy personality—although I know that wasn't true.

Ronnie continued the introductions. "And, Sam, this is Jenny Mitchell, C.J.'s personal assistant."

I turned on the charm for C.J.'s hired hand. "Hi, Ms. Mitchell. Nice to meet you, too. Welcome to Prospect, and Happy Groundhog Day." I thought I sounded irresistible.

Jenny Mitchell giggled.

"Hello, Chief. Good to meet you as well. It's my pleasure." She spoke with a slight southern accent. But not from Tennessee. My guess was western North Carolina or southwest Virginia.

Jenny seemed like a girl with manners and good taste. She might have had good legs, too, but I couldn't tell because she wore a navy blue pantsuit. I decided to look for a different new adage.

Ronnie spoke again, "Sam, as y'all know, C.J. grew up right here in Prospect."

I don't know why he assumed I knew that. I wrinkled my brow into a near scowl.

"She's come home now, so to speak," he continued, "to appear in the big benefit show at Dollywood in a couple o' days—ya know with Dolly, Kenny Chesney—that Knoxville boy, LeAnn, Tanya, and a few other *really* big stars."

I didn't have the heart to tell him that other than Dolly Parton, I didn't know who he was talking about.

"Sam, I'd like you to act as a bodyguard for C.J. for the next few days until she gets on her plane and heads back to Nashville."

I'm confident I didn't drool, but I must have looked foolish as I stood there with my mouth open in disbelief. I looked at Ronnie, who sensed my confusion, then at C.J. Profitt and back at Ronnie.

"I'm a cop, Ronnie, not the Secret Service. I don't know much about being a bodyguard. Is there a problem? Is Ms. Profitt expecting trouble?"

The mayor began to offer an answer when C.J. interrupted. "Look, I don't like this any more than you do."

She spoke without warmth or even an East Tennessee accent. *How quickly they abandon their roots.*

I took a moment to look out the window and stared into the bare branches of the big tulip poplars that rimmed the square. I focused on a lone squirrel sitting on a nearby branch that looked straight at me, as if to say, "Tough day, bud? Well, ya gotta take the good with the bad." Then C.J. spoke and broke my trance.

"In case you didn't know, I'm a lesbian," she said, as though it would explain everything.

I thought the statement sounded out of place. "Wow, that's neat. I used to be a Presbyterian when I was a kid."

I'm pretty good at reading facial expressions and guessed that if C.J. could have gotten her hands around my throat I'd have been lying face up with the mayor futilely administering CPR.

"You should stick to being a cop—you're not much of a comedian," she said.

Our relationship was starting out extraordinarily well.

"Gee, I thought that remark was somewhat clever," I said.

Ronnie grimaced and looked like I had just kicked him in the groin. Jenny Mitchell put her hand over her mouth to hide a smile. I liked her already.

"Ronnie, does this guy think he's going to be funny at my expense?" C.J. asked.

The mayor continued to look embarrassed and tried to mitigate my behavior. "Now, C.J., Sam means no offense. He'd just rather see the lighter side of life no matter how serious things get. Right, Sam?"

I ignored Ronnie's question and answered C.J. "Actually, Ms. Profitt, I've got more to think about in my life than what anyone does in their own bedroom. And I'm not one of those guys who fantasize about watching two women get intimate. Let's get that clear, shall we?"

C.J. huffed and shifted in her chair.

"Sam?" Ronnie repeated, and gave me a look that said, 'Jenkins, you bastard, back me up here, or I'll have a stroke, and *you* can deal with that.'

Always quick to respond to an emergency, I said, "Oh, absolutely, Mr. Mayor. That must have been a defense mechanism or something equally foolish left over from my adolescent days."

Without skipping a beat, C.J. jumped right back into the fracas. "I don't need sarcasm from him, Ronnie. I've got enough threats and crap from this so-called Family Values Group."

That piqued my interest.

"Has someone communicated a threat to you, Ms. Proffitt?" I tried to sound concerned, but thought if someone was looking for a hired killer, I might apply for the job. "Something more serious than the usual kook messages I'm sure all celebrities get?"

She flicked a hand dismissively in the air.

"When my publicist started spreading the word about me coming home to Prospect before performing at Dolly's Imagination Library show, I got a note from someone saying they didn't want *my kind* back in town. That's all. I didn't take it seriously."

Jenny Mitchell sat forward on the sofa and spoke up for the first time, "C.J., that's not exactly true. In two weeks, you got six letters, each one more nasty than the last. They went from just a quick note to more detailed letters saying how you'd meet your maker sooner than you think. They were all signed The Coalition for American Family Values."

I shifted my look to Jenny and waited to hear more.

"The writer may be a kook, Chief," Jenny said. "But there may be more than one kook."

"May I see the letters?" I asked.

C.J. changed position again and crossed her right leg over the left. She shook her head vehemently.

"I threw them away," she said. "People like that just piss me off."

I thought C.J. would be as helpful as a BB gun against a charging rhino. I looked to Jenny for assistance.

"Ms. Mitchell, can you help me reconstruct those letters? I need something to give me an idea how they speak, what they said, the words they used... You know what I mean?"

Jenny nodded. "Sure, I can help. I remember them quite well."

"Have you ever employed a bodyguard before, Ms. Profitt?"

Quick with a shake of her head, C.J. said, "I have not. I dislike you macho types. You think poor little ol' me needs your muscle to survive. I do quite well on my own, thank you very much."

That did a lot to make me sympathetic. I couldn't wait to act as her hired muscle.

"Ronnie, may we have a word, please?" I pointed my head toward the office door.

"O' course, Sam, o' course," he said, and began heading for the door.

"Ladies, please excuse us for a moment," I said.

I held the door for Ronnie, and we stepped into the reception area.

The mayor may have anticipated a scene and asked Ms. Connor to vacate the room. "Trudy, why don't y'all take a break and get you a nice cool drink?"

"Oh, thank you, sir, but I'm fine," she said. "I just had something ta drink."

"It's a lovely day, Ms. Connor," I added. "Why don't you go outside for a smoke?"

The dawn broke, and Ms. Connor gathered up her purse and coat, nodded to the Mayor and gave me a slightly dirty look for exposing her filthy habit.

I scowled at Ronnie. "Why are you giving this job to me? She's a multi-millionaire who can hire private security people to guard her body."

Ronnie looked exasperated. I think a hair even came out of place.

12

"Sam, she's an old friend. I know she's a little hard ta get ta know, but she's really a good person, and I felt sorry for her when she tol' me what was happenin'." His expression pleaded for help. "I do believe beneath all her tough talk, she's concerned—no, frightened. She's scared over what may happen... And I trust your abilities."

"She's got a funny way of making friends. Probably averaged a 4.0 in Obnoxious 101 in school. I've told you, Ronnie, I don't know how to be a bodyguard."

The mayor stuck a finger under the starched collar of his white shirt, trying to loosen his seventy-dollar red paisley power tie. After his next statement, I thought he'd been building up the courage for a confrontation.

"Well, now, Sam, I don't believe that's entirely true." He looked at me with a smug expression—like he had something on me.

I looked back, right in his eye. *Don't try and play chicken with me, Mr. Mayor*, I thought.

"After I interviewed you for the job, Sam, I needed to check your credentials, o' course. One of the things that impressed me was the amount of time you spent in the Army and in the Reserves."

I frowned, and he swallowed before continuing.

"A friend of a friend, you see, put me in touch with a retired general who lives in Knoxville." He began to look more relaxed. "That general knew of you and helped me get some information and opinions on y'all from Army people that I might not have heard from with a simple records check."

He paused to let that sink in as a faint smile crossed his lips. I kept looking at him, like a defiant little boy who knew what would come next.

"It seems, Chief, y'all were chosen several times to head up security details to be a bodyguard, so to speak, for some very important people— Generals Earl Wheeler and William Childs Westmoreland—both Chairmen of the Joint Chiefs of Staff at the respective times. Why, you even helped protect a Vice President once. Now, someone who didn't know how to guard a body wouldn't have been chosen for such jobs, would he?" He grinned and looked pleased with himself, the smug bastard.

13

I took a half step closer to him and picked an imaginary piece of lint from his shoulder, then pretended to flick it on the floor.

"I was chosen," I said, "when those people visited the place where I was stationed because someone thought I was the best shot with a handgun available at the time." I tried to muster up a maniacal expression before continuing. "Others were convinced I was mentally unstable and wouldn't hesitate to use a gun."

Ronnie's eyes widened.

"As far as the Vice President is concerned, I took him to a whorehouse in Seoul while his Secret Service guys laughed their asses off. I didn't have much of a career in VIP security."

Ronnie took a turn frowning at me.

"And, Mr. Mayor, who helped you gather all this information while avoiding the proper channels and requisite signed releases?"

"As I mentioned, Sam, a retired general, three stars as a matter of fact, who still has considerable influence in the active Army."

"Al Steinmetz," I said, while Ronnie practiced his poker face. "He's from Knoxville. I knew him years ago when he was a Brigadier. Now he's a politician, no offense, and does favors for a living." I snorted. "Be advised, Ronnie, any favor from Steinmetz comes with a big price tag on it."

"Now, Sam, he speaks highly of you. Quite highly indeed. He and some other notable Army officers thought you were one of the finest small unit commanders they ever knew. He said that's why they promoted you."

I gave him an almost silent snort. "They promoted me because I didn't want to be promoted. I liked my job. I was happy. I wanted to remain a captain and be left alone. That seemed too un-Army-like for the likes of them, so Steinmetz, the overall honcho of the people I worked for, called me into his inner sanctum at Fort Bragg one summer day while on my two weeks active duty. He told me to accept a promotion or step aside for someone else to have a chance. I had a pension to think about and while I loathed caving in to that guy, I also wasn't about to take my ball and bat and go home."

Ronnie said nothing. I wanted to have the last word so, I provided a final thought.

"Steinmetz was a good soldier, but he's not on my hit parade at the moment."

Ronnie's shoulders dropped two inches. He let out a sigh of defeat and tried his sales pitch again. "Sam, I'd consider it a personal favor if y'all would look out for C.J. for the next few days. The big show is on Saturday the 10th. After that, she'll be on her way back to Nashville. It's only for a week. Please, Sam."

I'm a sucker for people who sound desperate. "Humph. It's a good thing I like you, Ronnie. Okay, but I'll need two associates."

"O' course, o' course. Y'all can choose two o' your people ta he'p."

Okay, pal, let's see how committed you are.

"And since it's a busy time of the year and I can't deplete the patrol force from their regular duties, the people who volunteer for this will need overtime for the hours they spend on this detail. Other people will have to pick up the slack, so additional OT for other cops will also be necessary."

I wasn't going down easily.

"Busy time? Overtime?' He sounded shocked.

I glared at him thinking; let's just see how much this dear old friend is worth to you.

Ronnie sighed, "All right, Sam, we're over a barrel here. I'll approve the overtime."

"That's time and a half for their extra work, and double time and a half on their regular days off."

"Sam, you sound like a union man." That came out as a gasp.

"We accomplish our mission with happy troops," I said. "Overworked officers, who are not somehow compensated, aren't happy. Someone has to look out for these people."

"All right, all right. But you've got to promise me not to piss off C.J. Promise me, Sam." Another gasp.

"I don't usually *try* to piss people off. It just sort of happens. I'll do my best."

Chapter Two

Back in the Mayor's office, I sat down with C.J. and Jenny, trying to get a handle on the people who sent the threatening mail. I felt proud of myself. I didn't make any inflammatory statements or wisecracks. C.J., on the other hand, took advantage of every possible opening to make snotty remarks about me, cops in general, all the other members of the male persuasion on this planet and anyone else who didn't agree with her ideas or way of living.

But we did our best to reconstruct the messages in the six nasty letters C.J. received from the person or people who called themselves The Coalition for American Family Values. Jenny helped more than her employer.

Somewhere during the short time we worked together, Jenny mentioned that Ronnie had planned to take the girls to lunch that afternoon. It would have been prudent for me to tag along, but I claimed to have made a prior commitment. Sick of C.J.'s rhetoric, I intended to start another officer on his career in executive protection and used Ronnie's phone to call Bettye.

"Do me a favor and get Lenny Alcock to come in for a special assignment at one o'clock," I said. "Tell him to dress casual chic in civilian clothes."

Bettye snickered. "Casual chic?"

I figured at least one of the women would be listening, so I kept the conversation businesslike. "That's what I said. It goes with the nature of the assignment."

"Will do, darlin'," she said. "But he's gonna ask, so I may as well know. What do you have for him?"

"I need him to take the mayor and a couple of good-looking ladies to lunch."

"Well... Sounds like good duty. One of them wouldn't be C.J. Profitt, would it?" she asked.

The feminine grapevine in the municipal building impressed me more every day.

"Yes, it would." I turned toward the wall and lowered my voice. "And since I'm going to ask, you'd better think up a good reason why and how you knew about this before me."

Another snicker. "Bye, darlin'."

We hung up, and I refocused on my new assignment.

With our work finished for the time being and before going downstairs to get my reluctant ducks in a row, I said goodbye to the ladies. C.J. frowned; Jenny smiled. I thought batting .500 wasn't too bad.

Before I left, Ronnie took me outside. "Sam, during their first meeting in February, February 7th to be precise, the city council is going to approve, for the record, hiring the new police officer and that clerk-typist you asked for. You can sign those people on for the next pay period of the month or whenever you're ready."

I smiled. "Good. Thank you."

"I hear the state has an academy class scheduled for mid-April. Can y'all get the new officer a seat?"

All this sounded like Ronnie's quid pro quo for my bodyguard services.

I didn't want to sound too anxious. "Maybe. Depends on how quickly I can complete the selection process. It's difficult to work as a full-time bodyguard and police chief at the same time."

"I know, Sam. Please do your best."

He buttoned the jacket of his gray Joseph A. Bank suit and looked ready to leave.

But I still wanted his company. "I've got a few applications downstairs, and I'd like to advertise the PO's job and see if we can get some hidden talent to come out of the woodwork."

Ronnie unbuttoned the jacket and sighed.

"Uh... Sam... There's something about this y'all need to know," he said.

That didn't sound promising. Trudy Connor picked up a few sheets of paper and fled the office.

"Uh, as I'm sure ya will remember, the Human Resources committee approved this rather quickly."

I nodded, wondering what was coming next.

"That's because there's someone we'd like you to hire as the police officer."

I envisioned getting the shaft. Ronnie smiled like a hangman offering the condemned man a blindfold.

"He's someone who comes with recommendations from several important local people—people who would like to see this boy get the job."

Ronnie actually began to look embarrassed. I never thought that possible for a politician.

"The man we've got in mind is Dallas Finchum. He's the nephew of your predecessor, Buck Webbster."

I began to feel the shaft.

"I remember y'all met Buck at his retirement luncheon," Ronnie said.

I remembered Webbster, the crooked bastard.

"He's Buck's sister's boy," he added.

Ronnie's embarrassed look turned to sheepish. On the other hand, I felt like biting a chunk out of Ms. Connor's desk and spitting it on the floor.

I'd been progressing nicely with my education in local politics and how to behave when frustrated by the system. When Ronnie told me about a young political hack being shoved down my throat, I controlled my emotions. I didn't turn red, and steam didn't escape from my ears. I kept myself from dropping to the floor, flailing my arms and legs and screaming obscenities. I did nod slowly though and give the mayor my street-cop's evil eye. I think he knew I wasn't pleased.

"Okay, Ronnie, have Trudy tell this guy to get in touch with Sergeant Lambert. She'll give him an appointment to see me. I'll make arrangements for him to get medical and psychological exams."

The mayor nodded. I jingled the change in the left pocket of my chinos.

"I'll give him a job-related agility test myself, and get going on a background investigation and schedule a polygraph exam. I assume the county sheriff's man will do one for us."

"I know he needs a medical exam, but is all the rest necessary, Sam? Dallas is a local boy—he comes highly recommended."

I had no intention of letting Ronnie off the hook easily.

"Yes, sir, it is necessary. I would never hire anyone who wasn't fit and thoroughly vetted. We can't incur any major vicarious liability when we know everything about a potential employee and act accordingly with that information."

Ronnie listened and nodded thoughtfully.

"Of course, *sir*, if you order me to by-pass those prudent measures, I'll make the appropriate notes in the file and proceed as you wish." I emphasized *sir,* and my statement came dangerously close to being insolent.

He grimaced. I wanted him to remember how former Chief Buck Webbster had been caught by state cops selling confiscated handguns and pocketing the cash, and how Ronnie once told me to keep a guy named Murray McGuire on the payroll when I wanted him fired. Buck ended up getting indicted, and Murray turned out to be the cause of more problems than Prospect had ever seen.

"No, no, no, Sam." He shook his head like someone just punched by George Foreman. "I didn't say that at all. I was just askin'."

"Uh-huh."

"I know better than to second guess yer po-leece instincts." Ronnie tried to be nice, maybe being honest and sincere or perhaps just trying to schmooze me so I'd protect his bitchy old school chum. "Y'all need ta do whatever has ta be done."

* * * *

I walked downstairs feeling generally abused, like the victim of an elaborate flummery. As usual, the doors to Prospect PD were wide open. I stopped in front of Bettye's desk, spun her side chair around and sat with my forearms resting on the back. I frowned at her. She smiled at me. I struggled to look mad.

"I suppose you knew this C.J. Proffitt thing was going to happen?"

Her smile never faded.

"I had heard she was here to see the mayor."

"That's all?"

"Well..."

"Do you have any idea how obnoxious she is?"

My act seemed to be working. Bettye started to appear concerned.

"No, uh...well...I've seen her on the news."

"I am not going to lunch with her."

"Oh, he wanted you to escort them?"

I ignored the question. "He'll probably take them to some place with nothing but fried foods. No, ma'am, not me. Let Lenny look after her today. I'm not doing it."

Now she looked anxious.

"Sammy, are you mad at me?

I shook my head. "No. I'm not. I'm mad at the world and especially at that used car salesman of a mayor. I was expecting to celebrate Groundhog Day in peace, and what do I get?" I didn't expect an answer so I continued, making another play for sympathy. "As my hero Mel Brooks said, 'Life stinks'."

I explained the threatening notes and the Coalition, why we had to perform bodyguard duty and my general displeasure.

She moved her chair closer to me. "Oh, darlin' don't be mad. It's only for a week." Bettye's voice makes Scarlett O'Hara sound like a bag lady.

I thought sulking might be appropriate. "Yeah, just a week, but I'm not starting today. I'd rather do filing or something for you. You need help with anything?"

She smiled again and shook her head. Her ponytail swayed from side to side, and she blinked a few times.

"I don't think so, but thanks."

She reached over and put a reassuring hand on my forearm.

"You're sure?" I said. "I'm a trained and competent police administrator who's not afraid to get his hands dirty."

"I'm pretty well caught up here," she said. "But it's just that busy time of the year for me, you know. I've got a million things to do—two kid's birthdays, Momma and Daddy's anniversary coming up, and I need a Valentine's present for Donnie."

Donnie Lambert was her husband.

I took the hint. "You need time off?" I asked. "Want to do some shopping?"

She shrugged. I wondered who was in control of the conversation.

"Take my unmarked car and get lost for a couple of hours. I'll listen for the phone and the radio. C.J. Profitt can fend for herself."

"Well, if you're sure, I won't say no."

"Good."

"I spoke to Lenny. He'll be here at one."

"Good."

"I'll keep track of the time and make it up somehow."

Like I'd ask her to work more than she does already.

"Don't worry about it," I said, playing the benevolent despot. "The time's on the house. I'm sure I owe you for some unpaid OT. When you get back, I'm going to get lost."

When Bettye left, I ditched my jacket and settled into her spot, ready to answer the phone, dispatch the cars, and plan how to provide that obnoxious woman with personal security.

Lenny Alcock had been my first choice for the detail. A quiet and polished guy, besides being a good cop, Alcock served in the Marine Corps Reserve as an assistant platoon sergeant and knew how to take orders. He was competent with his weapon, and I could count on him to behave appropriately in a nice restaurant.

Picking Harlan Flatt as the second man came just as easily. Harley was big and tough and unquestionably the most well-armed member of Prospect PD. I called him at home and suggested he volunteer for the job. He sounded enthused.

The quiet morning had turned into a busy day. While Bettye spent time away from the office, I sent my cops to handle two motor vehicle accidents, a family fight and a pair of first aid cases.

Things like that are typical in police work. One minute you're bored and thinking about making Groundhog Day memorable and next you're

21

flimflammed into protecting a grouchy Grammy winner, someone who you would cheerfully drop down an elevator shaft. I felt concerned about hiring some politico's kid and wondered how to find a competent clerk-typist. I know the policeman's old maxim—crime never sleeps. On that day in Prospect, I wished it would have taken a snooze.

* * * *

My temper tantrum of earlier that morning had subsided, and I needed to get serious about my bodyguard job.

If I wanted to protect C.J. Profitt from a right wing, weirdo, family values group or even from just an irate fan, I'd need to know all I could about C.J. herself and how she might be vulnerable. I had no intention of going to the library and scouring back issues of *Entertainment* for answers, so I decided to try the less direct approach and ask a favor from the only person I knew in show business.

I called Rachel Williamson at WNXX, one of the four major Knoxville TV stations. Rachel had worked her way up from morning news girl to senior news anchor. She and I had become good friends.

Her answering machine kicked in, and the message beep sounded. I began my story.

"Your voice mail always answers, but I know you're there, hiding from the fans who adore you. Pick up the phone so I can start my heavy breathing."

The connection finally clicked in.

"Okay, you caught me," she said. "I'm here. What comes after the heavy breathing?"

"I say I'm hopelessly in love with you, you're the only girl I'd ever leave home for, and I'm looking for a favor from the only person I know in show biz."

"Aw, the truth hurts." She tried to sound disappointed and failed. "But I thought you'd come to the point sooner or later. By the way, it's good to hear from you. How are you?"

"Fine as fur on a frog, darlin'. How 'bout y'se'f?"

"My, my, don't you sound local today? I'm well, thank you."

Rachel spoke with a slight Pennsylvania accent, was a gorgeous forty-year-old with dark brown hair and eyes and the cutest little dimple on her chin.

"Can I believe any of that noise, or are you just looking for a favor?" she said.

"Believe every word of it, cowgirl. If we weren't married to other people, I'd gallop up Broadway on a white horse, scoop you onto my saddle and ride off into the sunset."

Am I cool or what?

"Yeah, yeah, promises, promises. What are you after, Sammy?"

"What do you know about C.J. Profitt? I've been assigned to keep her safe while she's hanging out in Prospect."

"Other than who she is and her public persona, not much. Why does she need police protection?"

I put her question on the back burner. "What can you find out for me? I need all the dirt. All the stuff the papers and fan magazines don't print."

"You need to call Mary Hart. I'm just a small town news girl. I know nothing about big time celebs."

"I don't know Mary Hart. I know you—you're my buddy in the entertainment world. I'm putting all my eggs in your basket."

"I hate to disappoint you, lover, but all I can promise is to make a few phone calls. Tell me why she needs a hot-shot cop like you as her bodyguard in sleepy little Prospect."

"She's gotten a half dozen threatening letters from who I think is the same person," I said.

"I hate to sound greedy, but what will I get for all the work I do?"

One of the reasons I like Rachel is because she can be as mercenary as me. "How about my undying gratitude?"

"Ha! You're hopelessly in love with me. I'd have that anyway."

"You're an evil woman. I'll tell you all I know, and maybe you'll see a story in this...when you can take it public."

"How about an interview with C.J.?"

"We're not exactly best friends at the moment. If I can charm her into not hating me, I'll ask."

She sighed. "Oh, all right, you're the boss. I'll take what I can get. Tell me about the operation so I can get to work."

I did, promising to call again with as much information as I could find on the Coalition for American Family Values. Rachel promised to call me with all the poop on C.J. Profitt a genuine investigative reporter could learn.

That completed phase one of my investigation. Next, I'd call my friendly neighborhood G-Man, Ralph Oliveri, at the Knoxville FBI field office, to see what the big computers of the Justice Department knew about the Coalition. I was just about to do that when my phone rang.

Chapter Three

I wasn't in the mood for any more mundane police work, and it showed when I growled into the receiver, "Prospect Police, Chief Jenkins. May I help you?"

The caller had a familiar voice—a Long Island accent I remembered from years ago.

"Hi, boss." The two words came out in an odd but unmistakable way.

"John?"

"Yeah, boss. How ya doin'?"

"I'm okay. It's been a long time since I heard from you."

"Yeah, boss. Must be sixteen or seventeen years."

"Sounds about right. How's it goin'?"

I knew better. There are certain people you never ask that question.

"Not so good, boss. That's why I'm callin'."

"Yeah, what's up?"

"I saw a couple o' the guys at the PD Alumni Association Golf Tournament last week."

"Uh-huh."

"Jimmy Baxter said you were workin' again. I need to ask about Tennessee."

People from the western half of Long Island all have a unique downstate New York accent. All except those from Brooklyn. They sound like they come from the Italian section of the Moon.

"Sure, but what's wrong?" I asked.

I had worked with John Gallagher for a long time. He retired several years before me and missed out on a lucrative contract and a few years of extraordinary overtime the rest of us cashed in on. Had he stayed, those factors would have added at least twenty-five percent to his pension.

John began telling me his hard luck story.

"We can't keep the house in Boca any more. The cost of living down there is going up so fast my pension can't keep up with it."

"Gee, I'm sorry." This was not going well.

"I had to re-mortgage the house," he said, "trade in the Caddy for a used Saturn and sell my boat, but even that didn't help. We got big-time money problems, boss."

For as long as I'd known him, John Gallagher always had money problems.

I hated to make him feel bad, but... "You bought a house in a subdivision where professional baseball players live," I said. "They make a couple million a year. Didn't you think that was a little extravagant?"

"I bought one of the smaller places on the block, boss."

He always had an answer, but not many solutions.

"John, next to you, the poorest guy in that neighborhood was a Colombian drug lord. You knew the place was out of your league."

"Yeah, I guess so, boss. My wife really likes the house, but I gotta ship up or shape out."

"You've got to what?"

He chuckled. "You know, boss... turn my life around."

"I've always said you had a black cloud hanging over you, John."

"I know, boss. It's a curse."

"Yeah, right, a curse. I hate to hear what's happening, but what can I tell you about Tennessee?" I dreaded hearing the reason for his question.

"Jimbo tells me you think it's nice up there. Is the cost of living easy on your pension? You think I'd like to live there?"

I felt a twitch in my right eye and a pain—like someone just spiked a roofing nail into my temple.

"Huh?"

"Could I get a nice house for a good price?" he asked.

Before I could answer, the radio squawked. Will Sparks, in unit 512, asked permission to out of service for lunch.

"Hang on a second, John. I've got a call." I keyed the microphone. "Five-twelve, affirmative on your 10-18."

I forced myself to refocus on John.

"You dispatch cars yourself, boss?"

"The desk sergeant is out to lunch."

"How many cops you got?"

"Twelve and me."

"Uh-huh," he said. "Not much of a crime rate? I'd like to live in a nice quiet place. Whattaya think?"

I had enjoyed most of the twenty years I worked in New York as a cop, but those days were over, and I didn't want my old squad moving in next door.

"Uh, yeah," I said. "I think you'd like it here. There are plenty of golf courses, beautiful mountain scenery, a big national park—lots to do."

"Sounds good. About those houses?"

I really didn't want to encourage him.

"Housing isn't cheap any more, but you still get a lot of bang for your bucks. Property taxes are reasonable, and there's no state income tax on your pension."

Why didn't I lie?

"No income tax? Maybe I could even put some money away."

I doubted that.

"Come up, and look around," I said. "What about your wife? What does she say?"

I shouldn't have asked that either. She might have wanted another house they couldn't afford.

"Oh yeah, she wanted me to ask you about the cultural things."

The woman wouldn't know culture if it attacked her in a dark alley.

"Cultural things? Who are you bullshittin', John? When's the last time you were at an opera or the ballet?"

"Well, you know what I mean."

"We've got movie theatres and some good restaurants. If you want to talk real culture, there's a symphony and theater up in the city."

27

"Oh, good. You know we like to eat out."

If I remembered correctly, three or four times a week.

"That's why your charge card statements look like the gross national debt of a European principality."

He laughed. "Still quick with the jokes, huh, boss."

"Yeah, that's me, Henny Youngman with a gun."

"What's the big town around there?"

"Knoxville is only thirty minutes away."

"Nice place?"

"Yeah, we go there often. You like sports, right?"

"Sure, watch'em all the time."

"UT has a football stadium bigger than the Meadowlands and a coliseum-sized thing for basketball. There's plenty in Knoxville for a guy like you to do."

He could find plenty of houses there. Maybe they'd like to live in Knoxville?

"How about a job, boss? Could I get a job? You hirin' any cops?" He ended the question with a short, uncomfortable laugh.

It was the question I had anticipated.

"John, you're what, sixty-five-years-old?"

"Sixty-seven."

"You want to be a street cop again?"

"A street cop? Working around the clock? I can't remember the last time I worked a midnight."

"Part of the job."

"You're not trying to use reverse psychiatry on me, are you, boss?"

I took a turn laughing at his unique language skills. "No, John, just telling you the truth. We don't have swashbuckling detective units at Prospect PD."

"What the hell, boss? I need a job, and I used to like working patrol." He paused, and I didn't comment. "I don't want to sell used cars."

He sounded desperate, and at times I've been known to be a hopeless schlep.

I've never known a good detective—and John Gallagher had been one—who couldn't hunt and peck on a typewriter at thirty words a minute or faster. I didn't think I'd sound insulting by offering him the clerk-typist's position, but I stalled and mentally grasped for a job title that sounded more up his alley.

"I can get you something here as an, uh...police operations aide. Would you want an inside job like that?"

"A POA job?"

He didn't exactly jump for joy so, for some stupid reason, I tried to make him feel better.

"You'd be my assistant, help out the admin sergeant and fill in for her at times."

"Your admin sergeant is a her?"

It was no time for John to get sexist on me.

"Yeah, she's a good cop." I sounded defensive.

"How much does it pay, boss? Could we live on the salary?"

"You had to ask, huh?"

John didn't answer.

"The people here don't make New York salaries," I said. "But with your pension and Social Security, this job and the friendly cost of living, you'd do okay."

"Big difference from my last job, huh, boss?"

I reminded him, "Your last job was helping a friend with his Roto-Rooter business."

"I meant our old PD job. Big difference from what we used to do."

"Yes, John, the old job could get pretty exciting." He had sparked a touch of nostalgia in me. "And the section was a good place to work."

"Had fun, didn't we, boss?"

"We could be a bunch of bad-asses, but even when we weren't acting like super-cops, we still looked the part."

"Yeah, boss, those were good times."

After talking myself into a corner, there was nowhere to go.

"So what do you say, John? You finished remembering your days as a detective? Wanna be a clerk-typist?" I slipped and used the job title Ronnie had in mind.

There was a short silence on John's end of the line.

"Sure, boss. What the hell? It'll be good workin' for you again."

The pain between my eyes spread east and west to my temples. I wanted to hold my head and scream.

"You'll need to come up and take a look at Prospect pretty soon. The job is open, and I'm ready to hire you."

"Uh...boss? I'm already here."

"What? You're where?"

"In a place called Lenoir City—a motel just off I-75. Know where that is?"

"That's only forty-five minutes from here. You drove up before calling me?"

"I guess so, boss."

"Same old John Gallagher."

He gave me another nervous laugh. "Uh, could I ask you another favor?"

I felt an involuntary shiver. "What?"

"You wouldn't have a place for me to stay while I looked for a house, would you? I don't think I could afford a motel for more than another night."

My head almost ricocheted off the desktop.

* * * *

John Gallagher had taken the trip from southeast Florida to east Tennessee alone, leaving his wife back in Boca Raton to close the sale of their house, pack their belongings and meet him sometime later— somewhere; neither of them knew where.

I should have been flattered that John trusted me to solve his financial and family problems, but for the next few days, or however long, I'd be stuck with him as a house guest. It would be like having a sixty-seven-year-old son coming home to get back on his feet. *Why me?*

I'd appeal to my wife's charitable side and ask her to introduce John to our neighbor, Mae Waddell, a real estate broker. Kate could dump Gallagher in Mae's hands with instructions to stick to reasonably priced homes, putting a realistic ceiling on what he might consider buying. I wanted Mae to find him some place to live soon—very soon, in a week or less.

Bettye walked in at quarter to one with Lenny Alcock only a few steps behind.

"Get all your shopping done?" I asked.

"Almost," she said.

"Good. After I take Lenny upstairs to meet Miss Personality, I'm leaving so his Highness can't find me."

Bettye made a face at my irreverence, and Alcock smiled.

Lenny is one of those clean-cut people who always look spit shined. Wearing a wool sport jacket and open neck dress shirt, he'd fit in at any restaurant Ronnie chose for lunch.

"You look like a detective," I said.

"Hoped ya might say that."

"Everybody wants to work in plainclothes."

He shrugged.

"Let's go and see Ronald MacDonald and his girlfriends," I suggested.

"Samuel, you are bad," Bettye said.

* * * *

Without ceremony, Ms. Connor announced our presence and Lenny, and I entered the mayor's rod and gun club.

To save time, I made the introductions. "This is Ms. Profitt and her assistant, Ms. Mitchell," I said. "Ladies, Officer Alcock. He'll be one of the men working with me to keep you safe."

C.J. was only two feet away in a green leather chair, and Jenny sat on the couch again.

Lenny took a step forward and extended a hand to C.J. "How do ya do, ma'am? Leonard Alcock."

C.J. looked at his hand as if it was a dead mackerel, but she shook it without enthusiasm.

"I do fine, thank you. How do you do, Leonard Alcock?" Her voice dripped with sarcasm.

Lenny let her rudeness slide and waved to Jenny. "Hello, Miss Mitchell."

Jenny smiled and waved back.

"Ronnie," I said, "can we speak outside?"

A look of concern and big question mark covered his face.

A spark of decency overcame me, and I offered something to lighten him up.

"It's about the new typist."

His entire body relaxed. "Oh, sure. O' course."

I laid a hand on Alcock's shoulder. "You know what to do. Call Bettye if you need anything."

"Yes, sir. Will do."

Ronnie and I adjourned to the anteroom.

That recent spark of decency left me as quickly as it had arrived.

"I assume you're picking up the tab for Leonard's meal?" I said.

He looked shocked. "O' course, Sam. You didn't think...?"

"I thought you'd do the right thing, but I didn't want Leonard put in an embarrassing position."

Ronnie looked hurt. "What have you done about the clerk-typist?"

"I'm hiring a retired detective who worked for me in New York."

The hurt turned back to shock. "A detective wants ta be a typist?"

"He's sixty-seven and decided to relocate here. He's happy to get an inside job."

"Really?"

If he told me the city council had another political hack slated to be my clerk-typist, I'd scream.

"Is there a problem?" I spoke with a little too much attitude.

Ronnie blinked a few times. "Sam, do you think it wise to hire a sixty-seven-year-old former detective as your clerk? I mean how much longer will he be workin'?"

It sounded as if he questioned my sanity.

I countered with the idea of changing job titles. "He's committed for a long haul. He likes to keep busy and needs the money. And I thought by having a man like that willing to accept the *low* wages you're offering, I'd keep him happy with a few more responsibilities and change the job title to police operations aide. That would be more descriptive of his actual duties."

That set Ronnie's mind into motion.

"Po-leece operations aide, ya say?"

"Uh-huh."

"Very professional soundin'. Very pro-fessional, indeed."

"Certainly is. We used to call them POAs."

Ronnie raised his eyebrows.

"They have POAs at the sheriff's office?"

"No. We'd be the only ones."

He used one of the smiles he saves for press conferences. If I had been holding a baby, he would have kissed it.

"Well then, that would make Prospect PD kinda special," he said enthusiastically.

"Yes, sir," I said. "That's us. I'm glad you thought of that."

"Right, an ex-detective as your operations aide. Excellent. Yes, sir, real fine. You're sure he's okay with the salary?"

"He is, but I wanted to suggest one more thing..."

Ronnie gave me a new frown when I said we should dispense with the six-month probationary period and start with the higher salary of a permanent employee.

"That's very unusual," he said.

"Do you know how lucky we are to get someone with John's police experience for only a clerk's pay?"

Luckily, I didn't have to say, "If I have to eat a young political hack as my new cop, I should be able to choose my new aide-de-camp without interference."

Ronnie shrugged and agreed. Then he almost passed out when I told him I wanted to give John the honorary title of detective—if nowhere else but on his desk name plate.

He croaked, "Make him a detective? Y'all don't have detectives on your table of organization."

"I thought it would add a little to John's self-esteem. And it's only honorary."

When the mayor began sputtering, I said, "If we hired a retired surgeon as our clerk, he would no doubt want his old title of doctor on a name plate."

"Is all this legal?"

"Of course. I'll swear him in as an auxiliary police officer and purchase his badge myself."

"B-b-badge?" I never knew Ronnie to sputter this much.

He finally agreed. I thought explaining about getting John a concealed-carry handgun permit or making any other demands might be pushing my luck.

Chapter Four

Since I claimed to be otherwise engaged at 1 p.m., the time the mayor intended for me to join him and the ladies for lunch, I thought it only prudent to make myself scarce for the entire afternoon.

Having concluded my business with Ronnie Shields, I drove home to see my wife and dog. The weather was exceptionally fine—fifty degrees, sparkling sunshine, bright, pollution free blue sky, and a smattering of puffy white clouds. As I drove through the subdivision gates, two pairs of cardinals flew past the front of my car and narrowly missed getting smacked by the grill. After parking the car, I walked to the front door, and let myself in. Bitsey, the wonder dog, wasn't expecting company and came thundering into the living room barking like a Tyrannosaurus who found an intruder walking through her neck of the woods. When she saw it was me, Bitsey rolled onto her back and encouraged me to scratch her tummy. My wife, Kate, followed, but didn't bark.

I left the dog on the floor and joined my wife.

"Hi ya, Kats. How's my favorite wife?"

She kissed my cheek. "Hi, sweetie. How many wives do you have, and what are you doing home at this time of day?"

"Trying to catch you messing around with the troop of Romanian acrobats I think visit occasionally. But since you seem to be alone, maybe a little lunch would do."

"Yeah? Well, Mr. Smarty-pants, the acrobats left fifteen minutes ago. And let me tell you, they were good today. I barely had time to comb my hair before you got home."

"It's nice to feel wanted."

I walked into the kitchen where I found left-over zucchini and rigatoni in the fridge.

"You look nice today," I said. "Going somewhere?"

I liked her outfit: jeans, a burgundy sweater with a floppy turtleneck, and a hound's-tooth tweed blazer. To that, add perfectly styled salt and pepper hair and an understated makeup job. She's really quite beautiful.

"Thank you. I just didn't want to walk around all day looking like Mammy Yokum."

"When have you ever looked like Mammy Yokum?"

"You know what I mean."

After heating olive oil in a wok, I added the main ingredients and mixed in white wine, garlic, oregano and capers. When everything was hot, I added Romano cheese and prepared to mangiamo.

Kate poured two glasses of Orvieto as we sat at the kitchen table.

"Hey, Katsy, guess who called today?"

"Henry Kissinger?"

"Try again."

"Your admirers are legion. How could I possibly know?"

"John 'Black Cloud' Gallagher."

"My goodness, the master of malapropisms. What is he doing these days?" She raised her glass and sipped.

"Actually, he'll be here this afternoon. I'm going to hire him as our new clerk-typist."

Kate almost choked on her wine.

"Oh my God, Samuel. Have you gone around the bend? You're hiring John Gallagher at Prospect PD?"

I nodded and stuck a forkful of food into my mouth.

"As a clerk-typist?"

I nodded again and continued chewing.

"What has come over you? What has come over him? Why is he here? John loved Florida. You think he'll like the Smoky Mountains? We're not famous for our beaches."

Kate was on a roll and not stopping for answers. I didn't even try to join the conversation.

"John Gallagher speaks a very strange dialect of English," she said. "Do you think anyone in East Tennessee will be able to understand him?"

"I think you're being a bit hard on him."

Before starting to prepare my lunch, I had turned on the satellite radio 60s station. In the background, Peter, Paul and Mary sang *Leaving on a Jet Plane*. It gave me ideas about a possible escape.

"Sam, I remember it quite well. John once made a big deal telling me about a vacation where he took his family to a wild game *preservatory*, a place with a *pamaranic* view of the countryside, and later that evening, they ate dinner in a New Orleans-style *Caucajun* restaurant. Do you *really* think the people of Prospect are ready for John Gallagher?"

"You're making that up."

"Hardly."

"He needs a job."

"So does ten-percent of the population. Don't you remember how his wife used to aggravate you?"

I swallowed half my wine. Kate took another imperceptible sip of hers.

"Sure, she was a pain in the ass, always calling the office asking if he could come home and handle one of her imagined emergencies. I'll straighten that out."

"She also blamed you and the other guys in the office for leading John astray."

"Who cares about her?"

"Why is he leaving Florida?" she asked.

"He's having a hard time making ends meet. They had to sell the house, his car and the boat. Maybe even his lawnmower. He needs help."

"Sambo, for a big tough guy, you're just an old softie."

Kate got up, kissed me on the forehead and topped off my glass of wine.

The next song from *60s on 6* came from Bob Dylan—*Rainy Day Women, Numbers 12 and 35*. When he sang 'Everybody must get stoned', I felt the urge to drink more wine.

"I thought maybe tomorrow you could take him to meet Glenda Mae, and she could find him a house they can afford," I said.

Kate frowned. "Okay."

"The quicker he gets his own place, the quicker he'll be out of our guest room."

Her big brown eyes popped open. "He's staying here?"

"Can't sleep in his car."

She loves it when I smile and shrug my shoulders. I think.

* * * *

Back at the PD—after I made sure Kate would allow me to return home with the Black Cloud, I found Len Alcock waiting for me.

"How'd lunch go? You fall in love with anyone?"

He sat forward in the guest chair and stared at me. "I do not believe that woman."

"Sorry I asked."

Lenny shook his head and finally spoke. "Halfway through the meal, this ol' boy walks up ta the table and says, 'Oh, Miss Profitt, my wife and me's big fans o' yours'. And he starts takin' somethin' outta his jacket pocket. By the time I got up and grabbed a hold on his arm, he said, 'Would ya mind signin' this?' and handed her a folded sheet o' paper."

"Could have been a gun."

He nodded. "Yes, sir."

"You acted quickly," I said. "The mayor should have given you a pat on the back."

"Not hardly."

"Did this fan look threatening?"

"I didn't know what was comin' outta his jacket."

"Sounds like you were pretty efficient. Did Ronnie give you a hard time?"

"Weren't the mayor I had ta worry about."

I shook my head and knew what he'd say next.

"Your Miss Profitt made a scene. Told me the man's just a fan, and I overreacted. What was I supposed to do? Most o' the people in the restaurant were lookin' at us."

"You did the right thing. A Secret Service agent might have blown the guy away. Don't sweat it. I'll go upstairs and have a talk with the boss and his guest."

"Mayor's upstairs, but we dropped the two women off at his house. They're stayin' there for the weekend."

"They're alone now?"

"Mrs. Shields is there. C.J. said she didn't want me around."

"Did she eat a bowl of stupid for lunch?"

Lenny smiled and looked less upset.

"Lord have mercy, but you got that right, boss."

"Let's go upstairs and iron out the rules."

* * * *

Lenny and I stood in front of Ronnie's desk, something dark, shiny, and just slightly smaller than the flight deck of the USS Ronald Reagan.

"Is C.J. going to call the shots for the entire week?" I spoke a little too forcefully.

Ronnie slumped in his chair and looked like he was getting ready for me to hit him. "Call the shots?" he asked.

"She told Lenny not to stay at your home."

"I, uh, thought she'd be safe. LaDonna's there. She or Jenny could call if..."

Ronnie had forgotten to unbutton the jacket to his gray pinstripe suit. The lower he slumped, the more the jacket bunched up around his midsection, making him look like a human Shar-pei.

I locked eyes with the mayor and without turning said to Alcock, "Give us a minute, Lenny."

He didn't comment, but raised his eyebrows, made a left face and walked from the room.

"I thought you trusted my abilities to handle this assignment," I said.

"I did, Sam. I surely did. I mean, I do."

We were all doing the mayor a personal favor, and I didn't want anyone involved to catch any flak from that woman.

"Then, Ronnie, for the rest of the week, there is only one person who makes decisions about C.J.'s safety."

He must have sensed my displeasure and sunk an inch lower in his overstuffed leather chair. The collar of his jacket almost touched his ears.

To be sure he got my message I added, "That's me."

He nodded vigorously.

"And she can't humiliate one of my cops when he tries to protect her."

Painfully, he said, "It was only a fan."

"Suppose the man produced a weapon or a bottle of acid?"

Ronnie winced. "I didn't think o' that."

"Alcock didn't shoot the man. He was justified in restraining him for the moment."

"I guess so."

"No guess. The law says so. Shall I read the statute for you?"

"Not necessary. You know yer bidness."

"We need to tell C.J. the rules."

"We?"

"You and me. I'm not having one of my cops questioned by her."

"Maybe I should talk with her tonight."

"Tonight you can reinforce what I say, but we talk to her now. And Leonard will be at your home until midnight when Harley Flatt takes over."

"Harley Flatt?"

"He's the other man I chose for the detail."

Ronnie squeezed his eyes half shut. "Harley is so...big."

"And since he started shaving his head, he looks very mean. That appearance is a plus for a bodyguard."

He nodded, reluctantly.

"Is she staying at your place all week?" I asked.

"The plans haven't changed. Sunday night after dinner, they're checkin' inta the Foothills View Mo-tel. Then, as ya know, she'll be spendin' lots o' time over ta Dollywood rehearsin'."

I took a step closer to his desk. He tensed up a little more.

"Alcock and Flatt will share the detail with me. And perhaps circumstances will dictate that other officers get involved. One of us will be with her at all times. Agreed?"

"Agreed."

"Ready to chat with the personable Ms. Profitt?"

He blinked several times. "Alright, Sam."

* * * *

I made a left onto Shield's Pond Road, through an arch of maples, past Ronnie's father's house, continued beyond the uncle's place, past a two-acre pond on the right, and into the driveway of Ronnie's home—a large, brick colonial across the street from his sister's. The dead end street was a virtual stronghold for the Shields clan.

I followed him around the house to the back door, where he resembled a teenager trying to sneak home after curfew. I wiped my feet on the rough mat, trying to make as much noise as possible so he'd get caught.

We found the three women in the living room where C.J. initiated a greeting.

"You brought him?"

"Hi, y'all." Ronnie tried to ignore C.J.'s question by walking over to give LaDonna a peck on the cheek.

"Hello, ladies," I said.

Jenny and LaDonna responded appropriately.

C.J. said, "What's he doing here, Ronnie?"

I answered for the mayor. "I've come for a powwow. If you don't mind, C.J. let's do it in the dining room. Mrs. Shields, Jenny, excuse us for a minute."

Never at a loss for words, C.J. said, "I do mind. We have nothing to discuss."

Before Ronnie could intervene, I said, "The hell we don't. Let's go!" I jabbed a thumb in the direction of the dining room.

Ronnie pleaded, "C.J., please, jest listen to what Sam has to say."

She rose brusquely and stormed out. Ronnie followed.

I looked from LaDonna to Jenny and smiled. "Sorry to interrupt." I backed out of the living room gracefully.

I pulled a chair from the end of the dining room table and sat. Ronnie took a seat on the side, leaving an empty seat next to me for C.J., who stood with her back to us looking out the window.

"Ms. Profitt, would you mind?"

She turned and folded her arms across her chest. I pointed to the chair next to me.

"Sit, please. I don't have much to say, but it's important."

"I'll stand, thank you."

I had no patience for her snit. "I'd like our eyes at a common level. Sit!"

Raising my voice worked. She huffed and puffed, but finally sat.

"I heard there was a misunderstanding at the restaurant."

"No misunderstanding. Your man behaved like a jerk."

Ronnie hung his head, looking at his clasped hands like a man praying this would all go away.

"Ms. Profitt, the mayor asked us to provide you with security. Do you want it?"

It took her a long moment to respond.

"Yes, but—"

"No buts. If you knew how to protect yourself, we'd be unnecessary. I think you don't."

"You can't expect me—"

She began to percolate. Her shiny, butch haircut accentuated her anger.

"Stop talking," I said.

Ronnie shot me a look of abject fear.

"Suppose that man had a weapon or a bottle of acid?"

The suggestion seemed to take her aback for a moment, but she responded in true C.J. Profitt fashion, "But he didn't, did he? Do you think—"

"This isn't a debate," I said. "We're going to clarify a few ground rules, and then you can make an important decision."

She tilted her head and folded her arms again. If body language could kill, I'd have been pushing up daisies.

"Do you own a gun?"

"A gun? Of course not."

"Then I assume if I gave you one, you wouldn't know how to use it?"

She glared at me. "No."

"Are you any good with your fists?"

Her expression told me C.J. thought my question might have been the most absurd she'd ever heard. "What the hell are you asking?"

"Can you personally defend yourself against an attack if the semi-literate imbeciles who sent the notes decide to get openly physical?"

She didn't answer, and Ronnie remained quiet.

"Few people can do it alone," I said. "Believe me. Now, here's your choice. Unless you allow us to do the job efficiently and without interference, and that means we determine what's necessary, go hire your own security."

"You can't expect me to allow you to manhandle an innocent fan just because you think he—"

I cut her off. "That's exactly what I think. Remember that bottle of acid. If we ruffle a few feathers, we'll apologize. But you'll be alive and well."

She pulled a face.

High above the house a pair of Army UH-1D choppers cruised the sky, their pilots and crews logging in the required airtime. The unmistakable sound reminded me of another time and place.

"Here's the deal," I said. "It's my way, or go find yourself a steroid sucking bodybuilder to keep you safe."

"It's a little late for that now, isn't it?"

"Go to a gym and pick the biggest guy with a copy of *Guns and Ammo* in his back pocket. You might get a good price. Everybody wants to be a private security expert nowadays."

"That's just stupid."

I shrugged. "So?"

Ronnie came alive. "Please, C.J., Sam knows what he's doing. Let him finish what he started."

"I will not be made to look like a fool," she said.

"Then you'll look like the most intelligent corpse in the morgue," I said.

She gave me a quick look. I thought she wanted to scratch my eyes out. Then she looked at Ronnie.

"Please," he said again.

"Damn it, Ronnie, you've almost got me over a barrel."

"Ms. Profitt," I said. "This is not painful. People are protected all the time. Just let my men do their job."

She looked at Ronnie, not me. "All right. I don't like this, but all right." She got up and left us sitting there.

After spending too much time at Casa Shields gaining C.J.'s acquiescence to my security plan, Ronnie and I returned to the municipal building, and Lenny Alcock returned to guard duty.

Chapter Five

"FBI Knoxville, Oliveri."

"Ralph, Ralph, Ralph," I said. "You're losing your Queens accent more every day. If you go back to South Ozone Park they'll call you a redneck."

"Your ass. I sound more like Nu Yawk than you, you hillbilly sheriff, Buford Pusser wannabe."

"You sound hostile," I said. "Is Carl breaking your chops? Need to clear more felonies? I'll help you make a bunch of RICO cases against half the churches in my county. Stick with me, kid, and you'll be an all-star."

"Yeah, right. If I stick with you, I'll be unemployed or the resident agent on the Blackfoot Reservation. I'd be going to work on a snowmobile from September to June."

"Hey, in the six months we know each other, you've seen more interesting stuff than J. Edgar Hoover could have shown you in a lifetime."

Ralph sighed and tried to make me feel guilty. "You're right about that, paisan. And I've got a feeling you want to make my life hell again."

I tried to sound insulted. "I'm hurt."

"My mother told me to be a CPA and open an office in Rego Park, but no, I had to get a job with the FBI and meet you. Now you're going to throw me into a pot of boiling gravy again."

"A pot of boiling gravy? Does your mother make her own pasta sauce? Forget it, of course, she does. Listen, I need some normal FBI-helps-the-local-cop kind of information."

"Yeah, what?"

"What do you know about the Coalition for American Family Values?"

Ralph let out a snort. "For chrissake, what are you getting involved with those assholes for?"

"Never heard of them, huh?"

"Of course I've heard of them. They're a home-grown group of right-wing nuts and weirdoes."

"Whoopee."

"Far as we know, they're only in east Tennessee. And you've got a few active members down in your area. What made you notice them?"

I told Ralph the C.J. Profitt story in its entirety. He gave me three names: Realtor Mack Collinson and his mother Elnora and a former national park ranger named Jeremy Goins. FBI files listed them as perhaps the most vocal specimens and placed them all as residents of beautiful downtown Prospect.

Thanks to Ralph, I'd have to expand my investigation to include those three and any of their cronies.

* * * *

I gave Bettye the names of Ralph's trio of all-American zealots. She spent a few minutes on the computer and found their current home addresses, dates of birth, driver's license photos, and any involvement with other police departments or the county sheriff's people. From what Bettye learned, I categorized them as genuine pains-in-the-ass, but probably not a dangerous cell of domestic terrorists.

At 4 p.m., I'd ask my road sergeant, Stan Rose what he knew about the Collinsons and Goins and question PO Vernon Hobbs, a thirty-year veteran of Prospect PD and the guy who knew just about everything that crept or flew in and around the city.

Since all of my suspects were linked to the real estate business, I'd walk across the town square and speak with their competition, Mae Waddell, who owned Walking Horse Realty. Actually, I'd kill two birds with one visit—see what she knew about the Collinsons and their henchman and save Kate the job of offering her a potential client in John Gallagher.

But before leaving, I thought it appropriate to tell Bettye about her new assistant.

I moseyed up next to the file cabinet where she stood looking into the top drawer. The khaki shirt and charcoal green uniform pants she wore looked as if they were tailor made. Most women would kill for a figure like Bettye's.

"You buy those uniforms off the rack?" I asked.

"Uh-huh. Why?"

"Just asking. You look nice."

She frowned. "What do you want?" And sounded suspicious.

"I can't say you look nice?"

"Of course you can." Less frown, more suspicion.

"Before I run over to see Glenda Mae about the real estate terrorists, I'll tell you about our new clerk-typist," I said.

"You hired someone already? Who is she?"

"Not a she, it's a he."

She lowered her eyes and looked at me over the tops of her granny glasses.

"A who?"

"No, a he."

"Yes, I heard that. You hired a man to be a clerk-typist?"

"I don't think he really wants to be a clerk, but he can type—a little. He needs a job in Tennessee and doesn't want to do manual labor or sell used cars."

She blinked several times. "What?"

Bettye closed the file drawer, turned to face me and put a hand on her hip. She does that while preparing to scold me.

"A guy called before—an old friend. Someone I used to work with...in New York. He's an ex-detective. Why are you laughing?"

I told Bettye about John's financial troubles and how he was trying to turn his life around with a move and change of lifestyle.

"I asked Ronnie to change the job title from clerk-typist to police operations aide."

Her smile continued. "Isn't that a fancy title?"

I sat in the chair next to her desk. She used her swivel chair.

"Yeah, we used to hire kids through the old CETA Program to fill jobs with that title," I said. "But it sounds good, and I thought it would make John, his name's John Gallagher, feel better about his new career."

Bettye just smiled and nodded. I think she's figured out how to handle me.

"It's a big step from retired detective to minimum wage office boy," I said.

"It is."

"You're going to be his boss, so I have to tell you, I'm going to give him an honorary title of detective."

She tilted her head and frowned at me again.

"He won't be a real cop," I added quickly, "just an auxiliary, but he was a squad dick for a long time. I'd like to make this as easy as possible for him."

"Uh-huh." It looked like she enjoyed seeing me squirm.

"John was a good cop for twenty-five years. He'll do well here. You'll like him. Everybody does."

"Does he look or act anything like you?" She gave me a look I didn't quite know how to interpret.

"No one looks like me except a few highly paid movie stars."

"Sam Jenkins, you're a vain man."

I didn't address the remark because it's probably true. "John's not a bad-looking guy. He just suffers from the Irish curse."

She rolled her eyes. "I'm afraid to ask."

"He's a couple of inches shorter than me and a few years older. That's not part of the curse. The curse is skinny legs, no ass and a pot belly."

She rolled her eyes. "Oh, Lord have mercy."

"Other than that, he's a nice-looking Irish boy. However, he does have a basic problem with the English language."

"I can't wait to hear this," she said.

"Kate says he suffers from what's called malapropism. You'll know it when you hear it. You can laugh if you want. I do. I used to carry 3x5 cards in my pocket and write down all the stupid things he said. I've still got an envelope full of them back at the house. You'll see."

"And you're making me his supervisor?"

"I am. You'll have more free time now."

"Thanks a bunch, darlin'."

She made *darlin'* sound like a four-letter word.

"Are you unhappy, Sergeant?"

Before Bettye could answer, we heard a commotion at the back door. I thought perhaps a rabid groundhog was trying to break in.

Someone slammed the door against the wall and set the stop to keep it open.

"Get outta the car, you sum'bich!" It sounded like Officer Billy Puckett was less than pleased with one of his clients. "Damn you, git outta my ve-hickle!"

"Grab his arm, Billy. I'll get his feet!" Officer Jamey Hawkins, the one who pushed the door open, added his two cents.

I looked at Bettye and did my Clarke Gable impersonation. "Frankly, my dear, I think two of the boys require supervision. You or me?"

"Sounds more like somethin' in your line, Sammy."

"Okay, but come and observe. It'll be good training."

We walked toward the rear entrance, past the detention cells, the squad room and the interrogation room and found two patrol cars parked at the back door, each with a handcuffed black man in the rear seat. The back doors of the first car in line stood wide open. The two uniformed cops pulled at one prisoner's flailing arms and legs trying to extricate him from the car with little luck and maximum effort. I decided to exercise my supervisory prerogative and lend a hand.

To get their attention, I spoke loudly. "Guys, you got a problem child here?"

"Got us a DUI, boss. Som'bich jest won't git outta my ve-hickle," Officer Puckett said.

Jamey Hawkins and Billy Puckett had served in the Marine Corps together in Afghanistan. Puckett was dark and stocky and Hawkins blond, tall, and thin. Puckett had lived in Prospect all his life. Hawkins came from Traverse City, Michigan and followed his buddy to Tennessee when he learned about the job opening at Prospect PD.

"You're not having much luck getting him out of the car, Billy," I said. "Mind if I give it a try?"

49

"Y'all's he'p would be cheerfully accepted, boss."

The sun was still shining, but at a lower angle. The bare branches of the decorative trees surrounding the municipal building cast intricate shadows on the blacktop and grass. The pattern looked as if someone blew black ink from a straw across the ground. It felt like a good day to have some po-leece fun.

"Okay, somebody keep an eye on your other guest in case he tries to run out of my parking lot. I'll have a word with this gentleman. Who is he, by the way?"

"Beats the hell outta us," Jamey said. "Got no ID on him."

I bent over and looked into the back of the patrol car and spent a few seconds staring at a big man who refused to make eye contact.

I figured him at somewhere between thirty-five and fifty. He looked like a well-practiced drinker, probably once a powerful man who had gotten soft around the edges. Little flecks of gray were mixed into his short, curly hair, and on that cool and beautiful day, beads of perspiration dotted his face.

"You're going to get out of the car sooner or later," I told the prisoner.

He turned and squinted at me, trying to fix me with the evil eye. Looking straight at my face, I recognized him.

"Burble Booker," I said.

He scowled, probably still trying to scare me off.

"Look, Burble, you *are* going to walk into that police station with me. Why not make life easy for both of us and get out of the damned car? I'll help you."

He looked away again, staring straight ahead, out the windshield. I figured it was time for my usually successful 'Plan B'.

"Burble, there's not a hell of a lot more I'm gonna say. You ready to get out or not?"

He showed no sign of cooperation.

That brought me to the distasteful part. Billy Puckett stood close to me, and I gestured for him to give me a little stretching room.

Burble had planted himself firmly in the back seat, so I reached in with both arms. Getting a tight grip on his neck with my left hand, I stuck two fingers of my right deep into his nostrils and started to pull.

"Jeezus Christ! Shee-it! Leggo my got-damn nose!"

Burble started talking, but still wasn't moving. I kept pulling and finally he conceded.

"Oh man, shee-it. Stop! Got-damn it, stop. Okay, okay, I'm comin'." He swung his legs out of the car.

I kept my fingers in his nostrils and guided him to the blacktop.

The two cops and Bettye began to applaud. Police officers have an odd sense of humor at times.

"Good man, Mr. Booker," I said. "Just keep walking, and you can have your nose back."

Once on level ground, we stopped, and I released my grip.

Burble, who stood two inches taller and more than twenty pounds heavier than me, sputtered out, "Man you don' play fair. Ain' nobody never did somethin' like dat to me befo'."

"Sorry if I stretched out your nose, but now that we know each other better, we'll get along fine."

He squinted at me, and then his eyes rolled back. He looked unsteady. I held an arm to keep him from toppling.

"Step inside with Officer Puckett, and we'll make this as painless as possible. By the way, are you taking a breathalyzer test?"

"Naw, I ain' takin' no damn test." He looked a little woozy again.

"You're not going to take a header, are you?"

He shook his head gingerly. "Naw."

"You're going to lose your license for six months if you don't take the test. That's automatic."

"Don' got no damn license," he said.

"You can't lose what you haven't got, my friend. Billy, he's all yours."

I stepped over to the second car as Bettye and Puckett escorted Burble Booker into the squad room to be logged in and processed.

Jamey Hawkins grinned and opened the back door of his patrol car. "You wanna grab this bull by the ring, too?"

"Might not be necessary. Let's see what the man says."

I looked into the car and spoke to a short chubby young man. "You coming out, or am I coming in to get you?" I asked.

"I'm comin' out," he said. "I ain't drunk and don' want no damn fingers in my damn nose."

Once our subject was standing on the blacktop, Officer Hawkins made an introduction. "Boss, this is Marvin Washington. I took him for obstructing. He tried to give Billy a bad time while he was cuffing the other guy."

"Does Marvin have ID with him?" I wanted to get a look at Marvin's face, which he conveniently hung very low.

"No, sir, nothing at all."

I could have sworn I knew that man, too.

"Look at me, Marvin." I took a long moment to study his face. "In a second, Jamey, we'll see just who Mr. Washington really is."

I unbuttoned Marvin's shirt and found a homemade tattoo of a flying bird with only one wing decorating the right side of his chest.

"Officer Hawkins, meet Harold 'Beaver' Booker, Burble's younger brother. We'll check him for a County Court assault warrant. I've met this guy before, and five will get you ten, there's a bench warrant for failure to appear."

Beaver dropped his head and moaned, "Aw, man."

"How do you know him?" Hawkins asked.

"A couple of months ago, Stanley and I went on a domestic call at Beaver's place. He and his live-in girlfriend, a woman everybody calls Tar Baby, were slugging it out. Beaver started winning, and she called 911."

Hawkins chuckled. "Tar Baby?"

I shrugged, and continued the story. "Beaver seemed reasonable enough at the time and volunteered to leave. But she said she wanted to file a domestic violence complaint, so we left her with the assault paperwork which she filed two days later. I guess she got pissed at him again when he came back home."

"How'd you know about the tattoo?"

"She had ripped his shirt open. I saw the tattoo and asked about the bird with only one wing. He said a few months earlier, Tar Baby did the artwork with a needle and thread and bottle of ink. But she had gotten so drunk, she passed out with only three quarters of the bird finished and she's never gotten around to adding the second wing."

"Unbelievable."

"Yeah. The tattoo looks pretty good for something done by a drunk."

"Billy gonna handle all the paper on these two?" he asked.

"I guess," I said. "You can hit the road again. I'll help Billy with these two and add your name in the appropriate places. But don't leave this afternoon before you sign a few court documents."

I removed Hawkins' handcuffs from Beaver's wrists and replaced them with my own.

"Will do, boss," Hawkins said. "See ya later."

Jamey Hawkins jumped into his car and drove out of the lot. I escorted the prisoner to our squad room, put him in a chair and locked one of the handcuffs to a big steel ring bolted to the side of a desk. Bettye met me with her log book, ready to take names.

She began to speak with Burble when I interrupted, "Excuse me while I find an autoclave to clean my fingers."

Bettye grinned. I doubt Burble knew what an autoclave was, but he grumbled anyway.

With my hands sanitized and me back in the squad room, I told Billy Puckett to check Beaver's name for a warrant in the county's system while I completed the arrest report on the drunk driver.

I brought up the appropriate computer screen and settled in for an hour of work.

"What's your real first name?" I asked.

"Burble," He yawned, acted tired and already bored with the procedure.

"Burble is on your birth certificate?"

"Uh-huh."

I wasn't in the mood for games.

"What kind of name is Burble?"

"My grandfather's name."

I shrugged.

"B-U-R-B-L-E?"

"Uh-huh."

"You have a middle name?"

"Naw."

He burped, and a cloud of sour breath invaded my personal space. I turned my head and made a face. Burble didn't seem to take offense.

"What's your date of birth?"

"Joo-lie twenny-forf, nineteen an' sixty-fo."

I did some quick arithmetic. "Makes you forty-two?"

He hesitated a minute and thought about that. "Uh-huh."

"Where were you born?"

"Right here."

"In the squad room?" My patience started to slip.

"Naw, in Knoxville."

"Thank you. How tall are you, and how much do you weigh?"

"Six-two, 'bout two hunnert, twenny."

I couldn't resist a little sarcasm. "Brown hair flecked with distinguished highlights of gray."

He scowled at me again. Not in a fun mood, I thought.

"Brown eyes?" I asked.

"Maroon."

"What?"

"I said maroon."

"What do you mean maroon? Don't screw with me, Burble."

"I said, I got maroon eyes." He sounded adamant.

"Look at me!"

He opened his eyes like two huge saucers, looked straight at me and burped a second time.

I recoiled again. "You're right. Color of eyes: maroon. You're one in a million."

"Uh-huh, dat's me."

I filled in several more blanks with the rest of Burble's personal pedigree. Billy Puckett sat at the desk across the room from where Burble and I were doing our thing. Beaver Booker slumped in a chair at Puckett's side, again hanging his head in shame. I assumed Billy had learned about the active warrant.

"Where was Mr. Booker when you saw him driving?" I asked.

"Goin' northeast on Sevierville Road, 'bout a mile this side o' Seymour. He was drivin' a brown '82 Chevy Caprice. Wait a minute."

He consulted his memo book.

"Tennessee tag BFR-349."

I started typing the court information, and after recording what I envisioned happened, I said, "Okay, Billy, listen up. *The defendant was driving northeast on Sevierville Road near the intersection of Prospect Road. The speed of the defendant's vehicle noticeably fluctuated, and on several occasions said vehicle crossed over the double yellow centerline. When stopped and confronted, the defendant's speech sounded slurred, his movements were unstable, and his eyes appeared vacant, watery and glassy*—and maroon."

I looked at Billy. He smiled.

"Forget that last one." I got serious and resumed business.

"*At close proximity to the defendant, his breath smelled with a strong odor of an alcoholic beverage.* Sound about right?"

Billy shot me a big grin. "Sounds like you were there, too."

"Good. Burble, my friend, sure you won't take a breathalyzer test? Judges don't like uncooperative drunks. You may go directly to jail, not pass go, and you definitely will not collect two hundred dollars."

Burble shook his head. "I done tol' ya I ain' takin' no damn test."

"Okay, suit yourself." I started to get up, but sat again, needing to satisfy my curiosity. "I have a question. Why do they call your brother Beaver?"

Beaver turned his head in our direction, scowling.

"Cause da man eat wood," Burble said.

"Why didn't I think of that? Whaddaya mean he eats wood? Like trees, two-by-fours, toothpicks?"

"Naw, man. When he a lil' boy he chew on wood. You know, da winnah sills, da bed post, maybe a chair sometime. You know—wood."

"So your mother called him Beaver?"

"Uh-huh."

"Real beavers eat living trees."

At least I thought they did. Burble frowned.

"She should have called him Labrador retriever," I said. "They chew everything."

Burble stared at me, probably not interested in my comments on his family history.

"Okay, we're done here," I said. "Sit tight, and wait for your prints and pictures. If you like the photos, come back and see me about having Christmas cards made. Good customers get a discount."

Burble exercised his right to remain silent. Drunks never appreciate my humor.

"Boss, you want me to charge Harold here with obstructing *and* the warrant?" Billy asked.

"Come outside for a minute," I said.

With more privacy in the hallway, I continued, "After you put Burble in a cell, talk to Beaver. Tell him the warrant stands. He's got to appear in court for that later today. But let him know you're willing to drop the obstructing charge, or at least hold off filing the court information if he's got something interesting to tell you in trade. Maybe Beaver is just another doofus, but maybe he's the informant of the decade. Let me know what he says."

I left Billy Puckett with his two prisoners cuffed to three-hundred-pound metal desks. I always saw that practice as something of a fire hazard, but brushed my concerns aside. No one forced them to get arrested.

I continued down the hall into the main office and sat next to Bettye Lambert.

"Lots of entertainment for a potentially quiet Groundhog Day," I said. "If we get a liquor store robbery, I'll feel right at home."

"Sam, we don't have a liquor store in Prospect."

I ended up wishing we did. Investigating robberies are a snap compared to the mess I was about to get into.

It was a little after five, so I called my wife to tell her I'd be late. My next stop, Glenda Mae.

Chapter Six

I left the municipal building through the front door and bounced down the fourteen stone steps to the street. As I reached the curb a marked police car with Officer Junior Huskey driving stopped for me at the cross walk. He looked over the steering wheel and flipped me a salute and a smile. If I wore a hat, I would have tipped it.

I strolled diagonally across the town square. Old tulip poplars void of leaves rimmed the city's center. A pair of crows perched on a bare branch provided contrasting silhouettes against the darkening blue-gray afternoon sky, while pair of squirrels hopped across the lawn seeking buried objects only they cared about. Cars circumnavigated the square making their way through town or attempted, with varying degrees of success, to parallel park. Prospect is never crowded or busy, but that was our version of rush hour. Officially it's a city, but it's not exactly what you'd picture if you heard a jazz quartet playing *Harlem Nocturne.*

I crossed a street, and, when I reached Walking Horse Realty, twisted the tarnished brass knob and yanked open the glass-fronted door. A bell attached to the wooden frame tinkled to announce my arrival. A blast of warm air hit me in the face like a soft pillow.

"Jesus, Maezy, I come here in the summer and freeze my butt off. In the winter, I feel like I just popped into a Finnish sauna."

Mae is blonde, somewhere over fifty and, as my wife describes her, drop dead gorgeous. She lives across the road from us in Walland. I think she likes me.

"Land sakes, Sammy, y'all are always complainin'. Come in here, and set yase'f down." She sat at her desk in a sleeveless blouse—in February.

I dropped into the chair behind the desk next to hers, opened my coat and knew in less than three minutes I'd take it off or witness a failure of my Right Guard. The three other desks in the office were empty. I assumed her sales personnel were still scouring the countryside for listings or had gone home for the day.

Since over familiarity has never been a problem for me, I leaned back, put my feet on the edge of the desk and crossed my ankles.

"Hey, lady. How's your love life?"

"Sugar, you don't want ta know. Or are you here to help me improve it?" She fluttered her eyelashes and flashed a million-dollar smile.

"Uh—oh, I'm here on business, and you put me on the spot. What's an all-American boy supposed to do?"

"I'd tell you, honey, but you'd only blush."

"I already regret changing the subject, but how about a little help for your favorite neighbor and the protector of your city?"

"Course, darlin'. Whatcha need?"

"What do you know about your competition, specifically Mack and Elnora Collinson and their hired hand, Jeremy Goins?"

"You mean Ku Klux Klan Realty? What do you want to know?"

"That said a lot, but tell me more."

I can't say I learned as much new information as I would have liked to hear, but Mae told me lots, often moving in and out of the realm of material facts. The Collinsons and company occasionally sold properties the conventional way, but absolute auctions were their stock and trade. The term meant properties offered to the highest bidder with no reserve prices, often a good way to buy cheap, unimproved land.

They also spent lots of time looking to list properties that would go into the multiple listing services showing them as the brokers of record. That way, when hard working realtors sold properties the Collinsons had listed, they got a piece of the action with no additional effort.

Other than that, Mae's information was all conjecture about their ultra-right-wing thinking and dislike of almost everyone.

I thanked Mae, got a platonic kiss on the cheek, put my clothes back on and hit the bricks. The temperate winter air outside the Walking Horse hot house wasn't very cold, but it reminded me of the initial rush of chilly water seeping into a wet suit and up my spine when I'd go scuba diving in the springtime, before the seas warmed up. I zipped my jacket, turned up my collar and retraced my steps back to the PD where the inside temperature felt more bearable.

* * * *

It was 5:30. Instead of sneaking into my office through the back door, I entered the PD through the lobby of the municipal building as most of our customers do during business hours. When I reached our doors, I found Bettye Lambert still at the desk and noticed a confused expression on her face. When I saw who sat in the chair next to her, I knew why she might feel bewildered.

"Black Cloud Gallagher," I said. "How the hell are you?"

John Gallagher stood and turned to face me. Aside from a bit more gray mixed into his reddish-brown hair and a few additional inches attached to his waistline, John looked the same as when I saw him at his retirement party many years ago.

"Hi, boss. How's it goin'?"

We shook hands, mumbled a few things old comrades might say and sat in the chairs around Bettye's desk. She forced a smile and still looked a little perplexed, probably from trying to interpret some of the things John said. I assumed she might be hoping for an excuse to go home, to save her from listening to two old cops shoot the breeze in her otherwise orderly world.

I gave John a date to start work, outlined what he'd be doing and took him on a quick tour of the PD. Then, I suggested he call the motel and check out. I assumed he already had, but mentioned it anyway. And I told him about his morning appointment with Glenda Mae to search for living accommodations.

I made a quick phone call and found Glenda Mae still at the realty, so to save my wife the trouble of introducing John, we returned to her office. I left him there to learn about the Tennessee way to buy a house, and I walked back to the PD.

59

Bettye had waited for me. After the initial exposure to her new assistant, I thought she might need a little therapy.

"So, what do you think of the Black Cloud?" I asked.

She blinked a few times and shook off the look of confusion. "He seems nice. I'm not sure I'll be able to understand everything he says, but I guess I'll learn."

"It may take a few days, but you're a smart girl."

She nodded, looking like she may never trust me again. "Why do you call him Black Cloud?"

"He's the unluckiest man on earth. If you're having a bad day, don't go near him."

Bettye wrinkled her forehead. "What do you mean?"

"Just keep an eye on him, and you'll find out soon enough. But here's an example. John's uncle died. He picked up his aunt and drove her to the funeral home. They parked and started walking across the street to the wake. When John realized he forgot to lock his car door, he turned around, leaving the old girl in the middle of the road. A few seconds later, the aunt got hit by a step van before she made it to the curb."

"Oh, my. But John was lucky he turned around."

"Maybe, but he's no longer Aunt Martha's favorite nephew."

"What happened to his aunt?"

"After a hip replacement, she lived."

"Oh, my," she said again. "Maybe it was just an isolated incident."

"Hardly. How about this one? One January he made a spur of the moment decision to take the family from New York to Florida. That's not easy between November and March without reservations. But John called around and thought he was really cool when he found the only available motel room within a hundred miles of Disney World. A pretty lucky break since snow covered the entire northeast, and everyone wanted to bail out.

"Seven days later, the entire Gallagher clan, mother-in-law included, jumped into his station wagon and headed for the Sunshine State. Eighteen hours later, they arrived at the motel. The room may have been a little crowded, but the kids didn't mind sleeping on the floor."

"Sammy, this sounds like it may take a while. You want coffee?"

"You buying?"

"O' course, darlin'. Be right back."

Bettye disappeared into my office and moments later returned with two cups.

"Thank you, ma'am."

She smiled. "My pleasure, sir."

When Bettye settled into her chair, I continued my story. "The next morning, they went to Disney World. Since Florida is often hot and sticky, after a day of palling around with Mickey and Goofy, the Gallaghers headed back to their room for a shower before going to dinner. What do you think they found at the motel?"

She blew across the rim of her cup and took a little sip. "I'm afraid to ask."

"A Piper Cub crashed directly into their room—the last room available in Florida. If John hadn't rented that room, the pilot would not have been killed, and the plane would still be flying. That's what I mean about the black cloud hanging over him."

"You don't know that's true."

"We could sit here until midnight, and I'd tell you more stories than you'd want to hear. Believe it."

"And you still want to hire him?"

"He's a good cop. And he needs a job. What can I tell you?"

"You may look like a tough guy, Sammy, but you're just an ol' pussy-cat."

"You're not the first to say that. What were you two talking about before I got back?"

"I was mostly listenin'. He does like to tell stories, doesn't he?" She picked up a pad and tossed it closer to me. "I had to write down some of the things he said. I thought you might be able to interpret."

"Good idea. He probably didn't notice. But if he did, it wouldn't bother him."

"If you say so."

"Hang in there, Betts. You'll learn to speak Gallaghese in no time. We all did."

I'm not sure she believed me.

61

* * * *

Bettye left for the day. I washed the coffee pot and then called the Chief at Pigeon Forge PD and the Sheriff of neighboring Sevier County and asked for a few police officers to help us keep C.J. safe. While Ms. Profitt's winning personality might not do much to generate enthusiasm for the job, I dropped a few names like Kenny, Tanya, and LeAnn to suck in any country and western fans. That ploy worked. The chief, sheriff and his chief deputy agreed to meet me at Dollywood early on Monday when we'd begin to coordinate our efforts.

At 6 p.m. Stan Rose stopped at the PD to pick up the gasoline sign-out sheets, and I discussed how the day went from boring to complicated and busy.

"You guys going to wear a little colored ball on your lapel, Oakley shades and talk to each other on wrist radios?" Stanley laughed at his reference on how to spot a Secret Service agent on detail.

"You're going to think we're something from the pages of *Soldier of Fortune* magazine when you see us in action," I said.

"I'll bet you're itching to slug it out with old lady Collinson, aren't you?"

"Sure, I'll knock her down and make her do the chicken."

"You sure you didn't work for LAPD once?"

"No, I'm just a big fan of T.J. Hooker."

Stanley shook his head. "Tell me more about the new clerk-typist."

I was about to when John Gallagher walked back into the reception room, gave us the same stupid, childish wave I remember from twenty-five-years ago and continued into my office.

"Hi, boss, how's it goin'?" He didn't wait for an answer, but turned to Stanley. "Hi, Sarge, I'm John Gallagher."

He and Stan shook hands. That completed John's meeting with the supervisors of his new employer, Prospect PD.

Chapter Seven

The weekend turned out uneventful, except for Gallagher driving Kate and me crazy. Thanks to his threats of us all being able to get together often, the future didn't look much brighter.

On Monday morning, I deserted my wife and dog, but didn't feel guilty about that because John was scheduled to spend the day looking for a house with Mae Waddell or one of her lucky sales representatives.

My first job on that sunny and mild February morning was to escort C.J. Profitt and Jenny Mitchell to Dollywood. The benefit show was scheduled for the next weekend, so for five days, all the Nashville stars would get together and begin rehearsals. At eight o'clock, Harley Flatt relieved Len Alcock. I found him at the motel, standing by with the two women.

We had no competent intelligence information on which to base our method of operation. Neither C.J. nor Jenny remembered any specific threats made by the Coalition for American Family Values. None of the notes said, 'I'll shoot you from afar', 'I'll burn down the motel with you in it', or 'I'll blow your rental car sky high'. No one in the law enforcement community knew those making the threats ever to have gotten physically abusive to the people with whom they took a dislike.

With luck, the marked police car escorting C.J.'s rented Lincoln Town Car would be enough to ward off would-be protesters or egg throwers. Without luck... Who knows?

Harley Flatt led the way, and I drove the Lincoln with the two women in the back seat. I chose to approach Dollywood by dropping down into Townsend, turning north into Wears Valley, past the small tourist community of Walden and enter the 'Forbidden City' where that leg of US 321 meets the Dolly Parton Parkway. From there it was only a short drive south to the service road and entrance to the Dollywood theme park.

We'd use a different route back to the motel in Prospect that night, and still another back to the rehearsal the day after—just my efforts to keep the opposition off guard.

As we clipped along at fifty-five, passing through the rugged Cutter's Gap approach to Townsend, C.J. asked, "Have you arrested any of those Coalition people yet?"

"I can't arrest someone when I have no actual evidence showing me who that someone is," I said.

"Well, they did sign the notes they sent."

Her statement smacked with annoyance and ticked me off.

Entering a sharp curve, I throttled down and after cutting the wheels slightly to the left, accelerated. The rear end of the Lincoln kicked around the turn as the wide tires hugged the centerline.

"I could be snotty and say, 'what notes?', but I won't. But I will ask you to consider this. Let's say you get annoyed with someone—anyone, it doesn't matter who. You send them a nasty note and sign it The Coalition of Country Singers. That person complains, and I lock up not only you, but Kenny, Tanya and LeAnn. Besides tromping on your 1st Amendment rights, would that be fair to your comrades?"

I thought not. C.J. remained silent and sulked.

During the rest of our ride, no one spoke except for Jenny making a few comments about the beautiful scenery and majestic mountain views she saw as we drove through Wears Valley.

I couldn't help thinking that she should have seen the same road twenty years earlier, before a dozen new real estate offices, peddling land and cabin rentals, desecrated the once quiet country lane. Before a dozen craft malls, offering everything from local woodcarvings to old-fashioned pottery to hand-dipped candles, brought in oodles of tourists with nothing to do but schlep from shop to shop and create more traffic than the two lane road could handle. Then, of course, there were the ubiquitous fudge stores that plague every touristy spot in the Smokies, offering enough calories and carbohydrates to make each visitor with a sweet tooth buy larger slacks at one of the Pigeon Forge outlet malls before they went home.

In this neck of the woods, popularity begets progress. Progress begets population, and population takes a beautiful place and makes it suck. Such was life. I remembered how Matt Dillon would look at a saddle tramp he didn't want hanging around his town. He simply told them, "Get outta Dodge."

I wondered if I could exercise my own form of population control by telling people, "Get outta Prospect," as I scowled and hooked my thumbs over my gun belt—if I ever wore a gun belt. My wife thinks I should be a hermit when I grow up.

As we made a right turn onto Dolly's parkway, a waiting Pigeon Forge PD cruiser spotted us, picked up the pace and escorted us the rest of the way into the theme park. The uniformed attendant at the kiosk where Dolly charges visitors to park as well as spend half their vacation budget on admission tickets, saw our little caravan and waved us through, flipping a salute as we passed. C.J. should have been impressed. I doubt she was.

Once we reached the narrow roads inside the park, a Dollywood Security golf cart led us at a snail's pace to one of the theatres. A few PFPD cops and a bunch of Sevier County sheriff's deputies and their cars were scattered around the building. If this were a military operation, I would have said our landing zone was secure and cold.

I wondered if the cops on the detail were there "on the arm"— working without overtime compensation, just to get a chance to meet Kenny, Tanya, LeAnn and the rest of those Nashville notables.

The chief, sheriff and their respective staffs seemed to have Dollywood sewn up tighter than a crab's posterior. I assumed C.J. would be safe for the rest of the day and left Harley Flatt to hang out with Jenny Mitchell and keep an eye on her boss.

I drove the Lincoln back to Prospect, stopped at the Best Western Foothills View Motel and parked the car in front of the office. The motel owner, Clay Plemmons, and I quickly checked the suite C.J. had reserved, and I called in another police officer to sit there all day, at time and a half, and watch the car and the room. I hoped Ronnie had a good story for the city council to explain away the extra expenses. The man would really owe me after this was over.

Then I got a great idea. I'd arrange for Katherine and me to have a few peaceful nights and John Gallagher to start making extra pocket money; I thought he'd love to be an additional bodyguard on the C.J. Profitt detail.

Shifting my thoughts to nailing the local Coalition members with having done something illegal, I called Junior Huskey to meet me at the motel and drive back to the PD.

"I've got some detective work I want you to do, kid." I said. "The timing has to be right, but for now, get together with Bobby Crockett and plan to interrogate the three hooples from Collinson Realty. When you get some time, see Bettye and the new guy, John Gallagher, about what we've got so far. I want you to concentrate on the hate mail C.J. Profitt received. I think one of those idiots wrote the notes—we just have to prove it."

"This guy John used to work with you?"

"Yeah."

"He was a detective? Full time?"

"Yeah, full time. We didn't have part-time cops in New York."

"Tell me again how many people were in your department up there."

"Three thousand cops and about five hundred civilians."

Junior smiled. "Shoot. I bet you had all kinds o' good jobs."

"You mean different sections? Preferred assignments?"

He nodded. "Uh-huh."

"Yeah," I said. "There was regular patrol in six precincts. Highway Patrol handled traffic enforcement on the major roads. Each precinct had a detective squad, and main office had all the specialized squads. There were aviation and marine bureaus, emergency services—all kinds of cops were running around getting into trouble. A young guy like you would probably like it."

"Where do I sign up?"

"Who said I'd let you go? You're my investigator-in-training."

"Thank ya, boss. I believe I could like bein' a detective."

* * * *

The second half of Monday consisted of interviewing our police officer candidate, Dallas Finchum. Bettye had given him instructions to be in my office at 1 p.m. Although Bettye was no fan of the former chief, Buck Webbster, she gave his nephew the benefit of any doubt about his fitness to be a cop at Prospect PD and scheduled him after I finished lunch. Bettye knew I'd be in a better mood after eating. She schedules guys like Charles Manson and Ted Bundy to meet with me between 11:00 and noon.

Prior to Dallas showing up, I took a complete set of police recruit applications and questionnaires from my old department, which I had squirreled away years ago for just such an occasion and photocopied them using Prospect PD stationery. I had gotten to be a real expert at 'desktop publishing' and was pleased with myself after seeing the finished products.

The personal history questionnaire looked just a little smaller than the Staten Island phone book. The medical questions called for documentation of every cold, mole and sore toenail he ever experienced during his lifetime. I also wanted Dallas to write out directions to each residence and each employer he'd had since high school so his investigator could easily find the places he had to visit. I didn't want the boy's job to be easy. Experience taught me that a little pressure can be a good weeding-out tool. Some people got fed up with the hassle and simply walked away. Those who really wanted to be a cop put up with all the work and chicken-shit and stayed with the program. I'd wait to see what kind of person Dallas Finchum might be.

I walked into the PD at five minutes to one to find Dallas, a handsome, dark-haired kid, waiting for me in the reception room, sitting at attention. Bettye left her desk and met me in my office.

"He been here long?"

"About ten minutes," she said. "He seems like a nice boy. Maybe you shouldn't bite his head off right away?"

"Maybe. Are you asking me to be gentle with him, Sergeant?"

She touched the end of my nose with her index finger. "Now don't go bein' mean and hateful with that boy, Sam Jenkins. He got all dressed up to see you and came in early. I know you like to see those things."

"Yes, ma'am, I'll be nice—because you asked."

She smiled at that.

"Joey Gillespie is on the way in," she said. "He'll watch the desk and answer the phone while I'm at lunch. I figured you'd like to interview the boy and not be disturbed."

"Lady, if I had a few more like you around here, I'd have nothing to do. Thanks. Take a long lunch if you want to do more shopping."

That generated another smile.

I was getting along famously with the woman younger people might call my workplace spouse.

I heard the back door open and close and watched PO Joey Gillespie walk in. Bettye left my office, and I stuck my head outside the office door.

"Dallas?"

He picked up his head and looked at me.

"I'm Chief Jenkins. Come in please."

I walked around behind my desk and sat. When I looked up, he was standing three feet in front of the desk with both hands holding a slim Naugahyde document case across his midsection. He wore a well-pressed black suit, white shirt, and a red and gray striped tie. If I had to guess, I'd say he had gotten a haircut fifteen minutes before he showed up in the lobby.

I stared at him. He waited. Had I been a candidate, I would have taken a seat, crossed my legs and hoped the interviewer read my thoughts: 'You gonna say something or what?' But I'm a sixty-year-old prima-donna with an attitude. When I was in my mid-twenties, I showed more manners, too.

"Sit down, Dallas," I said. "We're going to be here a while. Get comfortable."

He looked relieved.

Being the hard-ass I fancied myself, I wanted to see if I could get the kid stressed out by just giving him the silent treatment. Perhaps a little pressure would make Dallas crack. I doubted that Bettye would consider my next ploy as treating the kid gently. When I was twenty-five I knew enough to never let them see me sweat, but I'd been around the world a few more times than Dallas.

After a very long moment I spoke. "Let me share a bit of philosophy with you, son. It's about how I think a police department should operate."

He kept looking at me, unsmiling.

"If I'm to enforce the law impartially and expect the cops who work here to do the same, I need the system to work like the famous statue of Themis—the Lady of Justice—implies. She holds the scales and wears a blindfold, indicating that justice is blind, and everyone gets an equal opportunity and a fair shake. Understand?"

I stopped and stared at him. He swallowed hard and gave me an almost imperceptible nod to make me think he still followed. I wasn't sure he did.

"So, you come here loaded with the political horsepower I just learned about, telling me I'm supposed to give you a job when there may be someone else out there more qualified and more deserving of it than you."

I paused again, for almost half a minute, to keep the pressure on. But I had to give Dallas credit. From the intense, pained look on his face, he was behaving like a real mensch by not vomiting or walking out.

"What am I to think about my idea of a totally fair system when the mayor tells me to hire some politico's kid—the nephew of an ex-chief who left his position under a cloud of impropriety? How am I supposed to look at you, the guy who comes here without fairly throwing his hat in the ring and showing me he's the best man for the job after competing with all the others?"

Dallas blinked a few times, but didn't speak. I waited another long moment and continued, still in a calm and rational manner, but my words left no doubt that I wanted our relationship to be all business.

"You just walk in and *tell* me you want to be hired."

He began to speak, but I kept talking, and he closed his mouth.

"When it comes to honesty, Dallas, I'm a genuine pain in the ass. I believe society has the right to expect a higher standard of conduct from its cops than it does from itself. Like it or not, son, when a citizen tells us they pay our salaries, they're right. We work for them."

Dallas began blinking a mile a minute. Even I couldn't help feeling sorry for the kid.

"Guys like your Uncle Buck are crooks," I said. "Sorry if I offend you by casting aspersions on your family members, but I don't think he should have gotten off because The Blount County Good Ol' Boy System protected him. I think the fat bastard should have gone to jail. Because of Buck Webbster, everyone who works for this department now comes under a veil of suspicion. People may think if the guy at the top was a crook, what can we expect from his subordinates? It will take us years to have the other cops in this state and the people we serve forget about your uncle. Why remind them by hiring you?"

I might have been getting a little carried away with myself and certainly wasn't painting a bright picture for Dallas. Depending on his personal fortitude, he may have been on the verge of going in his pants. To the kid, I probably seemed on the brink of being out of control. Perhaps he was waiting for me to begin screaming. I couldn't blame him if he threw his hands up, told me I was nuts and ran out. But I still had his attention, so I continued.

"If a Prospect cop makes a mistake and it's something done because he believed it was the right thing to do and in the best interest of the job, I'd be stupid not to forgive him and do all I could to get him the slightest repercussion possible. But if a cop got caught doing something illegal for personal benefit, I believe I'd have to be restrained from killing the son-of-a-bitch. Is my philosophy coming across loud and clear, sir?"

Dallas nodded and muttered something I didn't hear.

I forced what I thought might appear to be a malevolent smile. "I guess I'm telling you that you're starting out with at least one, possibly two strikes against you. With me, my friend, it's only three strikes, and you're out. We've never met before, and I'm getting you shoved down my throat for political payback. For some reason yet unknown to me, I seem to be accepting that. Well, good for you—maybe. So, I'm giving you the benefit of the doubt."

He sighed and looked as if a three-hundred-pound barbell just slipped off his shoulders.

I wanted to replace a little of the weight. "This morning someone I respect asked me to keep an open mind and give you a chance to prove yourself. Okay, I will. For her. Not for you. You get no free ride and no gift in the job department. You are not hired yet. You have many things to do before you earn the spot you're looking for. Understand that?"

"Yes, sir," he croaked.

"Are you willing to suffer my tirade and then do what I request?

That may have confused him. He paused, but said, "Yes, sir."

I smiled again. Not like a friendly police chief, more like Hannibal Lechter. "Okay. Now I want you to put yourself in my position. Tell me why I should hire you rather than kick your ass?"

His eyes fluttered uncontrollably. He squeezed them tightly and tried his best to regroup.

"Sir, I'm sorry, really sorry things happened the way they did. I can't undo anything already done, but I can apologize to ya because someone, my mother mainly, did them. My other uncle, not Buck—his name's Claude Webbster—he made the calls for Momma. Sir, I see yer point. I'd be upset, too, and I do apologize. Lord have mercy, I apologize to ya. If ya want me to leave now and just go away, I will. I don't want to work somewhere I'm not wanted. But I'll tell you, sir, if ya give me a chance, I'll work hard for ya. I promise. I swear. I'll do whatever ya want if only you'll give me a chance."

That little speech impressed me. I'd met Claude Webbster and didn't place him much higher than his brother Buck on the food chain. But the kid may have been an anomaly in the family.

"Kid, I'm not sure if someone told you all the right things to say or you're naturally clever and they just came to you. We'll see. You listened to me rant and rave for a few minutes. Good, I hope you understand something about me now. I'll give you a chance—the same one everybody gets from me. If you earn the job, so be it. If you're unable to get over the hurdles I place in front of you—tough shit. Life is full of disappointments—move on. Starting now, I expect 110% effort from you. And 120% honesty. If I catch you lying or trying to beat me and the system, I won't hire you, and I'll do my best to see that no one else on earth will either. If you get by me and later on I learn you lied to me, I'll do my best to not only get you fired, but after you're terminated by the mayor, I'll kick you down the stairs of this building and jump on your back with both feet. Understood?"

He nodded, but didn't speak. I waited, but the boy only looked at me. I began to wonder how much of the stress I just dished out affected Dallas. It hadn't come close to what a street cop feels when they confront a six-and-a-half-foot tall construction worker holding a knife to his wife's throat.

"Are you interested in going further?"

He nodded again, swallowed and spoke clearly. "Yes, sir."

I handed Dallas the packet of paperwork I wanted completed and impressed upon him that neatness counted, and everything must be back within seven days. Then I drew his attention to page nine of the personal history questionnaire.

"Take a look at the question about arrests, Dallas. It asks, 'Have you ever been arrested for any offense.' Any is underlined. It doesn't yet ask if you were found guilty of anything—that comes later."

He blinked rapidly and nodded like a little doll with a spring-mounted head.

"Now, let's suppose you were arrested for something," I said. "Pick a charge. How about shoplifting, a simple larceny? You're a good-looking, clean-cut young guy, a first offender, and you buy yourself an expensive attorney who tells you to plead guilty and get a good deal from an understanding judge. The judge agrees to hold his verdict in abeyance for six months and then dismiss the charge against you if you've kept your nose clean for that period of time. After six months, the charge is dropped, and your lawyer tells you it's like the arrest never happened. He also tells you that if anyone asks you if you've been arrested, tell them no. And that's true. You can do that because your records have been expunged. Well, Dallas, old boy, if that ever happened to you and you decide not to tell me about it, I hope to hell your lawyer will give you a job because I won't. We clear on that?"

The blinking continued at warp speed. He was having trouble keeping himself from shaking, but he nodded, indicating he understood.

It looked like I hit a nerve and had certainly captured his attention, so I continued.

"Somewhere in that questionnaire I ask not only for information about any arrest but also any traffic violation and any parking ticket you ever received. Think hard. Go to the Department of Safety office where you get your driver's license renewed and give them a couple of bucks to print out your complete driving history. Tell me about everything. These things may not disqualify you from getting hired, but one little white lie will. If, after you sign an official document as being truthful, you get it notarized and submit it to me and I learn you lied, I will arrest you for making a false statement to a public official. This is where we find that the truth will set you free and a lie gets your ass collared. Enough said, right?"

His left shoulder twitched, and he nodded again.

"Are you cold? I asked. "You seem to be shaking a little. The climate control set too low for you?"

"No, sir. I'm okay."

"Anything you want to tell me about before you leave?"

"Yes, sir," he said and burrowed into his briefcase, coming out with a couple of typewritten pages. "I'd like to leave you with a copy of the résumé I prepared for you, if I could."

I stood and reached across my desktop for the documents he held.

Dallas swallowed with some difficulty and finally spoke. "And I guess I should tell you how I was arrested in college...for rape."

That sounded a bit more serious than shoplifting. I blinked and drew my head back an inch or two. "Were you convicted of anything that stemmed from the charge?"

"No, sir. All the charges were dropped."

I just couldn't wait to hear his explanation.

"As we discussed," I said. "You still have to list that one on the questionnaire. When you come back, I'll have you write a statement about the incident and give you a chance to tell your side of the story. I'll even teach you about writing statements before you do it."

His eyes looked overly wide as he nodded in time with my every word.

"Would you like to tell me something now?"

"Yes, sir. It was pretty simple. I was on a date, and we were gettin' along just fine. We went back to her dorm room, started kissin' and all,

73

and then we had sex. The next day the campus police arrested me. When the county police down there investigated, they spoke to the girl, and she didn't want to press charges."

"Did you forcibly rape her?"

"No, sir!" He snapped out the answer. "She was willin' at the time, or at least that's what I thought. I swear ta God, we were getting' along just fine."

I studied him for a few seconds and saw no guile or deception in his face. His words sounded vehement and sincere. They had what an interrogator might call the 'ring of truth'.

"Okay. I've heard stories like that before," I said. "And believe it or not, I have a heart. I'll give you an opportunity to tell your side—in writing. I'll give you plenty of paper."

I never thought my office felt like the Alaskan tundra in late autumn, but Dallas couldn't keep from shivering.

"Sure you're okay?" I asked.

He bit his bottom lip and nodded some more. "Yes, sir."

"You have our number. If you come up with any questions while you're filling out the applications, call. It doesn't matter how silly you think the questions are. It's better to ask. If I'm not here, speak to Sergeant Lambert. One of us will tell you what to do. When you return the paperwork, we'll give you dates to go for the medical and psychological exams. Anything else you need to know or want to say before you leave?"

"No, sir, I'm ready."

"Good. See you in seven days—or less."

And off he went.

Chapter Eight

At 4 p.m., Lenny Alcock stopped in and threw me a curve. He'd been scheduled to pick up the guard detail at 8 o'clock that evening, but asked to be replaced. His daughter was playing in a crucial basketball game against a rival high school. Lenny's wife and daughter wanted him at the game for moral support.

I couldn't blame him for being less than enthusiastic—overtime money or not—with the job of guarding an obnoxious recording star. I lacked a lot of enthusiasm myself. And he offered me the alternative of another cop who Lenny claimed to be enchanted with Ms. C.J. Profitt. He said PO Johnny Rutledge wanted me to know he'd like to pick up any time Len or Harley needed off for the rest of the week.

While Johnny wasn't the kind of kid who would ever set the world of law enforcement on fire, he was competent and always came to work willing to do whatever the radio dispatcher or a supervisor told him.

So, Johnny Rutledge was scheduled to relieve Harlan Flatt and partner up with John Gallagher for twelve hours of fun outside a not very populated motel during a dull winter's night in the Smokies. Excitement abounds when you're a cop.

After Alcock left, Gallagher showed up. I heard him greet Bettye.

"Hi, Sarge. How's it goin'?"

"Hello again, John. How did you make out today?" she asked.

"Pretty good. We saw a bunch of places. Boy, Sarge, they build nice houses around here. I shouldn't have a problem finding something good."

Aha, my hopes elevated.

"Boss in?" he asked.

"He is."

John walked over and knocked on my doorjamb.

"Hi, boss. How's it goin?"

"Hey, John. You buy a house today?"

"Not yet," he said.

My hopes sagged.

"I saw a bunch of nice stuff for between two twenty and two sixty-five. But there was one for three-fifty that was really nice. I mean *really*."

I frowned at three-hundred and fifty grand.

"I figger with the extra bedrooms, the kids could come all at once. It's only an extra hundred large. Whaddaya think, boss?"

I squinted at him for a long moment. He stood there smiling.

I didn't hide my displeasure. "John, are you fuckin' crazy? You sold your new car, sold your boat, and now you're selling your house in Florida to get out from under your bills. For all I know, you had to sell that little Maltese you owned."

"Boss, that dog died years ago."

"I hope it didn't starve to death because you couldn't afford dog food."

He let a fatalistic look cross over his face. "It just got old and died."

Gallagher rekindled the grin and stood there like the village idiot, but I wasn't finished with him yet.

"I won't even ask how many credit cards you have and how many of those are maxed out."

That must have jogged unpleasant memories. His smile faded.

"For as long as I've known you, John, you've spent money like a drunken sailor on shore leave. Why not give yourself a break and set a limit—a realistic one—and stick to it?"

He hung his head, then looked at me and smiled that same stupid smile he used when someone caught him in a ridiculous situation.

"Yeah, boss. I guess you're right. That was a nice house though. And when you think about a thirty-year mortgage, that extra hundred grand spreads out a lot."

"Jesus Christ, John, in thirty years, if you're still alive, you'll be pushing a hundred. Why not look for smaller payments?" I began to feel like two buffalo were bumping heads inside my skull. "See why I hate you, John?"

His wide grin returned. "Say it ain't so, boss."

As I finished lecturing Gallagher, Stan Rose walked into my office. He said hello to John, and I gave him an updated story about keeping C.J. Profitt safe. Stanley said he remembered a few times at LAPD when he'd gotten involved with celebrities and showed no enthusiasm for the bodyguard detail either.

"Hey, John, I'll help you make owning a new home easier. How about some overtime before you start the regular job? You can have twelve hours tonight and then cut back to four hours each night so you can look at houses or work in the office and still get enough sleep. It's easy stuff for you, VIP security for a country and western singer named C.J. Profitt. Ever hear of her?"

Of course he had. Florida enjoys shit-kickin' music almost as much as Tennessee.

"VIP security?" he asked. "I used to love those details. At time and a half? Sure, boss, count me in."

I let my emotions show. "Okay!"

John asked, "You remember how we guarded that Nigerian delegation to the UN when they stayed on the Island for a big party?" His faraway smile told me they were fond memories.

My elation of only moments ago began to fade with the thoughts of that incident. "Yeah, I remember. You and a couple other lunatic detectives ended up dancing the night away with the Nigerian women. That ain't gonna happen in Prospect."

He frowned. "Okay, boss. Don't get excited. I'll be good. But that Nigerian thing was all Frankie's fault. He was a bad influence on me. Baxter, too. Jimmy was the craziest of the bunch, always singing and dancing. I was just a victim of circumstance. Ask any of the other guys. They'll tell you."

I rolled my eyes and didn't want to discuss ancient history. "Do you have a gun?"

"A gun? No, not with me. It's locked up back home."

"Okay, you can use one of mine. But don't even think about losing it. If you do, I'll kill you. And don't leave it hanging on a stall door in the men's room like you used to do."

"Don't worry, boss. I haven't left my gun on the stall door in twenty years."

"John, you haven't been a cop in twenty years."

He grinned. "It's okay for me to carry a concealed handgun around here?"

"Tennessee is kind of loose about shootin' irons, especially when I swear you in as an auxiliary cop."

Stanley Rose shook his head. "Nigerian women? Armed auxiliary cops? I thought LAPD was strange."

John and I left headquarters just after 5 p.m. I wanted to get home, eat, relax and get back to the Foothills View Motel before eight. To make Gallagher an armed and dangerous bodyguard, I gave him my old Smith & Wesson revolver, a gun he'd be familiar with. I'd carry my Glock 19. I doubted John, the old-timer, could get used to a gun with a plastic frame.

At quarter to eight, I pulled into the motel parking lot. John drove up behind me in his little electric blue four-door Saturn, ready for twelve hours of VIP security. Johnny Rutledge waited for us in his marked Prospect PD cruiser. I made the introductions and headed for the office to get a key and thoroughly check out the second floor suite again and the adjoining rooms.

As I spoke to a part-time clerk named Alford Joiner, Harley Flatt called my cell phone to say rehearsal had run into overtime and they only left Dollywood at 7:45. In the interim, John and I gave the place another good toss, looking for anything inappropriate in the spotless, but affordable motel room. Johnny watched, learned and helped a little.

"You guys sure look like you've done this stuff before," Johnny said. "Pretty good for a couple of old retired cops."

"It's like falling off a bike, kid," John said. "Stick with me, and I'll show you all the strings."

Johnny looked confused.

I interpreted. "He means, for him, acting like a detective is like riding a bicycle, something you never forget. And if you listen to him, he'll show you the ropes."

Johnny smiled and nodded after the explanation. He was a guy anyone might call Mr. Medium—neither tall nor short, fat nor skinny. Even his brown hair was medium length—neither dark nor light.

"Gallagher speaks a strange form of English," I said, trying to further enlighten the young cop. "After twelve hours together you'll be totally confused, or you'll start to catch on. But you won't know until the shift is over."

Rutledge nodded again, but I doubted he understood.

At 8:35 Harley Flatt arrived at the motel with the ladies. He headed home to get almost twelve hours of rest, and I made more introductions. John must have sensed C.J.'s attitude and acted all business. He can be a real pro when he turns off the nit-wit act. Johnny Rutledge behaved like a star-struck fan. Unfortunately, C.J. didn't seem in the mood to make nice for her adoring public.

When C.J. left the room, I spoke to Jenny. "What are you guys planning for dinner?"

"We ate a late lunch and won't need much before breakfast. We'll just send out for something."

"Okay, tell the guys and one of them will get it for you."

I gave her a card with several cell phone numbers, mine and Stan Rose's included.

"These men will be outside—one always in front. Another may be moving around behind the motel at times. You probably won't hear or see them. John Gallagher's done work like this before. He's very good. Officer Rutledge is a good cop, too. You can rely on both."

I waved to Johnny Rutledge, calling him outside.

We stood on the balcony walkway overlooking the parking lot. "Listen to what Gallagher says. He knows what he's doing."

"Yes, sir, will do. Looks like a piece o' cake."

"I hope so." Then, unable to leave my curiosity unsatisfied, I asked, "You volunteered for this job?"

"Yes, sir."

"Having money problems? Need the OT?" I wondered if I had a second Gallagher on my hands.

Rutledge beamed. "No. sir, I'm a big fan o' C.J. She's awesome."

My second biggest fear proved true.

"You really like her?"

He nodded like a kid I just offered a new bicycle.

"Oh, jeez," I said.

I left my version of the Prospect Secret Service in place and met Stan Rose before going home.

Our cars sat close together, parked driver's side to driver's side. Stan sipped from a Styrofoam coffee cup. I didn't want to get anywhere close to caffeine.

"Rutledge volunteered for the job," I said.

He grinned. "I know."

"Poor misguided kid likes C.J. Profitt."

"He's not the only one. She sold millions of records last year."

"Rutledge said she's *awesome*. For chrissakes, he sounded like a valley girl. I hate that word."

Stanley already knew that and opted for his California smart-ass act.

"Whoa, dude," he said. "She's, like, bodacious."

I growled, "I'll tell you what's awesome, Stanley. A battery of 175 mm guns going off at night is awesome. A Tac-Air flight laying down a quarter of a mile of napalm, lighting up half the North Vietnamese Army is awesome. A cup of goddamn latte' or a grouchy singer is not awesome."

"Picky, picky, picky."

I growled again. Stanley laughed.

"You know what Mel Brooks said, don't you?" I asked.

"Not off hand."

"Life stinks."

Stan laughed again. "Yeah, I remember the movie with that name."

I dropped the gearshift lever into drive. He flipped me a salute, and I drove home.

* * * *

At 10:15 that night the telephone rang. Kate and I were watching a Law & Order rerun—I on the floor doing my forty-eighth sit-up, and she on the couch sipping a glass of Riesling. I got up and answered the phone. It was Stanley.

"I hate to bother you at home, boss... It's a long story. I just sent Johnny Rutledge to the hospital in an ambulance. He was poisoned."

"Poisoned? How the hell?"

"I'm getting there," he said. "When the women got the munchies, instead of telling our guys to order the food, one of them called Wah Lum for a delivery. I've already been there and learned that Mr. Lum's grandson was the delivery boy. He got stopped along the way between the restaurant and the motel by a guy who gave him twenty bucks to borrow his bicycle and take the order to the motel room."

"Oh, for chrissakes. No wonder the world can't exist without cops."

"The guy told the Lum kid he wanted to meet C.J. Profitt. The boy didn't care about meeting her, figured the guy was just a fan and agreed. This guy delivered the bag of Chinese food and took off immediately on the bike."

"And Rutledge acted like the royal food taster?"

"Gallagher didn't like the looks of the deal and took Rutledge into the motel room with him. John started to call 911 to get our cars looking for the guy who took off on the bike because C.J. said he wasn't an Asian. Then Johnny decided to see if the food tasted bad."

"Why did he do that?" I asked rhetorically. "He think she's the Queen of England or something?"

Stanley let that go and continued. "Johnny keeled over holding his stomach in less than a minute, obviously poisoned. Gallagher was already talking to the dispatcher, so when he saw Rutledge hit the floor, they had Rural Metro rolling right away."

"How's Johnny?"

"Last I heard, they pumped his stomach. He's alive but hurtin'."

"How about the guy who delivered the food... Anybody find him?

"No luck. He ditched the kid's bike behind the steak house and must have driven off. Between Gallagher and the women, I got the description of a medium-sized white guy between thirty-five and fifty-five."

"That narrows it down to a half million. Okay, I'll meet you at the motel in less than a half hour."

Twenty-two minutes later, I pulled into the lot of the Foothills View and parked my Ford next to C.J.'s rented Lincoln. A ceiling of low cloud cover hid the stars and half-moon. Tall mountains almost blocked the sky to the south, and only the motel security lights illuminated the parking area.

I talked to John Gallagher and learned that he thought something was amiss when a guy on a bicycle carried a brown paper bag up to the second floor and knocked on C.J.'s door. John first noticed that after getting off the bike, the man walked through the breezeway where the ice maker was located. Then, in less than two minutes he came back out front looking for the stairs to the second floor balcony.

The curious thing, according to John, was that this cyclist wore a pair of wraparound sunglasses in the darkness. Good old John. I'd trust his description most—five-ten to six-foot, one-sixty to one hundred eighty pounds, wearing an olive drab field jacket, blue jeans and a black or dark blue baseball cap with an unidentified logo on the front. Not bad for a sixty-seven-year old guy sitting in the dark almost one hundred feet away. Neither C.J. nor Jenny could add much to John's description.

When the food arrived, Jenny answered the door while C.J. remained on the couch watching TV. Jenny took the bag and tipped the man three dollars. C.J. had paid the restaurant with a credit card when she phoned in the order.

Jenny only added that the medium-sized man needed a shave—something John couldn't see from his position. And she hadn't taken notice of any emblem on his cap and didn't think his Army field jacket had a name tape or patch sewn onto it.

Oddly enough, C.J. had taken a liking to John Gallagher. When I finished speaking with Jenny, I found him sitting on the couch telling C.J. about Boca Raton. Before I left, he told me C.J. had invited him to spend the night on the couch, giving him several magazines to help him stay awake.

If I'd been poisoned, she probably would have called the local trash man to haul my body out of the way.

Stanley went back into service to supervise the other two road cops handling the calls, and I phoned the dispatcher for a county crime scene unit to look around the motel for clues. Then I drove to the Wah Lum Chinese restaurant where Mr. Lum had remained open waiting for me. I spoke to the old man and his daughter, Mai, first. Then Mai introduced me to her son, David Chan, the sixteen-year-old delivery boy and utility infielder at the restaurant.

David said he had taken the short ride from the restaurant on the town square toward the Foothills View where a man claiming to be a fan of C.J. Profitt stopped him at the end of the motel driveway. Apparently, David didn't think it was odd to meet a man waiting on the street corner who knew he was delivering the bag of food. As our astute president has often said, "Our children are our future." Maybe Dubyah had inside information that inspired more faith in the next generations than I've been privy to.

David hadn't seen the man come from a car, but since a strip mall with plenty of parking was across the street and there's a restaurant next to the motel, many cars were in the immediate area. The only emotion David showed was to express how 'totally pissed' he was that the man had ridden his bike down the steep hill behind the motel and ditched it in the parking lot of Johnny Milton's Paradise Found Steak House. He described the man who gave him a twenty-dollar bill as almost as big and almost as old as me, and he wore a green jacket. The kid plotzed when I asked for the twenty so we could check for fingerprints.

At the emergency room of Blount Memorial Hospital, I took out my badge and tinned the nurse at the triage area. I learned that Johnny Rutledge could be found on the third floor and would remain a guest of the hospital for at least twenty-four hours.

The elevator dropped me off fifty feet from the nurse's station called Three North. I used my badge and a friendly smile again, but the supervisory nurse behind the desk, a woman in her fifties who looked tough enough to toss me out the window, only scowled.

"I've come to see Officer Rutledge, the kid who ate the poisoned food."

She squinted at me over a pair of Dollar Store reading glasses. "You family?"

I really wasn't in the mood for an unwarranted inquisition, but tried not to lose my temper. I thought, badge trumps family any time. I remained calm and indulged her.

"I'm his boss, and I want to start an investigation on his attempted murder."

"Murder?" She sounded surprised. "I thought he ate some bad Chinese food."

"I think when you get your tox report back it'll say there was a recognizable form of poison present."

"Then shouldn't he have a guard on him?"

I *really* wasn't in the mood for her. "He wasn't the target," I said, "just an unlucky guy with a passion for General Tso's chicken."

The tough girl smiled.

"Lemme make sure toxicology puts a rush on this—if they're not already working on it." She picked up a phone and made the call.

After she cradled the receiver I said, "Thanks."

"Any idea what kind of poison?"

"I'm just a cop. You're the scientist."

"Not me, sugar. You wanna see the boy?"

"Please. I'd like to talk to the attending physician, too."

"I'll page him."

She picked up the phone again and spoke to someone who controlled the PA system. A moment later, something barely intelligible came out of the wall speakers. The only recognizable words were 'Three North.'

"Thanks again," I said. "How's the kid?"

"You ever have a stomach virus?"

"Sure."

"Figure ten times worse. Wait'll you see him."

"Yikes."

"You bet. He's outta danger, but he'll be one hurtin' cowboy for a few days."

"That'll teach him to eat fried foods."

She chuckled. "Yeah, right. He's in 318. Make a right, then three doors down and on the left."

"Appreciate it."

"Any time."

She went back to a Cosmo article about sex over sixty.

I did a right face and wandered down to Johnny's room.

A dim light on the wall behind his bed glowed in the otherwise dark room. The TV was off, and Johnny's eyes were closed. His face looked almost green. I stood next to the bed for thirty seconds or so before putting my hand on his shoulder. His eyes opened slowly. They, too, looked awful.

"Oh, hey, Sam, y'all didn't have ta come out tonight. I'm okay. Musta been somethin' I et." He made a halfhearted attempt to laugh.

"You know, kid, I keep telling old man Lum he's got to take that alley cat chow mein off the menu."

Johnny smiled again.

"You don't look so good, so I won't ask you how you're doing. But the nurse told me you'll be as good as new in no time, so you hang in there."

It looked like cracking a smile made him hurt.

"Can I do anything for you or get you something?" I asked.

"No, I'm good. Thanks."

"Stanley called your wife. I understand she's getting someone to cover for her, and she's on the way."

Johnny's wife worked as a nurse at Saint Mary's Hospital in Knoxville. He nodded again, almost half asleep.

"Okay, kid, I don't want to keep you up. When your wife gets here, she'll probably yell at you, so save your strength. I'm going to find your doctor and have a chat. I'll leave my number at the nurse's station in case you need anything. If you do, have them call me or Bettye back at the barn. Now, take care of yourself, and do what you're told."

He nodded. "Thanks for coming, boss. See y'all in a day or two."

When I returned to the nurse's desk, the woman with whom I'd spoken earlier introduced me to a young doctor who looked Filipino. From him, I learned that the toxicology people had gotten right to work on the analysis of the contents of Johnny's stomach. Their report said the General Tso's chicken they tested contained enough atropine to either treat half the county for exposure to anthrax or kill a large-sized water buffalo. Young Rutledge was lucky John Gallagher arranged for an ambulance as quickly as he did and the ER crew spared no time pumping the poison out of his stomach.

I felt a great compulsion to roust the local members of the Coalition for American Family Values.

Chapter Nine

John Gallagher walked into the house at 7:00 a.m., just as I came downstairs for breakfast. Harley Flatt arrived to relieve him an hour early because of all the excitement the night before.

Kate wore her most unrevealing and conservative robe in deference to our guest. She looked good after spending considerable time tidying up her hair before setting the table and making a large pot of coffee for the three of us.

My wife usually sits down to breakfast wearing a sexy, low-cut negligee and sporting a slightly tousled 'bedroom' hairstyle. I usually want to have sex before breakfast five out of seven days a week. That morning the sex had to wait; I behaved like the ultimate professional.

As I stepped into the kitchen, I heard John telling Kate about his adventure.

"Hey, Sam." John only calls me Sam in front of my wife. "How's it goin'?"

I kissed Kate for the second or third time that morning before cutting a slice of crusty Tuscan bread.

"Hi, John. How's the hero of Prospect doing this morning?"

"Oh, man, what a night!" he said. "How could that crazy kid eat the poison food?"

I shrugged. "Good work last night. I'm proud of you. You're right back in the groove—just like the old days."

He gave me a stupid grin while he poured a cup of coffee. "Want a cup?" he asked.

"Sure."

"John, have you been awake all night?" Kate asked.

"I snoozed a little, but I was reading magazines most of the night. C.J. gave them to me. I think she likes me."

I snorted. "You may be the only one. That woman's a misandrist."

"A what?

"She hates men."

"Yeah?"

"Yeah!"

John raised his eyebrows. "Maybe she just hates you?"

I glared at him.

"John, if you're going to meet Glenda Mae again this morning, why don't I call her and see if she can back up your appointment until later this morning?" Kate suggested. "That will give you a chance to sleep for a couple of hours."

"Okay, if you don't mind."

"What's going on?" I asked. "Isn't Mae going to send John out with one of her saleswomen at 9 o'clock?"

"Yes," Kate said," but it's a good idea for him to get at least a *couple* hours sleep."

I frowned at Kate.

"Maybe they can wait until eleven," I suggested, not wanting things to drag out too long. "You going to square that away for him?"

"I will." She rolled her eyes, but knew I wanted John to find a house ASAP.

"I'm gonna grab a quick shower," John said. "I'll get some breakfast later."

"Suit yourself, buddy. I'm leaving as soon as I finish eating. See you later."

John took a big sip of coffee and headed upstairs.

"Aren't you pushing him a little hard?" Kate asked. "He's not a kid, you know."

"He'll get enough rest. Besides, I thought you'd like your privacy back as quickly as possible."

"Yes, I would, but I don't want to find him dead in the guest room."

As Kate talked, I gobbled down pieces of ham and white cheddar from my plowman's breakfast.

"You're one of the world's biggest pessimists, sweetie," I said.

Kate threw her napkin at me. "Don't talk with your mouth full."

The cloth bounced off my forehead.

"People say you look ten years younger than your age, but that's no reason to behave like a child, Katherine—really."

She smiled. "You love every bit of me."

"I do. Wanna have a quickie in the pantry while John is in the shower?"

"Eat your breakfast, and go to work."

* * * *

When I walked into the office at 8:10, Bettye didn't give me a chance to get my jacket off.

"Sam, have you seen Johnny? Stanley left me a note. Is Johnny okay?"

I explained the situation and made her feel better about things. Bettye not only plays the role of desk officer and administrative sergeant, but den mother to the eleven men at Prospect PD.

For the next hour, I tended to the logistics that go with a fiasco. Bettye said the radio had been quiet, and only a few requests for police assistance came in on the phone line. So, it looked like my pair of would-be gumshoes could take a break from their patrol duties for part of the morning. She called in Junior Huskey and Bobby John Crockett, and I briefed them on how to handle the Collinson gang.

"I'm sure you've heard the scuttlebutt about what happened to Johnny Rutledge last night," I said. "So far he's doing okay and should be released in a day or two."

They said they had heard, made a few comments and asked a few general questions.

"I want to treat the old written threats and the new poisoning as separate and maybe unrelated things for right now," I said. "You two concentrate on the notes."

Junior and Bobby nodded.

"Be sure not to mention the poison to the Collinsons and Goins until you've got an idea where these people are with the notes."

Junior frowned, and Bobby looked impassive.

I tried to clarify. "If you think they are the ones responsible for writing the notes and intend to send more threats."

The pair nodded again. A light had gone on.

"I want to work another angle with the Coalition to see if they say something about any plans to harm C.J. This crew may think it's their 1st Amendment rights to verbally attack her, and they might make a specific threat."

"Harm her?" Junior said. "Don't ya think poisonin' sorta makes it attempted murder?"

"Sure, that's what I'd charge them with, but that team isn't made up of three great intellects. If they hear the M word or even attempted M, they may get spooked and lay low. The Coalition has no history of violence or even personal confrontations. These morons may have only wanted to make C.J. sick enough to drive her out of Prospect. They're stupid enough to think a couple of ounces of atropine in the chow mein would only cause a tummy ache."

"I don't like chow mein myself," Junior said.

"Naw, it ain't spicy enough for me," Bobby told him. "I'm kinda partial to any o' that Kung Pao stuff."

"Guys?" I interrupted. "I just used chow mein as a generic Chinese term. It was actually General Tso's chicken."

They smiled and re-focused.

"I suppose Goins may be working in the park today," I said. "But I'm not sure. The maintenance crews work seven days a week, and I don't know his schedule. So, you two concentrate on Mack and his mother. Walk into their office like you own it. If there's a customer, tell them to get out and come back. Do a good cop—bad cop act. But for God's sake don't smack an old lady around. Think of yourselves as nasty cop and sweet, understanding cop."

"We kin do that," Junior said.

"I've never liked Mack Collinson, that hairy-faced booger," Bobby said.

"In case you weren't told," I said. "Jenny Mitchell, C.J.'s assistant, said the notes looked like they were typewritten, not printed on a computer. So if these ya-hoos have an old conventional typewriter... Work with that. Any questions?"

90

"Y'all want us ta check with you before we do anything?" Bobby asked.

"I won't be around for most of the day. Do what you think is best—within reason. If you have any doubts, ask Bettye—or John Gallagher if he's here. As another famous New York detective used to say, 'Use your intelligence, guided by experience'".

After Junior and Bobby left, I briefed Ronnie Shields on the incident of the night before. The mayor never thought such villains could transact their illicit business in his quiet little city. After telling him my tale and painting John Gallagher as the unlikely hero, Ronnie approved John's official employment date to start before the next pay period began and promised to get the Finance section to struggle through the extra work of a single person on a special payroll run.

When I finished my sales pitch, Ronnie believed that he'd have to look far and wide to get a former hundred-thousand-dollar-a-year senior detective on board for clerk-typist pay. John had retired long before anyone from our department made such a salary, but Ronnie didn't need to know that truth.

After taking a short breather back in my office, I called the county health department and booked dates for Dallas Finchum to get medical and psychological exams. Once he passed those, I'd schmooze the sheriff's polygraph examiner to make room for him and administer a standard pre-employment test.

Next, I touched base with the chief of Pigeon Forge PD and the sheriff of Sevier County. Although I asked Harley Flatt to alert the cops detailed to assist us with C.J.'s security about the attempt to poison her, I spoke to the big guys personally and asked for a little help tracking down any members of the Coalition for American Family Values in their jurisdictions.

Then I called Ralph Oliveri. I didn't know what he and the FBI computers could find to help me, but I brought him up to speed on last night's event and asked for the most recent chatter they heard from the coalition of self-proclaimed guardians of truth, justice and the American way.

* * * *

My first telephone call to WNXX didn't find Rachel Williamson in her office, so I tried her cell phone. On the seventh ring the voice mail kicked in. My patience for voice mail is not something I'd brag about, but I waited for the beep, thinking the woman could drive me to drink early in the day.

"Come on, Rocky," I snapped, "if you're not at work, you must be at home or someplace where you can hear your cell phone. Unless you're doing your hair, call me as soon as possible."

She picked up a second before I broke the connection.

"Boy, I wish my mother never told you about the nickname those kids gave me in high school." She sounded a little out of breath.

"Yeah, mothers say things during times of stress best left unmentioned. Don't worry, I won't tell anyone unless I have to."

"You wouldn't dare!"

"I might, now that I know how much the secret means to you. It's amazing how I learn things."

"You are so mean."

"I have a history of playing the bad cop."

"You're worse than that."

"Yes, but I'm cute and cuddly, and Mizz News-lady, I call bearing gifts. How about an exclusive on the attempted poisoning of C.J. Profitt?"

That stopped her cold.

"What?' she asked. "What happened? This I've got to hear."

"Yes, my lovely friend, now that I've got your attention, you do."

I gave her all the gory details and ended with, "And my cop, even though tasting the food was stupid, had C.J.'s best interest at heart. He's just a hopeless fan, so maybe you shouldn't mention what he did and that he ended up the hospital."

"Why?"

"Because he'd only be more embarrassed than he already is."

"What do you want me to say?"

"Tell everyone that when our cops thought something didn't look kosher with the food delivery, they sent it to the lab at Blount Memorial who discovered the poison and leave it at that. Will you do that for your old buddy?"

"Kosher Chinese food?"

"Don't get smart."

"Of course, old buddy. I just love it when you owe me another one."

"And Johnny Rutledge owes you one, too. The kid isn't really stupid. He just should have listened to his more experienced partner."

"You mean your new clerk-typist?"

"Police operations aide. John has feelings to consider. Actually, I've sworn him in as an auxiliary cop and plan to make him an honorary detective—for old time's sake."

"You're a piece of work, Jenkins."

"Thank you."

"I won't bother to ask how you pull off these things because you'd only give me some line about trade secrets. But I want to know how you think up some of this stuff."

"It's why I get the big bucks, baby."

"Okay, hotshot, I hate to report I've had no luck finding any dirt on C.J., but it's the truth. I'll try again in Nashville. There's a reporter at our affiliate there who's been around the city for twenty years. I'll check with him. If he doesn't know, he may know a cop who does. I promise, I'll get you something."

"Or your name isn't Brenda Starr."

"If I dye my hair red will you wear a patch on your eye?"

"That's a nice thing to say, and I'd love to be your mysterious boyfriend, but I was going to be snotty and call you Rocky again."

"Hey, mister."

"Bye, Mizz Williamson."

* * * *

The forty-five-minute drive to Dollywood took me along a north-bound leg of Highway 321, through the mountains on a winding two lane road with only a few other vehicles traveling in either direction. Most of the rental cabins dotting the landscape were closed up, waiting for the vacationers who come to the Smokies for the spring wildflowers. Many of the small businesses along the road were also boarded up, their proprietors having fled to Florida to escape the expected cold temperatures we had yet to receive.

When I reached the intersection of the Dolly Parton Parkway, I turned right and mingled with the vehicles driven by people shopping in the hundreds of outlet stores that make Pigeon Forge what it is today. I turned left into Dollywood and found the music hall.

After speaking with two deputies parked outside, I entered the building to find Harley Flatt and his partner from Pigeon Forge PD. Harley pointed at C.J., sitting in the third row, center stage, watching a skinny young guy with a big black cowboy hat singing to a cute blonde who made more money in a year than my entire budget for the police department. I saw Jenny Mitchell standing in one of the aisles talking to a man and walked over.

"Hello, Jenny," I said. "Everything going okay?"

"Oh, hi, Chief," she said. "So far everything's fine. How's the policeman doing?"

"Got a stomachache, but he'll be okay in a couple of days. Right now he's getting pampered in the hospital."

She smiled like someone who genuinely cared about Johnny.

"Chief, I'd like you to meet my father. Chief Jenkins—Robert Mitchell."

We shook hands. He had a firm grip

"Sam Jenkins… Nice to meet you."

"Call me Bob. Good to meet you, too. Thanks for looking out for my little girl. She called last night to tell me what happened. Hell of a thing isn't it? I started driving right after we spoke and got here a short time ago. It didn't take too long."

"I'll do my best to protect Jenny and C.J. while they're here," I said. "I just hope when they leave, the threats stop and so does all this mischief. Though, I tend to think it won't."

"Why do you say that?" Mitchell asked.

"Just a feeling at this point. I may know more after I talk with someone who's trying to develop a few leads for me. And I plan on picking up a few members of this Coalition who signed the notes. I'll see what they have to say for themselves."

"So, you've already identified someone?"

"Not exactly," I said. "We've got a few suspects, but no proof yet. I think poison is a drastic measure to get C.J. out of sleepy little Prospect, but it looks like someone has a genuine desire to harm her—here or elsewhere."

Bob Mitchell shook his head and looked at his daughter. She put her arms around him.

Mitchell looked to be in his mid-fifties, about five-foot-ten and well put together. He had short gray hair and a ruddy complexion, suggesting lots of outdoor activity. He seemed intelligent, but more from a blue-collar background than a grown-up rich kid. From the way he moved, I guessed he was either ex-military or a cop. His actions suggested more than just an athletic bearing. He did simple things with little wasted motion.

"You know how to take care of your daughter," I said. "You got here when she needed fatherly support. Did you take time off from work, or were you on vacation?"

"Right now, Sam, life's one big vacation for me. I recently retired, and I'm enjoying it living in Virginia. I've got plenty of time to help you keep an eye on my daughter."

"You look pretty young to be retired," I said. "Did some civil service system allow you to do that?"

He shook his head and smiled. "I was an engineer and lucky enough to be financially able to pull the pin before I got too old to enjoy myself."

I knew the feeling. I used to hear people say I'd been too young to retire. Well, good for him. So far I liked Bob Mitchell.

"I can't help asking, Bob, but do you think we've met before? You look very familiar."

"I don't think so. I believe I'd remember you."

"Have you lived in Virginia all your life?"

He didn't speak with much of a southern accent.

"I was born there, but moved around a lot with my work. How about you? You don't sound like a Tennessee native."

"No, I'm a New Yorker. I retired myself and came here fourteen years ago."

"I'll think about it," he said, "but I don't believe we've met. I didn't get to New York very often."

"I will as well. Of course, I'm getting pretty old and experience more than my share of senior moments to impede my thought process." Bob laughed.

Jenny said, "I can't believe that."

"I've got to get back to the other side of the mountains," I said. "Bob, good to meet you. Jenny, make sure your boss listens to Harley and does what he says. See you folks again."

I left through the lobby entrance.

All the way back to Prospect, I wondered how I would approach the three Coalition members about the poisoned Chinese food. I ran several scenarios through my head, but still wasn't sure of the best method. Then, as I traversed the section of US 321 called the Inez Burns Parkway, a stretch of steep, winding road close to Townsend, I knew what I'd do—or what I'd have someone do for me.

Chapter Ten

When I arrived back at the Prospect Pickle Factory, I saw that Bettye had everything under control.

"Just to let you know what's happenin', Sammy darlin'," she said. "Johnny Rutledge was released this mornin'. His wife is takin' a few days off until she thinks he's okay to be on his own."

"Sounds good."

"He'll get his own full-time nurse for as long as she thinks he needs one. Your friend Ralph called and has some information for you. Y'all need to call him before too long."

"Yes, ma'am."

"John Gallagher called and wanted to know what's the story about earnest money. He'd never heard of it before. So I told him. Sounds like he may have found a house.

"That may be the best news I've heard all morning."

She gave me a quick nod and continued. "And Stanley called askin' about Johnny and all, and wanted to know what you had planned. Y'all need to call him, too."

"Yes, ma'am, again."

"And a few minutes ago Junior was on the radio sayin' he's made an arrest of a woman and is on the way in."

"I could go on vacation and not be missed."

"Not so, sugar. "How's your day been goin'?"

She made me feel superfluous.

Before I answered Bettye, a bearded man wearing a wrinkled, brown wool sport jacket and brown shirt buttoned at the neck burst into the lobby. From photos periodically shown in local newspaper ads, I recognized Mack Collinson.

"My momma's sixty-five-year-old. Jest whot in the hell's them cops doin' arrestin' her?" he yelled.

Junior's radio transmission interrupted Mack's bluster.

"501 ta headquarters, me an' 507 are 10-36 at the back door with that female 10-32. Mileage 56,441. Time check, please."

Bettye acknowledged the call and stated the correct time for the record. I assumed Mack Collinson hadn't finished squawking yet.

"That mean my momma's here now?"

"Uh-huh," I said without enthusiasm.

"I wanna see her, damn it, an' I wanna see her now!"

"Mr. Collinson?" I asked.

"Damn rot!" he said." An' don'chew think y'all kin push me around none! I wanna see Momma an' I wanna see her *rot now*!" He stretched out the last two words for emphasis.

I figured Mack must be thinking: *Ain't no Yankee po-leece-man gonna push Mack Collinson aroun', nosir.*

I smiled, outwardly, to look like the friendly civil servant, but mostly to annoy him. "I'm Chief Jenkins, and I might let you see your mother...if you calm down and keep quiet."

"You ain't gonna git away—"

I lost the smile. "Hey!" I yelled.

He stopped.

"You either shut up, or I'll take you to see Momma in handcuffs. Capiche?"

Mack started to open his bearded mouth again when I cut him short. "One more word and I'll lock your ass up for disorderly conduct. My last instructions were for you to shut up." I scowled. "I insist. Understand?"

He nodded, blew out a big breath and put both hands defiantly on his hips. All three buttons of his jacket were closed, but when he moved his arms, I saw his pants belt had at least a dozen holes, more than half of them crudely added with a Phillip's head screw driver or some other not so sharp object. I guessed that as old Mack lost weight—from the span of excess belt, perhaps thirty or forty pounds—he added holes. I tried to imagine him that much larger and wondered if he had been twenty-five percent more obnoxious.

"Okay," I said. "I'm going into the back room to see your mother and the two officers who arrested her."

Mack tried to speak again, but I held up a hand to stop him.

"Goddamnit, what part of *shut up* don't you understand?"

He blew out another breath and made a face showing his disgust and frustration. After a long moment, he looked at Bettye and then back at me.

"Once I know what's happening," I said, "I'll get back to you. And if you behave yourself, I may let you speak with her. But maybe not. It depends on you. We clear so far?"

He kept staring at me in a way a melodramatic writer might call *with venom in his gaze*. But to me that snake was just a mook in need of intense supervision.

"Have a seat out here, and wait." I pointed to a row of chairs against the wall.

I walked back to the squad room and met Elnora Rae Collinson. She seemed calmer than her son and from my first impression not as stupid. But one look at Ma and any cop worth their salt would see her as a potentially nasty customer.

"Officer Crockett, would you begin the arrest report?" I said. "Officer Huskey, step outside, please."

Junior and I went into the juvenile interview room for privacy. I closed the door.

"I hope you plan on charging her with more than being ugly," I said.

Junior laughed. "Yup, gonna charge her with six counts o' aggravated harassment."

"No kidding? Explain."

"Well, me an' Bobby, we goes inta the office there, and that hairy-faced fool, the son, is out front. So, I tell him we wanna see him an' his momma. She musta heard me 'cause she yells somethin' like 'I'm in here,' and somethin' else. So me and Bobby and stupid goes inta her office."

"Sounds like you're really impressed by Mack Collinson."

"I'd like ta beat the fool outta him."

Junior is a pretty easygoing guy, but he sounded serious.

"Steady there, big feller. Finish your story."

Junior grinned and continued. "Then Bobby starts tellin' them we wanna talk about this Coalition o' Family Values business, and while he's doin' that, I see this closet door open jest a little."

I wish I had a nickel for every time a cop told me that one.

I smiled. "Open just a little?"

"Yessir. So I take my toe an' opens it jest a little more, and I see this tan case that looks like an ol' portable typewriter."

"Wow, convenient."

"Yessir. So I pick it up and says 'What's this?' The ol' lady, she says, 'What's it look like, son? It's a typewriter.' So I says, 'I'll bet when I take a sample o' typewritin' I can match it up to them hateful notes C.J. Profitt got in the mail.'"

"Very sharp."

"Thank ya. Well, sir, then Mack, the stupid one, he goes, 'Don' say nuthin', Momma.' But the ol' lady, she ignores him and says, 'You damn rot I sent them notes. Ain't no one else done took the bull by the horns ta keep that ungodly lesbian outta Prospect. I figgered I would.' Then I arrested her."

"Was that a verbatim account of your conversation?"

"If ya mean is that exactly like it happened, yessir."

"Good job, kid. Only forget the part about your toe helping the plain view doctrine. The closet was open wide enough for you to have seen the typewriter case, right?"

"Yes, sir, I hear that."

"Did she make that remark about the notes spontaneously, or did you ask her something first?"

"Didn't have to ask nuthin', she just said it like she's proud of herse'f. Anyways, she can say she wasn't advised o' her rights and can take back the statement. I don't care." He smiled and waited for my inevitable question.

"Okay, I'll bite. Why don't you care?"

"Cause, I figgered if I check on the typewriter ribbon, I might could find evidence o' what she typed. What do ya think o' that?"

"I'd think it would be outstanding po-leece work if you found something."

"I shore did. Looks like mebbe two different notes, fer as I can see, mebbe more."

"You guys are like Batman and Robin. I'm impressed. Now I'm going to speak with her shithead son. Bettye will do the booking page, and then I want to talk with the old lady again. Hang in there, kid. You and I can get together when you write the prosecution worksheet. And I'll see who I can send the ribbon to so we can get a lab technician's take on how many hate notes they can trace to the same machine."

"Sounds like a favor from your FBI friends."

"Nothing gets past you, Junior."

I returned to the lobby, and Bettye adjourned to the squad room to officially book in the prisoner. I decided to face the music and confront Mack, the mutt.

"Mr. Collinson, I understand your mother admitted to sending C.J. Profitt several pieces of what we call hate mail. That's a serious crime."

He jumped up, looking just as agitated as before. "I ain't sayin' nuthin' 'cept that lezbian bitch ain't got no rot bein' in this town with the rest o' us good Christian people."

I shook my head. "Gee, I guess you missed the part about love thy neighbor in Sunday school."

"Do whot?"

"Forget it. Your mother's under arrest for aggravated harassment. When we get finished processing the arrest, I'll give her the choice of getting arraigned today or being released on bail to appear in court sometime in the future. You understand what I just said?"

"I heard ya."

"Good. You don't need to see her before we're finished."

"Damn you, Jinkins! Y'all thank you kin push us around 'cause you ain't from around here. Big shot po-leece chief, ain't ya?"

I wanted to stick out my tongue and give him the raspberries, but remained the consummate professional. "You finished?" I asked.

He assumed the same posture as before, with his hands on his hips, shook his head and blew out a big breath.

"If you think she wants to get bailed out—and I'm guessing she will—she'll need $150.00. That's $25.00 on each of the six charges. All things considered, I think that's a bargain."

He screwed up his nose and snorted.

"If you haven't got the cash, go and get it. We'll wait patiently for your return."

He snorted again. Maybe it was his impression of a feral Smoky Mountain hog.

I heard Bettye walk back to her desk and return the booking log to the top drawer.

Mack needed to have the last word. "You thank yer somethin' special, don'cha, Jinkins? Ya know whot? Yer nuthin' ta me, mister."

With that said, the nitwit stormed out, perhaps to find the closest ATM.

I turned around and looked at Bettye. She flashed a big smile and said, "Well, Jinkins, whotcha thank o' that?"

"Oh, I could have just slapped him so hard."

* * * *

While waiting for her witling of a son to fetch the bail money, I listened to Ma Collinson's manifesto on the evils of lesbianism and other unnatural and ungodly behavior—her words, not mine—and how someone *needed* to protect the citizenry of Prospect from *those* people.

After we had gotten to know each other better, I asked why her friend tried to poison C.J.

"Well, it weren't no friend o' mine," she said.

"You know who did it?"

"Don't know what yer talkin' about."

"C.J. wasn't poisoned, you know. One of the police officers guarding her tasted the food."

I wanted to see if she reacted. Nothing.

"He felt sick and got his stomach pumped," I said.

Still not a flicker.

"You see how long it took to pin the hate mail on you. If I learn you or your son or Jeremy Goins or any Coalition member poisoned the food, I'll come down on you like a ton of bricks."

Elnora shook her head and snorted like an old sow.

"I ain't sorry someone tried," she said. "But I am sorry that young po-leeceman done took what was in-tended for that lesbian. But it was his own stupid fault. Mebbe he learnt him a lesson."

"You think C.J. Profitt deserves to die because of her sexual preferences?"

"All queers an' lesbians need ta be kilt."

I think my eyes popped at that one.

"It's all con-trary ta God's law," she said. "Us good Christian folk shouldn't oughta be subjected ta the likes o' her or others o' the same kind. Whot's our chil'ren gonna think if'n these people's allowed ta walk our streets an' do whot they wanna do?"

She waited for an answer.

I shrugged and tried to look genuinely stumped. "Beats me."

I guess that was the wrong answer.

She snapped, "You ain't one, are ya?"

I couldn't resist that opportunity, so I put on a serious look and asked, "One what?"

"Oh, Lord have mercy."

"I know I'm going to hate like hell to ask this, but philosophically speaking..."

I spent fifteen additional minutes talking with Elnora. When my head felt like it was about to explode, I stopped, cursed myself for ever starting the conversation and stomped out to the lobby to collect the bail money from Mack. While Bettye wrote out the bail receipt, I downed a half-dozen Advil. Bettye took the promise-to-appear form into the squad room and obtained a signature from Elnora Hitler. While Bettye was enjoying Ma Collinson's company, her desk phone rang.

"Prospect Police, Chief Jenkins speaking, may I help you?"

"This here's Hub Welchance. Lemme speak ta the chief."

I sighed, dropped my chin on my chest and spoke again.

"This *is* Chief Jenkins. What can I do for you?"

"Ya kin quit questionin' my client, that's whot."

"To whom am I speaking, please?"

"Hub Welchance," he repeated.

"Well, Hub, ol' buddy, who's your client, what kind of client do you have, and what do you want?"

"Jinkins, ya say? How'd y'all spell that?"

Tough question, but I answered.

Then he said, "I represent Mrs. Elnora Rae Collinson. I want ya ta cease and desist any futher questionin' of her rot now, hear?"

I just love guys like that. I figured it was time to implement Jenkins' theory of how to annoy an attorney.

"And your name again, sir?"

"Do whot? Oh, Hubble A. Welchance, esquire, attorney at law, specializin' in civil rots vi'lations—pro-tectin' the civil and God-given rots o' white folks."

"Is that Welchance with one L or two?"

"Huh?"

"How do you spell your last name, sir?"

"You never heard o' me?"

"No, sir. Have you not heard of me?"

"You? No, I don't know ya."

"Oh, too bad. One L or two?"

"One."

"What kind of a name is Welchance?"

"What kinda name?"

"Uh-huh. I'm interested in genealogy."

"Lord have mercy, my family's been here fer, I don't know, more'n a hunnert years. It's a Tennessee name."

"Thanks. How many Bs?"

"Do whot?"

"Spell Hubble for me."

He did.

"Thanks again. Whaddaya need, Mr. Hubble?"

"Damn, son! It's Mr. Welchance, and I already done tol' ya! Y'all are ta stop questionin' my client till I git there."

"Where are you coming from?"

"Why, Knoxville, o' course."

"Don't bother. My sergeant is about to release Mrs. Collinson on bail. Talk to your client later, and you can represent her at arraignment. She'll tell you all about the arrest."

"Well, why in the hell didn't ya say so, son?"

"I just did. Have a nice day, Hub." I hung up.

Five minutes later, Ma Collinson used our restroom, Junior and Bobby John came to the lobby, and Bettye asked who I'd been speaking with. Without obvious emotion, I told her.

"Hubble Welchance?" she said.

"Uh–huh."

"The Hubble Welchance?"

"Gimme a break, Blondie."

She wrinkled her nose at the nickname. "Well, aren't you honored?"

"Am I?"

"Yes, sir, you sure are. Hubble Welchance has represented just about every extreme right-wing idiot that's come up on charges in East Tennessee for years. He makes a living at it."

"He any good?"

"Depends on your point o' view. You'd say he's a butt-hole."

"I'd use different nouns, but I understand."

I looked at Mack Collinson who stood a few feet away watching us.

"You have something to say?" I asked.

As if I had flicked a switch, his eyes widened, and Mack went into action. "You ain't heard the last o' this, Jinkins!"

I shook my head, barely able to believe his act. "Mommy will be out in just a minute." I pointed to his previously occupied chair. "Now sit down like a good little boy, or I'll comb your beard with a chain saw."

The oaf mumbled something, but sat again. Bettye covered her mouth to hide a snicker, and I dropped into the chair next to Bettye's desk.

After Elnora emerged from the powder room, the pair of miscreants left the lobby, and I spoke to Bettye. "You're a lot better than Junior."

"Hey, whadda ya mean?" Junior asked.

I ignored the question. "He giggles all over the place when I talk to people like those two. You're a real pro. You keep a straight face no matter how humorous I get."

"You were trying to be funny?"

"Pfui. Now excuse me while I practice being mean so I can do battle with the F. Lee Bailey of the Skin Heads."

Chapter Eleven

After our happy little police department returned to normal and I went back into my office, I noticed a report from Neal Brickman, the sheriff's crime scene technician who checked out C.J.'s motel suite and the grounds around it. He found nothing to identify a subject responsible for the poisoning—not a latent fingerprint, shoe impression or thread of physical evidence to link a certain someone with the attempted murder, should I ever find a decent suspect. A few minutes later, I heard a familiar voice in the lobby.

"Hi, Sarge, how's it goin'?" John Gallagher sat on Bettye's side chair.

As time marched on and they were still talking, I felt neglected and walked out of my office and stood in the lobby. I cleared my throat.

John turned in my direction. "Hi, boss. How's it goin'?"

"I'm good, John. How's by you?" I imitated his dopey delivery.

"I bought a house today, boss. I was just tellin' the Sarge about it."

"Good for you. Where is it?" Before he could respond, I added another thought. "More importantly, did you stay within your budget?"

He described the area of Prospect where he'd be living and assured me he had gotten a good buy. I was proud of him again. My sixty-seven-year-old surrogate son would soon be moving out.

"I'm glad you found a house," I said. "Now you're going back out there to look at some more. Follow me."

From John's reaction, it looked like I just asked him to walk down Main Street naked. But he better understood my intent when I explained that I wanted him to go to Collinson Realty and tell them he needed a house. He'd use the same story he told Mae Waddell, but keep his price range much lower so they wouldn't look at the same houses a second time and chance being recognized by a seller he had already met. That shouldn't have been problem because the Collinsons weren't famous for selling up-scale properties.

"Tell these right-wing lunatics you're a retired New York cop," I said. "They're in favor of law and order and everything that would make the country revert to the innocent days when America was a better place."

"Innocent what?" John's confused look prompted me to elaborate.

"You know, the days of slavery, no votes for women, segregation and McCarthyism. Get the idea?

"Sure, boss. You want me to scam them. Make them admit something."

"You're such a smart boy."

John Gallagher was a natural for the job. Even if he walked into their office and told those sociopathic reptiles he was a cop working undercover, they would never believe him.

* * * *

Tuesday turned out to be uneventful for C.J. and Jenny. Harley Flatt stayed with them all day, and Len Alcock worked the overnight shift watching the motel. John Gallagher offered an extra pair of eyes and entertained Lenny with his inane stories from 8 p.m. until midnight.

I also felt better knowing Bob Mitchell had booked a room at the Foothills View for the rest of the week, staying close to Jenny. I'd take as many friendly eyes and ears as I could get.

Ralph Oliveri faxed several clear surveillance photos of my gruesome threesome and information on and pictures of a few additional members of the Coalition for American Family Values that FBI photographers had taken at a demonstration held on the previous Martin Luther King Day. Mack and Elnora Collinson showed prominently in that group, too, as did Jeremy Goins.

Other than Ma's recent arrest, Mack and his mother had no criminal record. Jeremy, on the other hand, had an interesting past. Once a federal ranger in the Great Smoky Mountains National Park, Goins lost that position after he got jammed up for beating two gay men he found one night parked in a lonely area, engaging in consensual sodomy. While this act, most often a simple misdemeanor, still remains on the books in many states, the Supreme Court has ruled that sex between two consenting adults, regardless of their respective sexes, is not a crime.

Apparently, that premise, acceptable to the nine wise jurists of Washington, was not something Jeremy chose to allow in his patrol sector. When one of the embarrassed gentlemen questioned Ranger Goins' decision to collar them, Jeremy viewed the act as resisting arrest and proceeded to tune up both defendants, causing them to require emergency treatment at the Fort Sanders Medical Center in Sevierville.

Ordinarily an incident like that could have gotten Ranger Goins not only fired, but criminally prosecuted in the state courts for assault and possibly in the Federal system for perpetrating a hate crime. But homophobic Jeremy had a lucky day. One of the individuals was married and didn't want details of the incident getting back to his family. The second arrestee went along with his newfound partner.

The park manager happily paid the freight at the emergency room and obtained signed statements from the two men ensuring the Department of the Interior that they held no one to blame for the tragic misunderstanding which took place on government property.

Shortly thereafter, Jeremy's political 'rabbi', a Blount County commissioner, came to his rescue and arranged for a transfer to the maintenance division in lieu of losing his job. With the generous overtime available to those assigned to the maintenance crews, the reassignment amounted to a sizable raise in pay. Injustices like that are not uncommon in government work.

When next I took my daily ride to Dollywood, I'd show the FBI photos to C.J. and Jenny and see if any of the faces rang a bell.

* * * *

I stepped through my office doorway heading for lunch when Dallas Finchum walked into in the lobby. He had again dressed in a jacket and tie and came close to being spit-shined from ear to ear. As I watched him speaking with Bettye, she held up a hand indicating he should wait and picked up the receiver from her telephone console. Just before she pushed the intercom button, I spoke.

"Looking for me, Sarge?"

"Yes, sir. Dallas is back already with the applications and other paperwork."

She smiled, and her expression almost said, 'See I told you he's a nice boy.'

"He's all finished," she said. "I thought you'd like to see him."

"I would, thanks. Dallas, come into my office."

He followed me and remained standing until I invited him to sit.

"I've got everything finished, sir." He sounded enthusiastic.

I reached across my desk, and he hopped up to hand me a 9x12 manila envelope stuffed with the completed forms. His navy blue blazer and gray slacks looked like something I'd wear. I took the papers out and laid them on my blotter. I sat and pointed toward his chair, again inviting him to plant it.

"Jesus, kid, it's only been twenty-four hours since I saw you last. Did you stay up all night to finish this stuff?"

"Almost all night, sir. I worked on it since I left you yesterday." He allowed himself a smile. "But I did get a couple hours sleep."

I thumbed through the applications and the questionnaires, scanning his work. Everything looked neat and complete. Dallas impressed me.

"This looks good. And that's a good start."

He beamed at the compliment.

"I've got you scheduled with the health department for one day late next week. Stop back at Sergeant Lambert's desk before you go, and she'll give you the exact times. Once you pass those tests, you'll go for a polygraph exam at the sheriff's office."

He nodded enthusiastically.

"We'll do your background investigation here. A man who just started working with us has a lot of experience with candidate investigations. You'll be hearing from a Detective Gallagher. Do I have all the phone numbers we'll need to contact you?"

"Yes, sir. I got me a cell phone now so ya can contact me any time ya need ta."

"At your first interview with Detective Gallagher, he'll show you how we want the statements written and teach you how he expects any additional work submitted."

"Yes, sir. I'd like ta learn."

I nodded, and Dallas looked so happy, I thought he'd burst.

"For right now, I think you're good to go. Thanks for all the effort."

"Yes, sir. You're welcome, sir. Thank ya for givin' me the chance."

We shook hands, and he stopped to speak with Bettye before he left.

To fortify myself for the ride to Pigeon Forge, I went to Howell's Pub for a barbeque pork sandwich, a pint of Bass Ale and a stimulating conversation with the English bartender, Reginald Smethurst. Had I anticipated the hassle C.J. would hand me, I would have drunk two pints.

* * * *

Floodlights illuminated the stage, orchestra, and first three rows of seats in the music hall, but the rest of the audience area remained dark. Bob and Jenny Mitchell sat in aisle seats in front of a Pigeon Forge cop named Rusty Filmore. A piano player and guitarist practiced something that could have been the theme song from an old cowboy movie. C.J. Profitt and Harley Flatt were not yet in attendance.

I said my hellos and learned I could find C.J. in her dressing room; Harley was standing guard. Two minutes later, I walked down a hallway and found him sitting on an uncomfortable-looking folding chair just outside C.J.'s room.

"What do you say, bud? Miss Personality in here?" I pointed to a door with a five-pointed star hanging three-quarters of the way up.

He nodded. "Mornin', boss."

"She alive and well?"

"None too friendly, but she's alive last time I seen her."

"Is she studying her lines, sleeping or eating Chinese take-out?"

"Beats the hell outta me, I'm jest the hired he'p."

A holstered .40 caliber Glock hung on his right hip. When he crossed his legs, I saw a half-sized version of the same gun strapped to his ankle.

I banged the side of my hand on the door.

"C.J., open the door. I need to speak with you." I sounded loud enough to wake the dead.

"I'm trying to sleep. Go away."

"You had all night to sleep. If you haven't got your clothes on, get dressed. In sixty seconds I'm opening the door." I turned toward Harley and spoke with less volume. "This job gives me plenty of other aggravation and a hell of a lot to do. I don't need her being such an uncooperative pain in the ass."

Harley looked at me and grinned like the Cheshire Cat. The door swung open, and Miss Attitude greeted me.

"Who the hell do you think you're talkin' to?" she yelled.

I moved the arm she had stretched across the doorway and walked into her dressing room. It was a mess. Like something a teenager might live in. And I always thought gay people would be neat.

I snapped at her. "You and I have business to transact."

She snorted, picked a couple articles of clothing off the chair from in front of a vanity table and tossed them across the room.

"I don't need to battle with you today, C.J. I may have a lead on who tried to poison you, so don't give me grief."

She screwed up her face in disgust. "Yeah, right. You're more concerned that your cop got poisoned. Just go away."

I let that go and focused on business. "I want you to take a good look at some photographs."

"You know, the other cops leave me alone. You are a *pain in the ass*," she said.

I didn't feel happy, but I smiled anyway. "I get the most money, so I offer the extra service. If it wasn't for one of us pains-in-the-ass, you'd be choking on your moo goo gai pan."

"General Tso's chicken."

"Who cares?" I said. "Sit down, and look at these pictures."

She wrapped the belt of a light robe around her waist and stuck out a hand. I offered the envelope of photographs. She snatched them and sat.

"The FBI took them at some anti-everything rally. These are the local members of the coalition who wrote you the love notes."

"You found out who did it?"

"Uh-huh."

"Did you arrest them?"

"The one who did the typing."

C.J. made a face and shifted on the chair. She crossed her legs and pulled out the 8x10 glossies. She took a reasonably long look at each, shaking her head before going on to the next. Then she held one, nodded and poked an index finger on one of the figures.

"I know this one," she said. "Sure, that could be him. I'm going back a long way, but I remember this guy from high school. If this is Jeremy Goins, and I think it is, he was a year or two older than me, but I used to be friends with his sister. Myra was my age."

"What should I know about Jeremy?"

"Other than being an asshole and a bully, what do you want to know?"

A saint could lose patience with that woman.

"Start by explaining *asshole* and move on to how and who he bullied."

"Humph." She tossed the photos onto the vanity and folded her arms across her chest.

"One explanation should fit all. He ran with a bunch of hard-ons. You know the type." She paused.

I nodded and spoke nicely. "Sure, but tell me anyway."

Her expression and body language told me she felt like I was taking advantage of her. "They bullied anyone weaker than them—didn't matter who. Collectively, that group had no more than a double digit IQ."

She paused again, let that sink in and continued. "I used to sing in school—in music class. Nothing serious at first, but later, I joined the high school chorus. Myra had been in my home room, and she was a pretty good singer, too. I encouraged her to try out for chorus. We were friendly and hung out together. Then one day, Jeremy came up to me at my hall locker and told me to stay away from his sister and stop filling her head with lies, making her think she could be a professional singer."

"You tell Myra that?"

"No, what did I know about the music business then? I tried to explain that I didn't tell her she could sing professionally, just that it would be nice if we could. But that idiot wouldn't listen. He got really close to me." Her expression said she wasn't recounting a pleasant

113

memory. "I remember his hot breath. He pointed a finger in my face and told me I'd been warned. Then he knocked my books onto the floor and walked away with two of his idiot friends. All three laughed like fools. I guess bullying a girl half his size was a real hoot."

I tried to picture C.J. as a teenager, without the celebrity hype and glitzy persona.

"Did he leave you alone after that?" I asked.

She nodded. "He never bothered me again."

"Besides being friends from chorus and hanging out together, what more can you tell me about you and Myra?"

She put a nasty scowl on her face. "You mean were we teenage lovers? Why don't you just come out and ask?"

I bit my tongue and didn't yell at her. "I didn't mean that specifically, but if you were, tell me about it. Or did you get mad as hell one day and smack the shit out of her for some reason?"

She shook her head, looking impatient.

"Or did you humiliate her in front of other students," I asked, "or, hell, I don't know. Did you ever do anything that would make her half-wit brother want to kill you?"

The nasty look disappeared. She stared into my face and then dropped her eyes and shook her head.

"No, none of that," she said

It looked like she was getting tired of perpetuating the tough dyke act.

I pulled a chair close to her and sat.

I tried to use the most soothing, friendly voice I could. "C.J., I'm not the enemy here."

She didn't respond, and for a few seconds, I thought about what I'd say next and decided on one of my greatest strengths—say something stupid. Generally, the girls love that.

"Look, it was hard for me to believe, but when you didn't immediately fall in love with me, I was shattered."

She shook her head, but I saw the beginning of a smile.

"Let's start over," I said. "As far as I'm concerned, being opinionated isn't a killing offense. And you don't deserve to be threatened. And you shouldn't have to live in fear. I'm here to help. *Please*, let me try."

She nodded. "Sorry I got nasty. I get that way more often than I should. I'm really sorry."

"Okay, it's forgotten. You're not the most evil woman I've ever met. I could tell you about a police commissioner's secretary I once knew. She really hated me. But never mind about her."

That caused a genuine smile.

"If we work together, I'll try to keep you safe until next Monday morning when you fly back to Nashville, but I believe there's someone out there who genuinely wants to harm you. I doubt going back to Nashville will persuade them to leave you alone."

She nodded. "I think you're right."

"We either have to learn who this bastard is or you'll live your life in fear and want to employ a full-time bodyguard."

"What do I have to do?"

"If I knew that, I'd be making a lot more than Ronnie Shields pays me. But we can put our heads together and try to solve this. Want to try?"

She sat forward, rested her elbows on her knees, and nodded. "Yes, thank you."

I placed my hand on top of hers and gave a gentle squeeze.

"Good. Is there anything else about Myra Goins that would make Jeremy want to kill you? Anything personal?"

"The last time I saw Myra, she told me her father forced her drop out of chorus. He made her get a job after school and give him the money. After that, we went our separate ways. I never thought she could be a professional singer." She began to raise her voice. "I was seventeen-years-old, for God's sake. I didn't know what it took to be a pro." She flipped her hands in the air in a gesture of frustration. After a long moment, she sighed and settled down. "I knew I wanted to make it big. More than that, I had to learn for myself."

I assumed my next question wouldn't be an easy one and anticipated resistance. "Now, don't chew my head off when I ask," I said, "but we have to talk about your sexual preferences."

She paused for a moment, took a deep breath through her nose, but then nodded. "Okay."

"Did you know you preferred girls back when you were in high school?"

"That was phrased very diplomatically. Thanks." C.J. shook her head and let out another sigh. "It's hard to explain. After dating, I knew boys didn't interest me. I wasn't sexually attracted to Myra, if that's what you mean. I didn't come out of the closet in high school because I didn't know I was in a closet. All that happened later."

"You think Jeremy and his Coalition friends are just asshole homophobes?"

She shrugged. "I don't know what else to tell you. You think they'd kill me because of what I am?"

"It doesn't sound like an intelligent decision on their part, but stupider things have been done by smarter people. I have someone looking into them right now. Two of my cops arrested a woman for writing the notes. A sharp kid named Junior Huskey found the typewriter she used, and she admitted writing and sending the hate mail."

"Who?"

"I'll get there, bear with me. The cop actually read parts of the messages on the typewriter ribbon. We only charged the woman with six misdemeanors, but at least she knows we're looking at the Coalition."

"You think there's more than one person actively involved?"

"Yes, but who knows? In a day or two, I might round them all up for a serious talk. I'll see what they have to say for themselves when I get the additional information I hope to have soon."

"You really think they'll admit trying to kill me?"

"No. She already told me she didn't have anything to do with the poison. And her son called a rather infamous right-wing attorney, so I'm guessing that unless I have a smoking gun and can offer them some kind of deal for a confession, they'll tell me to go pound salt."

We looked at each other. I thought some very thick ice had been broken. And I doubted C.J. and I would be antagonizing each other again.

"Please tell me. Who is this woman? Do I know her?" she asked.

An arrest is public information. I had no reason to withhold the name.

"Her name's Elnora Collinson. She's the woman in the photo, and..."

A big light came on in C.J.'s head. She clamped her mouth tightly and began nodding.

"And her son's name is Mack. Sure, I know them. Mack was one of the idiots Jeremy Goins hung with. Mack was as big a bully as Goins, as long as they had friends along to outnumber whomever they wanted to intimidate."

I picked up the stack of FBI photos and flipped through them. "Here, look. This is her son, Mack today. Remember him?"

A sardonic smile crossed her face. "Sure, that's him. I didn't recognize him with the beard."

"Let's forget about the Coalition for now," I said, wanting to broaden our area of interest. "Is there anyone else who would have a warped need to do you harm?"

"I guess over the years I've pissed off more than a few people, but I really don't know anyone with enough hate to kill me."

"Think about the people who you've been closest to. Is there a husband, father, brother or other woman who objected to you getting friendly with someone they know?"

"I've never had any confrontations with families." She shook her head. "And I've been lucky. No persistent stalkers or weirdoes until this Coalition thing came along."

"Okay then." I stood up. "Listen, kid, hang in there. We're all looking out for you. Harley Flatt is a real good man. He'll eat someone alive before he lets anyone hurt you."

"He looks like he could."

"Believe it."

She showed me the biggest, most genuine smile I'd seen from her yet.

"I'll see you either later tonight or tomorrow," I said.

"I'll walk out with you," she said. "I shouldn't hide in my dressing room all day. I'm not getting paid for this, but I've agreed to sing and may as well practice a little so it sounds good."

I gave her a light tap on the shoulder. "That a girl. You're a real soldier."

"Don't push your luck, lawman. I'm not too familiar with being friendly."

I laughed.

When C.J., Harley and I reached the auditorium, we found Bob Mitchell talking to Jenny, Rusty Filmore and two people from the crew who I didn't know.

The last words I heard him say were, "...so, I've taken it easy ever since getting out of the racket."

I didn't know the subject of his statement, but the last phrase he used made something click for me. I knew where I had previously known Bob Mitchell."

* * * *

I handed Harley Flatt my keys and asked him to fetch the small digital camera I kept in my briefcase. Several other performers wandered into the auditorium. A few of the musicians carried sheet music.

I turned to C.J. and whispered, "Go along with anything I say, and as soon as Harley gets back, don't argue with anything you hear. Ad lib if you have to."

She frowned and got a questioning look on her face.

"Just do this for me," I said. "For us."

From her look, I thought I'd made my point. When Harley handed me the camera, I started my pitch.

"Hey, folks." I said. "I've got to leave for the day, but before I go, I want to take a few snapshots. Who knows, I may toss out my Beach Boys albums and get to be a country and western fan. Come on C.J., get over here with Tanya. You too, Harley, Bob, Jenny. Make a tight little group."

"Thanks for the offer, Sam, but I never take a good picture," Bob said.

"Come on, man. You're one of the team—almost another paid bodyguard. Come on now, let's go."

Then C.J. took over, "Stand up, Bob. You'll be the only man I hug this year. Get over here."

Bob shook his head again, but offered a good-natured grin.

"Jenny, tell your daddy to get over here, or you're fired."

"You better do it, Daddy. I think she means it."

And so, my group formed for a few casual portraits. Then, C.J. asked several more of the singers to join us for additional photos. She even called over the skinny kid with the big black hat, whatever his name was, I can't remember. My final shot was a zoomed-in close-up of Bob Mitchell.

"Folks, I appreciate your cooperation. Thanks for the pictures. See you all sometime later."

Before I left, Harley asked to speak with me. We walked up the auditorium aisle together.

"Jest what the hell was that all about?" he asked.

"Uncontrollable urge. I have this thing about family photos. Got it from my old Jewish mother."

"I thought your mother's name was MacDonald."

"Sure, and her father was Irving MacDonald, the famous Scottish/Jewish diamond merchant."

"Do what?"

"Forget it. You know I'm just a big ol' liar."

"I do now."

"I'm only guessing right now, but keep an eye on Bob Mitchell. He said something that bothered me. I'll start checking him out thoroughly."

"That don't make me feel any too comfortable," Harley said.

"If he's who I think he is we could use him on our side."

Harley looked perplexed.

"It's probably nothing," I said. "But let's not get caught with our pants down."

Chapter Twelve

Back in my office, I fired up the computer, popped the memory card from my camera into a nifty little card-reader and came up with a screen full of pictures from Dollywood. When I selected two photos to print, I saw that the machine was out of photo paper. So, I consulted my source for everything hidden in the closets and drawers of Prospect PD.

"Hey, Betts, do we have more photograph paper somewhere?"

"Sure, darlin'. Y'all hang on, and I'll get some," she said.

While I waited, I made an E-copy of one of the group photos, and then cropped it to give me another close-up of Bob Mitchell. I'd print that one and the zoomed-in head-shot I took of him alone.

It only took a minute for Bettye to bring me a small stack of glossy 4x6 print paper. I placed the stack in the hopper while Bettye looked over my shoulder at the pictures I'd taken. I clicked on the first and enlarged it. She pressed her hand on my shoulder like a little kid peeking over a fence. Her perfume smelled nice.

"You took these?" she asked.

"Yes, ma'am. They call me Flashgun Casey."

I advanced to the next shot.

"Lord have mercy," she said. "That's Harley Flatt standin' there with Kenny Chesney."

"I know Harley Flatt, but who's Kenny Chesney?"

"Who's Kenny Chesney?"

"That's what I said."

"Well, he's just as famous as C.J. Profitt. He's a big, big, big star, Sammy. And he's from Knoxville."

"A big star, huh? You'd think he could afford a hat that fits him."

I advanced through a few more pictures.

"Sam, that's LeAnn Rimes and Tanya Tucker with C.J."

"Oh yeah, you know them? I thought they were cute so I asked them to pose for these pictures."

"You asked them?"

"Yeah, they're nice girls."

I advanced to the next shot.

"Who's this guy standing next to Harley?" I asked.

She slapped my shoulder. "Lord have mercy, man, that's Toby Keith."

"Toby needs a shave. And talk about hats—Jeez, that thing he's wearing is disgraceful."

"Sam Jenkins, I hope you know I want copies of these pictures."

"Sure, Betts, you can have as many as you'd like," I said.

She bent over and kissed my forehead.

"Since you know all these people," I said, "you might like to work on the security detail Saturday night. Leonard, Harlan, and I will be there. And since Ronnie is going to spring for overtime for us to protect his high school sweetie, I can't see why you, Stanley, and John shouldn't be there, too. Print up the pictures, and I'll get these people to sign them for you."

"I'd love to go." After that offer, she kissed my cheek, a big long one. "Ooh, this sounds excitin'. I think I'll wear..."

I interrupted her thoughts. "Hey, lady, personally I think you're cuter than all of these Nashville chicks, but this is work, not the Easter Parade. Wear something that hides your Glock. Okay?"

"Whatever you say, darlin'." She half ignored me and swung her hip to push me further out of the way. After finding a spot in front of the keyboard, she punched a few keys and then began putting checks on the photos she wanted printed. "Can I get a little room to copy these pictures?"

"Who's stopping you?"

She put a hand on my shoulder and pushed me and the chair totally out of her way.

"Would I be sexually harassing you if I said you smelled good today?"

"No, sir, I'd think that was a compliment. Thank *yew*."

"That smells familiar. What is it?"

"Cristalle. I love it. Give me a little time here, would ya?"

"Sounds familiar, too. I must have bought that once or twice."

"I'll bet you did. I'm uncomfortable bent over like this. Can I use your chair iffin y'all are finished?"

I stood up and pushed the chair back in place. She sat and clicked another key.

I sounded petulant saying, "I never wore perfume when I was a sergeant."

"I never handcuffed suspects to gravestones like you did."

"You're getting to be a real wise-guy."

"I learn from the best, sugar. You said I can make a few sets of these pictures?

I knew when I couldn't win. "Be my guest."

"Momma would just *love* to have them. And so would Aunt Charlotte."

"Gotta keep Momma and Aunt Charlotte happy."

"Move, darlin', move. I'll forget what I've done if I can't concentrate."

* * * *

A few minutes later, while I loitered in the lobby waiting for a phone to ring, John Gallagher walked in. Then Stan Rose joined us. The computer in my room kept buzzing, Bettye's photos still printing away.

"Hey, boss," John said, "you sent me to meet two guys from the KKK."

"Just what I wanted to hear," I said. "Come into my office, and keep talking. What happened?"

"The first one I talked to was the old lady, *Eldora* or something," John said. "I told her I was looking for a house and explained what I wanted. I couldn't believe it. First thing she asked me was if I picked a church yet. What kind of question is that?"

I shrugged. I'd heard things like that before.

"I told her no, but I was a good Catholic boy. Then she says, 'Oh, I thought you were a Christian.' You believe that?"

"Welcome to Appalachia, John-Boy. Someday I'll take you to see the snake handlers and foot washers."

Stanley laughed.

Bettye heard me and said, "Sam, don't you be hateful now."

"You keep saying that, Betts. And I thought I was a nice guy. Okay, John, what's next?"

"She sends me out with that bearded doofus son of hers. Man, he smelled funny. Must use turpentine or something for aftershave. What a weirdo. And that other guy, Jeremy. What a pair of losers. First house they take me to see is up on the four lane highway, right behind the Seventh Avenue Advantage Church—like right in the backyard, behind the parking lot."

Stan interrupted, "The what kind of church?"

"Seventh Avenue...? Advantage? That's not it?"

I assisted with a translation. "He means Seventh Day Adventist, as in Jehovah's Witnesses."

"Oh, sure," Stanley said.

Bettye smiled and kept watching my computer.

"So, next we go to see a cabin in Townsend," John said. "Nice neighborhood, lots of hills and trees and stuff. The cabin was small and needed work, like new appliances, new fixtures in the bathroom and..."

"John! Forget the condition of the cabin? What did you learn from those two idiots?" I said.

"Oh, yeah. So, we're standing on the porch looking down at the road. It's gotta be seventy-five or a hundred feet below us. And Mack, the guy with the beard, he asks me what I did in New York. So I tell him I was a cop. They look at each other and the other guy, *Jerry*, he asks me if I worked with lots of blacks and Spanish. So I say yeah. And he says it's much better here in this county where it's mostly white." He turned to Stan. "No offense, Sarge."

Stanley shrugged. "No sweat."

"Then Mack says he bets that if I bought the cabin, I could have fun sitting on the porch with a rifle. Said I could shoot any spicks or niggers that went by. No offense again, Sarge. He used those words, not me."

123

"It's okay, John," Stan said. "They really said that?"

"You bet, Sarge. And they only met me an hour before. I guess they trusted me."

"Nice guys," I said.

"I just grinned," John said, "and they went on making all kinds of *dispatchatory* remarks about black people and the Mexicans who've been moving into the county."

"Dispatchatory?" Stan asked.

"Yeah, Sarge, *dispatchatory*. You know, like not nice."

"Sure, John, I understand." Stanley seemed to be picking up Gallaghese.

Bettye laughed, and I smiled. Stan was learning quickly.

"Then we looked at a couple more places," John said, "and Mack starts talking about what he calls the New World Order. He mentioned people in a place called Telephone Plains. Strange name, but I figure these are weird people."

I interrupted. "How about Tellico Plains?"

"Yeah, could be. Sounded like telephone to me. But anyways, these people belong to a group called The New World Order, and he says they hate the way family values are going to shit." He looked over at Bettye who had turned her attention from the photos printing and listened to John's story. "Sorry, Sarge. Pardon my language, but the boss likes to get *merbatim* reports. Anyways, Mack said how he hated Bill Clinton and wanted to know how anyone in New York could have elected Hillary senator. I told him that in down-state New York, a French poodle could get elected if it ran as a Democrat. They made some remarks about New York Jews and other people, and he told me how he *knows* there'll be a revolution if a Democrat gets elected in 2008. I heard more about political crap than real estate."

"By God, John-Boy, y'all done good t'day," I said.

"Thanks, boss. I try."

"I'm just sorry they didn't recruit you to whack C.J. Profitt for them," I said. "You being an ex-gunslinger and all. But you're only scratching the surface with these people. I almost want to bring the morons in and sweat them to see if they really know anything about the poison. But I think you should play them along some more."

"Okay, boss, can do."

"Stan," I said, "get driver's license photos of Jeremy Goins, add five look-alikes and show them to the Chan kid. See if Goins was the guy who took the food from him and brought it up to the motel.'

"Okay."

"John, I think we're going to tell the FBI about your new friends and see if they want to finance an undercover operation."

"You trust somebody from the FBI, boss?"

"Yeah, a nice kid from Queens. He's a good guy."

"Whatever you say, boss."

"Bettye," I said, "shine your sensible shoes. We've got a date Saturday night."

* * * *

Later that afternoon, I walked up to the mayor's office. Ms. Connor gave me no opposition or tap dance to keep me from going right in. I gave Ronnie an update on Johnny Rutledge and the situation in general and mentioned the crew I intended to take to the Dollywood Imagination Library Benefit. I included my wife and learned something I should have guessed. Ronnie and his wife, LaDonna, would be C.J.'s special guests. Then I told him what he could do to help. Without explaining too much detail to him, I put the mayor to work for me.

"I need you to dip into your bag of political tricks, and get me a big favor."

Ronnie frowned.

"I believe it may shed some light on these threats and the attempt on C.J.'s life."

The mayor lightened up a little.

"Why certainly, Sam. If it's in my power, I'd be happy ta he'p y'all anyway I can."

"What I need will put you in a deeper hole, and you'll owe someone a second favor."

"Sam, don't ya worry 'bout that. I been there before. What is it ya need?"

"Call Al Steinmetz. This afternoon would be best. I want to see him as soon as possible. Suggest early tomorrow morning. I need some of his

Army horsepower to help identify someone and see if Army CID or Military Intelligence can connect him with a dissident group which keeps popping up. I believe the general's help is crucial to the investigation.

At first, Ronnie didn't answer and took a long moment to think about what I had asked. The mayor had never been in the service, and the idea of tapping a three-star for a second favor may have seemed a little daunting. I was about to say, 'Suck it up, Mr. Mayor. If I have to, I'll call myself,' when he nodded.

"Okay, Sam, if ya need General Steinmetz's he'p, I'll call. Just promise me y'all will be on best behavior with the man."

"I'll be as respectful as a PFC looking for a weekend pass."

"I assume that means yes?"

"Sure. Well, within reason."

"Sam."

"Jeez, Ronnie. Sometimes you're so easy, I can't resist."

He gave me a pathetic look.

"Okay, okay," I said. "I'll behave. Trust me."

He frowned again and didn't look all that sure he'd believe someone who said, 'Trust me.'

Then I said, "I'll call before five o'clock and see how you made out. Right now, I've got to speak with my man at the FBI and check on this right-wing group of yahoos."

* * * *

Ralph Oliveri and his boss, Carl Harmon, were together when I called. I felt honored when Ralph suggested putting me on the speakerphone—how very Federal of him.

I explained how John Gallagher had 'infiltrated the mob' and scheduled another meeting with Mack Collinson where he'd resume his search for a home.

Carl Harmon asked, "Sam, the man you have working on these people is a middle-aged clerk-typist?"

"Police operations aide, Carl—with a lot of experience—an ex-detective."

"Ralph told me he used to work for you back in New York. When was the last time he did any police work?"

"Not long ago—twenty years, maybe."

I heard Carl take in a long breath and slowly let it out. I envisioned him shaking his head.

"Sam, we don't know a lot about these coalition people. This Jeremy Goins has an independent history of violence. Collinson may have someone else close to him who is equally violent. Is Gallagher up to dealing with this group?"

I was about to answer when Carl continued.

"You know, if he encountered trouble, it might be a few minutes before backup could get to him."

"So far he says yes. I'll ask again, and I'm sure you'll make the situation perfectly clear when you speak to him."

"I will. I plan on having Ralph and Bonnie Rowatt as the backup team. They can pose as a couple on vacation doing some sightseeing."

"That's good. The only problem I envision is when the locals see Ralph looking around, they'll say, 'There goes the neighborhood.'"

"Hey, I heard that. I have feelings, too, you know."

"Of course you do, Ralph. Even goombahs from Ozone Park need love."

"That's South Ozone Park, buddy."

"Sorry, I know it makes a difference. Carl, I'm trying to connect with someone tomorrow morning who may help me with a big question. Can I bring John Gallagher into Knoxville and meet with you in the afternoon?"

"I have nothing going tomorrow. Call, and let me know when you two can be here."

"I'll do that. Thanks. Ciao, Ralphie."

I hung up as Stanley walked back into my office. He handed me a six-pack of head shots, one being Jeremy Goins.

"The Lum kid didn't seem as stupid as I first thought. Actually, he's a pretty good boy when he starts talking," he said.

"You must have the magic touch."

Stan shrugged that one off.

"Anyway, he didn't think he'd be much help if I sent him to a sketch artist, but he knew none of these six was the guy he saw the night he made that delivery."

"Why are we so lucky?"

"I even pointed out Goins and got a definite no. So, unless Collinson could shave and then re-grow that bush on his face overnight, there are additional personnel involved here."

"I hope the guy I have negative thoughts about isn't on the roles of the Coalition. If he is, we might have some really professional talent to contend with."

"Pros we don't need," Stan said.

"I'm still only guessing," I said. "I have no reason to connect him to the Coalition, but I think I've seen him before and wonder why he may be lying about his past. Maybe I'm all wet, and he's what he claims to be. With luck, I'll know something tomorrow after asking someone a few questions. I'd rather have the guy working with us than against us."

"Do you enjoy complicating our lives?"

Stanley can be bitchy at times, and I ignore some of his questions.

"And maybe John can learn more the next time they go out house hunting," I said.

"You sure John isn't getting in over his head?"

"The FBI is interested in helping out. They'll wire up John and send a backup team to stay close to him. Aren't these hate crimes just dandy? The Feds have all kinds of money to spend on investigations."

When Stanley left, Ronnie Shields called. He had arranged an appointment with Lieutenant General Alfred Steinmetz for 0930 hours the next morning. Ronnie gave me an unlisted phone number, an address and directions.

I hoped Steinmetz was in a giving mood. I'd spit-shine my jump boots for the occasion.

Chapter Thirteen

I hit the road at 8:30 the next morning. The drive to Knoxville wouldn't take an hour, but I would encounter a crowd of dashing commuters on Alcoa Highway while heading into the city and didn't know how long I'd be winding through the side streets of Sequoyah Hills before finding Casa Stenimetz.

After passing the Cherokee Drive exit leading to UT Hospital, I ascended a hill—the hospital visible on my right and Fort Loudoun Lake, a long, wide swell in the Tennessee River, to the left. The sun had risen just over the trees to the east and created sparkles on the rippling water. At the top of the hill, just before crossing the Buck Karnes Bridge, a herd of two dozen horses grazed on a field reserved for the UT School of Veterinary Medicine.

Merging into the right lane, I passed the exit for Neyland Stadium and took the off-ramp to Cumberland Avenue. At the traffic light, I turned left where Cumberland changes its name to Kingston Pike. Another three quarters of a mile and I turned left again toward the river and into Sequoyah Hills. I've always liked that part of the city, but couldn't afford one of the houses. With the proliferation of large stone and brick *Olde English*-style homes and half-timbered Tudor cottages, it reminded me of Garden City, an affluent town on Long Island, not far from where I grew up.

I arrived at the address Ronnie had given me twenty minutes early, but didn't pull into the driveway right away. Instead, I circled the block and parked at a curb down the street from where the general lived.

There was no reason to believe my visit was other than a social call, sanctioned by Steinmetz himself. But this business had me feeling paranoid, and old habits die hard. I wanted to see if anyone else might be looking for me or if other visitors were calling on the general. I didn't want Steinmetz to surprise me and introduce some spook who'd tell me to leave Bob Mitchell alone, saying no more than Bob was on special assignment, and I had no need to know more than it was none of my business. Things like that tend to happen when you work in the more unconventional corners of the United States Army.

So, I indulged myself and kept an eye on the general's house. It seemed that anyone going to work had left home long ago. For the first ten minutes, no one drove or walked by. My mind began to wander. I thought about how I came to find my parallel career with Uncle Sam's finest.

Early in 1918, my grandfather, Samuel W. Jenkins, joined the Marines at age fifteen. He looked older and because America needed fighting men in Europe, the recruiting sergeant never asked him for a birth certificate. I've been told that my great grandmother, accompanied by a neighbor and family friend, a New York City police sergeant named Gordon Campbell, stood on a dock at the Brooklyn Navy Yard and watched the troop ship carrying young Sam to France steam out to the open waters of Long Island Sound and continue on to the Atlantic Ocean. A twenty-four-year-old Marine Corps lieutenant stood next to them. No one could stop the progress of the ship or the fate of my grandfather.

My father, Eddy Jenkins, had been a soldier in the 3rd Infantry Division during World War Two. My Uncle Al, the other male role model in my life, was a belly gunner on a B-24 in the same war. I grew up hearing stories from these three men and had no choice but to carry on the tradition.

So, when the Vietnam War escalated and a girl I knew, who worked for the Selective Service System in Hempstead, New York, told me I was scheduled to be conscripted, I contacted a recruiter and asked for my draft to be pushed up. Why wait and tamper with fate?

I completed basic combat training at Fort Jackson, South Carolina, went on to advanced infantry training at Fort Gordon, Georgia, experienced an infusion of lunacy, and volunteered for airborne training and spent a few additional weeks at Fort Benning, Georgia.

After assignment to the 508th Parachute Infantry at Fort Bragg, North Carolina, the weeks whizzed by. I saw soldiers walking around post wearing green berets. They looked sharp, and I thought I'd look pretty cool in one of those hats. And their mission intrigued me. Special Forces' lineage came from as far back as the French and Indian War and more recently, the OSS teams of World War Two. I spent time in the library learning about men like Robert Rogers, John Mosby, Wild Bill Donovan, Frank Merrill and Aaron Bank.

I had grown up hearing stories about Audie Murphy and watching the movies of John Wayne and Richard Widmark, Burt Lancaster and Lee Marvin, who received a Navy Cross for heroism in the South Pacific. For God's sake, even Captain Kangaroo was a decorated war hero. I was doomed.

All these things influenced my thoughts, and I volunteered for special warfare training. We were engaged in a 'limited' war, and the Army needed advisors in Southeast Asia. So, in no time my application was approved, and I began my 'S' course at the John F. Kennedy Center for Military Assistance, a euphemistic name for the Special Forces school located just down the road from my temporary home with the 82nd Airborne Division.

There I met guys like Alfred Steinmetz. I became someone not unlike Steinmetz and the cadre of men who did things the average American male looked at as manly and heroic, but in truth, never wanted to experience. If the average suburban husband and father valued their sanity and the ability to sleep and diddy-bop through life with relatively few cares, lacking those military experiences was a good thing.

I looked at my watch.

No cars were parked on the street in front of or behind the home. Not a creature was stirring. So, at 9:30, I pulled into the driveway, locked the Ford, walked to the front door and pushed the bell button.

Westminster chimes announced my presence, and in less than a minute an attractive woman in her mid-sixties opened the door. She looked well-dressed in a sweater and blouse and pair of expensive slacks that may have come from the classy, high ticket Talbot's store a mile or so down Kingston Pike.

"Good morning," she said.

I smiled and said, "Hello, my name is Sam Jenkins. I stopped by to see the general."

Then she surprised me. "Yes, of course, Major. He's expecting you. Come in please."

Three cheers for Big Al. It's always best to keep the staff fully briefed on your guests and the happenings of the day.

On the outside, the house and grounds looked impressive. Inside, the place was exquisite. A faint odor of wood smoke traveled to the entrance from within the house. It complimented the décor of English country antiques and furnishings.

The trim, gray-haired lady, Mrs. Steinmetz I presumed, led me through the living room, past the dining room with the kitchen visible in the background and into a great-room or library with his and hers desks, leather upholstered chairs and love seats and enough volumes sitting in built-in bookcases to accommodate a platoon of knowledge-crazed Franciscan monks.

When I stepped into the room, Mrs. Steinmetz said, "Enjoy your visit, Major. I'll bring you gentlemen coffee shortly."

The general had been looking out a tall leaded glass window. When he heard his wife's voice, Alfred Steinmetz turned and looked in my direction, showed me a big smile and walked over.

He extended his right hand. "How the hell are you, Major? Always good to see one of the old bunch. Come in here, and get comfortable."

As always, the general's handshake said lots about his character—firm, with enough strength, but never overdone.

"Good to see you, too, General, but since last we spoke, a couple of years before I retired, the Army had the bad sense to promote me again."

"Excellent." he said. "I'm glad to hear it. Where did you end up?"

"I left the 11th Group early in '86 and took an unpaid billet in a Civil Affairs brigade with the promise of a promotion. Two years later, I retired a half-colonel."

"Well, I'll be damned. Congratulations, Sam. No telling how far you could have gone if only you started drinking with the right people." He laughed. "But I remember you were the guy who got attached to that A-team of yours. We had to use a crowbar to get you out and promote you to major, didn't we?"

I smiled and nodded. Sure, he remembered. He personally used the crowbar.

"I was damned surprised when that Mayor Shields of yours contacted me about you—early last summer, I'd say. You had dropped off the radar for a long time."

"I always thought low profile was best."

"Sure, a lot of guys in the racket did. Nothing wrong with that." He shook his head and smiled again. "You were all good soldiers—accomplished a lot and sometimes did the impossible. I'm glad so many of you combat vets stayed in the part-time Army."

He pointed to one of the well-worn wingback chairs that flanked the fireplace. The smell of vintage, quality leather reminded me of an old British sports car. Several oak or hickory logs burned slowly in the wide firebox and occasionally crackled and sputtered. I took a seat, and he chose the chair opposite me, across a leather-topped coffee table. Behind me, the row of tall casement windows overlooked a back garden.

Al Steinmetz was in his late 60s, a couple of inches shorter than me, but heavier by ten or fifteen pounds. Still a solid, barrel-chested man, he looked fitter than three quarters of the local boys only in their twenties. His mostly gray hair, once worn in a GI crew cut was now like mine, too long for the Army and shorter than that worn by most civilians.

Steinmetz was one of the more affable and approachable general officers I'd ever known, but as I always told others, underestimate him at your own peril. If push came to shove Big Al was all business—a genuine tough guy.

"I always enjoy seeing someone from the old Army," he said. "But I know you're here on police business. How can I help?

I gave him a brief account of the C.J. Profitt story and then brought my purpose for seeing him into perspective.

"I'm just doing a little recon by fire, so to speak. But someone who's become a frequently seen player in all this, I believe he's an ex-soldier, is denying that fact, and I can't understand why. When first we met, I thought I recognized him, but couldn't say for sure or from where.

Then he made a remark that triggered my memory. I'm almost certain I ran across him on one of my trips to Fort Devens."

Steinmetz only offered a, "Hmmm." We both knew who took up a lot of space at that military installation.

"I'd bet a pension check he was one of the NCOs at 10th Group involved with training Special Forces reservists. But he claims to have been a civilian engineer."

I handed two photos of Bob Mitchell across the table.

"He uses the name Robert Mitchell and says he's from Virginia. Can you use those pictures to see if anyone knows him and can confirm his identity?"

The General looked at the pictures and nodded. "I think you're right, Sam. he looks GI to me, too. What did he say to jog your memory?"

"The very same thing you just said, General. He referred to our former work as 'the racket'. That's not much to hang my green beret on, but it clicked for me, and now I'd swear I remember him up at some training area on Devens. But that's more than twenty years ago, so I'd need help to confirm my suspicion."

"You think he's involved with these threats and the attempted murder?"

"I don't know. I believe he's not telling the truth, and that bothers me. If he is who or what I think he is, then of course he's capable of taking out a female singer whenever he wants. I can't imagine him involved with a bunch of right-wing weirdoes like this Coalition, but if he is—as a hired hand or simply philosophically in tune with them—I have more to worry about than an old lady and her two stupid henchmen."

Steinmetz nodded and tossed the photos on the coffee table.

"If he's acting independently, I have to learn why. Of course, *he* may just like a low profile, too, and doesn't make it a practice of telling war stories to the general population. If that's so, I'll let him know I'm not one of the rank and file and demand an explanation. I'll try not to hurt his feelings."

Steinmetz chuckled. "I agree with you on those points, entirely. I'll see what I can find. When do you need this?"

I've been accused of carrying my balls in a bowling bag before, and this was no time to adopt timidity as my policy. So, I told Steinmetz exactly what I wanted.

"Day before yesterday, General."

He laughed. "I won't be the first one to observe that Sam Jenkins has no problem pushing someone into working for him—regardless of their rank. You're a piece of work, my friend, a real piece of work."

"Yeah. I've heard that before, sir."

"Sam, I remember holding a staff meeting one morning at Bragg. I don't know how we got into this side conversation, but you came to mind when I coined a phrase everyone seemed to like. I told them some of you mavericks were well-versed in being 'charmingly insolent'. You guys were masters of upward discipline, and we were all the better for it."

I was saved from the necessity of being either more charming or more insolent when Mrs. Steinmetz entered the library with a silver tray and coffee set.

"We're finished with business, Ruth," he said. "Why don't you join us?"

"I'll get another cup and be right back," she said.

I spent the next half hour socializing. When I left at 10:45, I felt confident that Al Steinmetz would be faxing Bob Mitchell's photos to several people. Then in a couple of hours, Al and Ruth might head to the nearby Cherokee Country Club, sit at a table overlooking the Tennessee River and sip bourbon old-fashions before lunch arrived. Wealth and power are good.

* * * *

I found John Gallagher waiting for me when I returned to the office. But he hadn't been sitting around wasting time. A second desk had been moved into the reception area just behind and to the left of Bettye's. A three-drawer file cabinet, swivel chair and armchair surrounded the old desk, and even a vase of old, dusty-looking artificial flowers sat on the desktop. I walked up and stopped next to Bettye's desk.

"Mornin', Sammy. Everythin' okay?" she asked.

"Howdy, Betts. Yep, okay so far." I gave her a smile and asked the traditional East Tennessee question, "You doin' aw rot today, darlin'?"

She shook her head and smiled back. I looked at Gallagher who grinned and looked like an old pot-bellied leprechaun.

"Hi, *Sammy*, how's it goin'?" John emphasized the Sammy part.

I ignored his comment and pointed to the new office furniture. "Where'd you get all this?"

"The Sarge told me who to see. That old guy, George Files, showed me the supply room in the basement. I picked this stuff out. He brought it up, him and his helper, that black kid, *Sturgeon*."

"Spurgeon, John. The boy's name is Spurgeon."

"Right. So, now I'm all ready to go. When do I get a badge?"

"Don't push your luck, bean-belly. You and I will get together with the Feds this afternoon so you can meet your new hillbilly terrorist friends and go on looking for a house and more information."

"Okay, boss. You want me to teach the feebs how to do it?"

"Why not. They're all younger than us. They can only benefit from your experience."

"I love stickin' it to the feebs," he said.

Bettye stifled a giggle. I gave her the evil eye. She made sure I saw her smile, but ignored me,

"Tell me about this house Glenda Mae found for you. As usual, I'm the last one around here to hear the news."

"Oh yeah, nice place. All brick, three bedrooms, two and a half baths, screened-in porch. They took two-thirty-five. I'd pay a lot more even in Florida for something like that. And can you believe it? We can close in two weeks."

"Sounds good."

"Yeah, and it's in a good neighborhood, nice and quiet, last house on a *culver sack*."

"A culver sack? Like on a dead end court?"

"Yeah, a *culver sack*. You oughta get a dictionary, boss."

I glanced at Bettye, who smiled again. I didn't get a chance to yell at John before Vern Hobbs walked in.

"Hey, boss," Vern said, with his usual deadpan expression. "You doin' aw rot t'day? Hey, Miss Bettye." He eyed up John and the new desk setup in the lobby.

"Whaddaya say, Vern?" I poked a thumb in John's direction. "This is John Gallagher. Maybe you've heard... He's going to work here as our new Operations Aide. John used to be a cop back in New York."

Vern looked at John with the same humorless expression and a toothpick rolling around in his mouth.

"Hey, John." He extended a hand. "Vernon Hobbs."

The two shook hands.

"Hi, *Vermin*, how's it goin'?" John asked innocently.

I quizzed Vern, the guy who knew everything about the citizens of Prospect, on the Collinsons and their Coalition. Vern was impressed with neither the people nor the organization.

"Mack Collinson mentioned The New World Order," I said. "He may just be using that term, or he may mean the actual organization. They seem to be a nationwide bleep on the FBI's radar and have an active group in Tellico Plains. Ever hear anything about these local fools being part of a genuine and serious, right-wing crew?"

"Shoot, ever'one knows 'bout The New World Order." He moved the toothpick from the right side of his mouth to the left. "You ever meet Mack Collinson?"

I nodded.

"He's jest a damn fool. He ain't, or I'd be damn surprised if he was, in the real New World Order." He waved his hand dismissively. "Mack's full of it—jest likes ta hear hisse'f talk. Ma Collinson, now she's been around ferever. Got her a big and nasty mouth, too. Thinks she's kindly like somethin' special 'round here. Ya know, like someone who's got the right ta pass jedgement on others." Vern hooked his thumbs over his gun belt and began a new topic. "Now, that Goins boy—I believe he's one sick puppy. He might could join The New World Order, The Aryan Nation, Skin Heads—anyone o' those bunches. Don't know that he has, but he could. If ya's lookin' fer someone who'd hurt this woman, it might could be him. Goins is a bad apple."

* * * *

That afternoon, John and I drove to Knoxville and the FBI offices at 710 Locust Street. For most of the drive in, he told me more about the house he bought. A few blocks from the parking lot, John started a new conversation.

"I guess they didn't have a height requirement when *Vermin* came on the job."

"Vern is pushing sixty," I said. "When he came on the job thirty years ago, I don't think they had any requirements down here. He might be the shortest cop in the world."

He shrugged. "So much for civil service standards."

As John spoke, he swiveled around looking at the Knoxville sights.

"Not much traffic for a city," he said.

"Yeah. Clean, too."

"I wonder how much the houses cost in here."

It seemed like John liked the downtown section.

After an hour with the Feds, we had a game plan in place. On Friday morning, John would start another day of house hunting.

Chapter Fourteen

When I pulled into my driveway and parked the Crown Victoria, I noticed Kate had not opened the garage door for me. Generally, I found it up and that allows me to enter the house through the laundry room, please my wife by wiping my feet on a mat and not contaminate the Berber carpet she loves so much. Tonight I'd have to walk around to the front of the house. It presented no great problem, but when someone in the neighborhood just tried to poison the famous singer I was protecting and put one of my cops in the hospital, I didn't like to see uncommon things.

The walk from the gravel driveway, over the concrete apron and along the narrow path to the porch seemed endless. The air smelled more like springtime than winter. Almost three months of more than usual rain and dampness had caused the layers of leaves, stacked one upon one upon one, in the wooded area surrounding the house to begin to compost and give off that familiar odor usually associated with the aftermath of the late snows of March. I resisted the urge to unsnap the safety on my holster. I felt tension in my forehead and told myself I was overreacting.

My apprehensions quickly disappeared after I mounted the porch and passed the dining room window. Kate stood over what looked like thousands of jigsaw puzzle pieces spread out on the big oval table and worked diligently to assemble the frame. Our Scottish terrier, Bitsey, offered support by sleeping on the floor near Kate's chair. All seemed well, so I didn't kick open the door with my gun drawn and roll across the floor to a position of cover. Kate turned around, and Bitsey made the short trip to the foyer, rolled onto her back and expected a usual greeting.

139

"Hi, sweetie. How did things go today?" Kate asked.

"Hi ya, Kats. Not so good. I'm still confused. No information on my country and western assassins. How's by you?"

"You think you're confused. I just spread out this 1500 piece puzzle—ugh!"

"Ugh? Poor girl. I know the fate of the free world rests with you finishing that thing in record time, but have you thought about dinner for your hard-working and always hungry husband?"

"Of course I have, sweetie. How's cavatelli and chicken parmagiana sound? I've also got a nice salad and fresh bread for my hungry boy."

"Super. What are you and Bitsey drinking?" I pointed to a round, stemmed glass sitting among the unassembled jigsaw pieces.

"The cabernet-merlot blend you picked up last week. Like some?"

"Yeah, but with dinner. It's damp and chilly and feels like a Laphroaig night."

I grabbed the familiar green bottle from the liquor cabinet.

"You actually opened a bottle of wine yourself?" I said. "I'm impressed."

"Of course. I found an old-fashioned corkscrew. My husband would never buy wine with a screw-off top."

"I'm doubly impressed. Good work for a girl who stays away from technical things and manual labor. But screw tops aren't a sign of poor quality anymore."

"Two snide remarks in one night. I should give you a TV dinner and Gatorade."

"For that, I'd steal pieces from the puzzle and drive you crazy."

"Bitsey, bite your father… He's mean. By the way, where's John? Is he going to be here for dinner?"

"John-Boy is working again. It's amazing how a middle-aged, money-hungry guy can live on junk food and little sleep. He must be going through his second childhood. Although, knowing Gallagher, he probably never left the first."

I poured a ration of single-malt whisky over a couple of cubes and stood behind Kate while she looked for puzzle parts to join. It took me a few minutes, but I found two that fit.

"I wish you liked to do puzzles. It would be more fun than watching TV reruns."

"I watch old *Law & Order* episodes for training purposes. Besides, Fred Thompson wants to be president. I need to record all his shows before they get a new DA. They'll be collector's items like Reagan's shows on *Death Valley Days*."

"Do you really think he'd get elected?"

"Who knows? America needs another actor in the White House. All these years of a guy who barely speaks English are too much." I took another sip of scotch and found another puzzle piece to fit.

"See, you're good at this." She knows flattery goes a long way with me.

"My whole life is a puzzle. I have to rest my brain when I'm at home."

"I thought you knew the people who wrote the notes to C.J."

"I know the local members of The Coalition for American Family Values. One of those lunatics typed the notes. I'm just not convinced they tried to poison C.J. Two of the locals are probably just bigoted blowhards. The other seems like a possible psycho, but he's not the one who spiked the food Lum's grandson was delivering. So, we've got a mystery guy somewhere out there, and I don't know who he is."

"You're looking at the bad guys for a clue? Why not look at C.J. herself?"

I slapped my forehead with the heel of my hand. "Ah, Watson, what a fool I have been! Why didn't I think of that? My dear woman, what would I do without you?" I spoke in my best Sherlock Holmes accent.

"See, you need me," Kate said.

"Of course I need you, Katsy, but I have tried to look at C.J. And I'm still looking, but so far no one has sent me any juicy stories or revelations. I'm hoping to get some dirt directly from a Nashville guy in the know."

"Well, good luck," she said, just as a kitchen timer chirped. "Aha! The chicken parm is done. Why don't you turn the heat under that water up to high? The cavetelli will only take a couple of minutes."

"Aha! I can do that."

* * * *

I checked with Len Alcock later that night and learned that Harley Flatt and company spent an uneventful Thursday at Dollywood. Len's previous overnight shift was equally unremarkable. John left him again at midnight, and all remained quiet between then and eight in the morning. I couldn't help feeling a false sense of security, but thought about an unseen ax getting ready to fall.

The next morning, John Gallagher and I walked into headquarters together. Bettye was already working away, doing her part to keep the city of Prospect safe for democracy. John stepped behind her chair and toward his desk. She looked at me and smiled.

"Good mornin', gentlemen. You two getting' ready for the big show on Saturday?"

"Morning, Betts. I can hardly wait." I sounded less than enthused.

John offered his usual greeting. "Hi, Sarge. How's it goin'?"

I said, "I can't help thinking Saturday night is when the balloon may go up."

"Balloon?" Bettye questioned my euphemism.

"Yeah, balloon. You know, when the balloon goes up we're under attack. When the you-know-what hits the fan. When the bad guys come over the hill."

Still no comprehension.

"It's an Army thing."

"Oh," she said.

"Maybe someone will try to clip C.J. at the concert."

"Think positively, boss," John said.

"Easy for you to say."

"Sam, I meant to ask you," Bettye said, "did you show those pictures of this man Mitchell to David Chan yesterday?"

I slapped my forehead, but didn't do my Sherlock Holmes act again. I had forgotten to give copies of the Bob Mitchell pictures to Stan Rose, who met with David Chan at the restaurant after school. But then again, I had no evidence that Bob was anything but a concerned father. Rationalization comes so easy for me.

"You know, boss," John said, "you never used to forget anything back on the job. You might want to get checked for old timer's disease."

"You mean Alzheimer's perhaps?" I asked.

"Yeah, old timer's…where you lose your memory and can't recognize anyone."

I closed my eyes and shook my head.

"Thanks for the advice, John," I said.

"You know, Sarge, back on the Island, we all thought the boss had a *photostatic* memory."

Bettye giggled. I wanted her to stop doing that.

"Lord have mercy!" I said, and headed to my office.

At ten after nine, Bettye buzzed my phone.

"There's an Alfred Steinmetz on the phone for you." She connected the call.

"Sam, I wish I could tell you that I worked my fingers to the bone to get you this information," the general said. "But I didn't. A couple of phone calls and a fax of the photos you gave me to the right man and I got an immediate recognition on your subject."

Hot diggity, I thought.

"My contact knew him from his time with the 2nd of the 10thSpecial Forces," Steinmetz said. "Your man's name is not Mitchell. It's Robertson, Robert Robertson, a retired master sergeant. He did thirty-five years active duty. Started out with the 82nd, went to the 2nd Division in Korea, then some time with the 101st and finally into Special Forces, where he stayed for more than twenty years."

"I knew he had the look about him," I said.

"He should. I hear he was a good soldier."

"Great job, boss. Tell me more."

Like cops, certain soldiers like the respectful familiarity of the term *boss*.

The general continued. "Prior to the promotion to E-8, he was an engineer NCO—a qualified master blaster. So you did see him up at Fort Devens, probably teaching basic demolitions. He was stationed there several times between overseas stints at Bad Tolz. If you met him twenty years ago, he was probably a staff sergeant. Of course, you may have run across him at the JFK Center, too, but that's not important."

Bettye stepped into my doorway and turned two palms up. I took that to mean she wanted to know if Steinmetz had offered any useful information. I gave her the international sign for okay.

She went to Mr. Coffee at the side of the room and poured two cups. She placed one next to me and hers on the outside edge of my desk. Then she disappeared, only to return with two chocolate chip cookies the size of small manhole covers resting on a napkin. She put the cookies next to my coffee cup and sat in a guest chair to listen to my phone conversation. I winked at her.

The general continued his monologue "As far as connecting him to this Coalition of yours or any domestic extremist group, I got nothing from either MI or CID or even Homeland Security, for that matter. I thought you'd like me to check with them as well."

He paused to let that sink in and impress me with his ability to access some of the more confidential government databases.

"Sounds like you covered everything, General. Want a job as a detective?"

"I'm too old to play cops and robbers." He chuckled "Should you need more information, I suggest you contact Command Sergeant Major Tibor Szabo at Head and Head, 10th Group. They've moved from Devens to Fort Carson."

Ha, I knew that.

"You ready to copy?" he asked. "Here's his contact information."

He gave me several phone numbers.

"General, I appreciate your help. I don't understand why Robertson has assumed a new identity, but perhaps your input will help me get a leg over with our mystery here. I owe you a favor."

"Why yes, sir, you do. You surely do."

I had just sold part of my soul to the devil, and he signed the invoice.

"Good luck, Colonel," he said. "Let me know how you make out. I'll be in touch." He hung up.

"Son of a bitch!" I said.

Bettye stopped sipping her coffee and looked at me with wide eyes.

A term Steinmetz used, master blaster, stuck in my mind. Robertson was an explosives expert. I hoped to hell he was on my side. I buzzed the intercom to tell John. He walked in, poured his own coffee and took a seat, then I gave them the news.

* * * *

The late morning temperature had already reached the upper forties, and the weatherman predicted at least another ten degrees before the end of the day. I walked across the town square, crossed the street and waved to Mae Waddell who sat looking out her window. I continued toward the Foothills View Motel and after turning into the driveway entrance, walked another hundred and fifty yards before reaching the blacktop parking lot and office. Finding no one behind the reception desk, I slapped an old-fashioned bell sitting on the raised counter. In less than a minute the owner, Clay Plemmons, came out from the back room.

"Mornin', Chief," he said. "What can I do fer y'all this mornin'?"

I told him I needed the information from Robert Mitchell's registration form. He photocopied the 5x7 handwritten index card and gave me the Visa number Mitchell used to pay for his room.

Mitchell, or Robertson, had provided a home address in a village between Fredericksburg and Fort A.P. Hill in eastern Virginia, not far from Interstate 95. That made sense. A retired Army man would settle near an active installation to take advantage of the commissary, Post Exchange and medical facilities.

He listed his vehicle as a Saab 9-5 with Davidson County, Tennessee plates. That sounded a little more interesting until I called Bettye, who ran the plate and found it registered to Jennifer Mitchell at a Nashville address. Not terribly unusual, Tennessee plates are less expensive than those in Virginia. I walked into the lot, found the car parked there and checked it out. The exterior looked clean, and the interior uncluttered. Very military. I learned nothing from it.

I decided to have a serious chat with Robert Robertson after lunch when I drove to Dollywood. Remembering one of my cardinal rules for detectives, I'd never conduct an important interview on an empty stomach.

Back at the PD, I began barking orders. "Hey, John, I want some company. You up for an early lunch?"

"Sure, boss. What do you recommend?"

"The easiest is Chinese. Wah Lum's just across the square."

"I can't do Chinese any more, boss. Can you imagine? I'm allergic to *suitamol maglucinate* now," he said.

"You're allergic to what?"

"*Suitamol maglucinate.*" He repeated it slowly, as if speaking to a dimwitted child. "You know MSG."

Bettye laughed. I growled and shook my finger at her.

"Don't laugh at him, young lady! You only encourage him."

She made a gesture of wiping the smile from her face, but couldn't keep from grinning.

"What?" John looked baffled as to why anyone would question him.

"Okay, John, how about Mexican? El Jibarito is a short drive away. Good food and cold cerveza. What do you say?"

"Sure, boss, sounds good. Anyways, the Chinaman might poison us. Want us to bring anything back for you, Sarge?" he said.

"No, thank you, John. I can't afford to eat as much as the boss." She looked at me again and burst out laughing.

My police department was turning into a segment of *Laugh In*.

"Remember what I told you about keeping 3x5 cards," I asked Bettye. "When I'm gone, you'll be glad you have something to remember all this."

John said, "Whattaya talkin' about, boss?"

I pointed toward the back door. "Go, John."

Alberto Mendez, the owner and host at El Jibarito, ushered us to a booth. The back of John's seat showed a brightly colored, hand carved toucan sitting on a tree limb, among a mass of leaves and tropical flowers. Behind me, a carved, machete-wielding farmer harvested an agave cactus in preparation of making tequila.

The waiter dropped off two menus and took our drink order. I asked for a draught of Dos Equis, and John wanted a Miller Lite. A dark-skinned little girl gave us a basket of tortilla chips and a small pitcher of salsa while we looked at the menus. John munched on a chip.

"Hey, boss, wanna get a bowl of that dip they make?"

"You want something more than the salsa?"

"Yeah, let's get some of that, whaddaya call it, green *gwock-a-motos.*"

"What the hell are you talking about?"

"You know, green *gwock-a-motos*," he repeated, almost sheepishly.

"Sure, John, I do know. And you know what really disturbs me?"

"Whatsa matter, boss?"

"You say something stupid like green gwock-a-motos and I know exactly what you mean. That's just sick, John. Sick."

When the waiter returned, I ordered shrimp enchiladas with rancho sauce. John picked a combination number five—chicken, cheese and beef enchiladas. I added a side order of guacamole for my mentally challenged colleague.

"Besides the thing you'll be doing with Ralph Oliveri this afternoon," I said. "I've got another job for you. We have a kid who's applied for a PO's job. He's already returned his paperwork and is getting his medical and psych exams from the county. Want to do a background investigation on him?"

"Sure, I love doing candidate investigations. Can we give him a poly?"

"Yeah, the county examiner will do one for you after we know the kid's passed the med and psych. If you have any specific questions after you interview him, write them up for the sheriff's guy."

After lunch, John went his way, and I drove to Pigeon Forge.

* * * *

Being in no particular hurry, I took the route through the national park. I snaked along the narrow road paralleling the Little River, wishing I had driven my old Austin-Healey and not the Crown Victoria land whale. When I reached the connecting road to US 441, I turned north and ran alongside the west prong of the Little Pigeon River until reaching the Dollywood turnoff.

The uniformed attendant at the parking lot kiosk waved me through without stopping me and asking to see a badge. I guess he'd gotten to know my shiny gray car.

I walked into the music hall and again found it dark at the rear, with the stage area well lit. C.J. stood in the spotlight on the platform, singing into a hand microphone, with three girls providing backup.

I stopped walking and watched her for a few moments, but didn't recognize the song. Her voice sounded husky and sexy, the music a little bit country and a whole lot blues. Under a washed-off demin shirt, she wore a low-cut white tank top over a black mini-skirt. Even with the spiky hair, she looked exquisite and sounded great.

I continued down the aisle and as C.J. wrapped up her song, I gave Harlan Flatt a poke on his shoulder, took him aside and explained my pending conversation with retired Master Sergeant Robertson. I wanted the interview to be just between Robertson and me, but wanted Harley in close visual contact in case the good sergeant decided to pull something drastic. Rusty Filmore, the young Pigeon Forge cop with hair to match his name, was again part of the detail, so I asked him to keep an eye on C.J. while Harley and I conducted business elsewhere.

C.J. had finished the blues number, and the piano accompanist began warming up a new tune while C.J. and her girls prepared to sing their next song. I stepped up next to Bob Robertson and got his attention.

"Can we have a word in the lobby where you'll be able to hear me without any competition?"

"Can we wait until C.J. finishes this next song?" he asked.

I shook my head. "No, we need to talk now—about Bob Robertson."

His friendly smile changed to a poker face. He nodded. I stepped back about three feet and motioned for him to lead the way up the aisle. Harley stood at the top of the carpet where the seats ended, his right hand resting on the butt of his Glock. He backed up a little and let Robertson pass, then followed me and took up a spot against a wall not far from where I began the conversation.

"I've just learned about a retired Master Sergeant named Robertson. Seems he looks a hell of a lot like you," I said.

"Yeah, well, I guess I need to explain."

"You think?"

"To start with, you're right. Robertson is my name. Mitchell is Jenny's married name. She's divorced now. The marriage only lasted a couple years. I used her name because I drove her car, and I'm on her credit card account. She looked at this as a business expense and wanted to pay for my room with her card."

That explanation didn't satisfy me.

"A business expense? You want to explain that one?"

"As you seem to know, I just retired from the Army. I've had a lot of experience with, ah...security matters. She asked me to tag along because C.J. was threatened. I thought I could offer a little extra protection for my daughter while you guys were concentrating on C.J."

"Sort of pick up the slack for us shit-kickin' local cops?"

He put on a friendly smile and shrugged. "I meant no offense. I just wanted to do the best I could to keep Jenny safe."

"Did C.J. know you went on the payroll?"

He kept his delivery soft and cordial. "I'm not getting paid. Jenny's just picking up expenses."

I pushed a little harder. "I asked if C.J. knew."

He didn't waiver. "Far as I know, she doesn't. Jenny has the authority to write checks and take care of expenses, no questions asked." He turned two palms up and shrugged again. "In the world of show business, the cost of my room isn't a drop in the bucket."

"Why tell the story about being a retired civilian engineer? Why not a retired NCO?"

"If you knew the business I was in, you'd understand. Most of us like to keep a low profile."

How many times had I heard the expression 'low profile' in the last week?

"I do know the business you were in. I was there myself for twenty-one years, full and part time. How do you think I saw through your scam?"

He shrugged and shook his head.

"I recognized you from somewhere," I said. "Finally, Fort Devens came to mind, and someone checked for me. Less than a day later, I knew who you were."

"I'm sorry," he said. "I didn't mean to deceive you. I shouldn't have wasted your time."

"I still don't see the need for a new name."

"Stupid mistake."

"Do you need to tell me anything else about yourself or your current affiliations before I call a guy named Tibor Szabo and ask about you?"

"Tibor Szabo?" Robertson smiled. "He's a good man. Look, Sam, I'm telling you the truth." His grin got wider and looked sardonic. "If you spent twenty-one years in the racket what makes you think Szabo would say anything to betray me?"

"I'd make another phone call first. Pave the way, so to speak."

"I could make a phone call, too."

"You could, but I'll guarantee my friend outranks your friend—unless you've got the Chairman of the Joint Chiefs on speed dial."

He lost the grin.

"Friendship goes only so far in the Army," I said. "Szabo's still on active duty. I have enough horsepower behind me to make him think about himself and his pension first."

"Then you've got me." His wide smile came back, like a kid caught with his hand in the cookie jar, trying to charm his way out of a jam. "My story's true. You won't learn anything else about me. I'm only here to keep Jenny safe, in case the people who threatened C.J. intend to get violent."

"I assume you're carrying at least one gun."

He nodded but didn't move his hand. "Just one, holster's on my right side."

"I'm sure you don't have a concealed carry permit that's valid in Tennessee."

"No, sorry."

I found myself in a quandary. Do I let Robertson continue to march? Retain his gun and help us keep Jenny and C.J. safe? Trust him based on his military credentials? If I wanted an easy job, I should have learned to fix small appliances.

"I won't arrest you on a weapons charge—a favor from one old soldier to another. But I want the gun. You'll get it back after the concert Saturday."

He nodded again. "Fair enough, but are you sure you don't want another competent helper armed and ready to rock and roll?"

This time I grinned at his use of language. "I'm sure, and just so Harley doesn't get nervous when he sees a pistol, take it out with your left hand and pass it to me slowly."

Bob Robertson did exactly as I requested. He knew the drill. I stood there and received a Beretta model 84F, a fourteen shot, .380 caliber automatic—a compact, well-made pistol that would make a competent shooter a dangerous person.

"Nice gun." I pushed the release button and dropped the magazine. I slipped that into my jacket pocket, racked the slide back and caught the ejected shell in my left hand.

"I hope I won't need that," he said.

"Makes two of us. I wish you had introduced yourself days ago. If I knew who and what you were, I'd have put you to work."

"I am sorry for the confusion. I'll help you anyway I can."

"Okay, I'll let you know. But for now, trust Officer Flatt. He's good with his weapon, too."

"Good to know," he said.

"Thanks for your time, Top." I used the Army expression for a Master Sergeant. "You can go back inside and sit with your daughter now."

He looked at me and nodded. "Yes, sir, I'll do that." He stood and walked into the music hall without looking back.

"What the hell was that all about?" Harley asked.

"You heard what he said. You believe him?"

"Hard ta say. Mebbe—mebbe not. Like ya asked, I've been watchin' him and ain't seen nuthin' out o' place."

"That's good, but continue to keep an eye on him. If he had one gun, there's no reason he won't have at least one more. Consider this guy potentially dangerous—very dangerous. I hope he's just here being a good father, but as you said, who knows? Tell Rusty and anyone else on the detail about this, but make sure the news doesn't get spread all over the county. I'll see what more I can learn."

Chapter Fifteen

I'd grown tired of driving between Prospect and Pigeon Forge and resigned myself to leave the Crown Vic at home and take my '67 Austin-Healey the next time I drove that winding, mountainous portion of US 321. If I had to make the trip, I wanted a few kicks along the way.

On the drive home over the mountain, I did something I chastise other drivers for doing. I used my cell phone while in forward motion. I asked Ralph Oliveri to search his databases for any information he could gather on Bob Robertson. Bettye had already obtained the Virginia driver's license information on the man and retrieved his exact dates of service in the Army. By giving Ralph his date of birth and e-mailing him the two photos I'd taken, Ralph could do a good job of seeing what the Justice Department and other sides of the Federal law enforcement knew about my subject.

I walked back into the PD and didn't get a chance to take off my sport jacket when I saw Beaver Booker sitting on one of the chairs in the reception area off to Bettye's right. "Hi guys," I said to Bettye and John. "Beaver, you waiting for someone?"

"Sergeant tol' me Mr. Puckett ain't here t'day. I need ta talk wiff y'all if dat's okay."

"Sure, about what?"

"Mr. Puckett axed me ta come in if I knew anythin' y'all should need ta know, if ya unnerstan' what I'm sayin'."

"Okay, I know what you mean. Come inside." I pointed to my office. "Hey, John, I want you to sit in on this."

152

John got up, and the three of us went into my office. I made the introductions.

"Beaver, this is Detective Gallagher. John, Beaver Booker."

They shook hands.

"Okay, Beaver, what have you got for us?"

He elaborated on his original statement. "Mr. Puckett tol' me if I come up wiff somethin' good, he make that new arrest go away."

"I understand," I said. "We're looking for something good, not kiddy stuff like pot or some other bullshit. Know what I mean?"

Beaver nodded. "Yessir, I ain't bringin' y'alls no bullshit."

"Whattaya know?"

"I know dis guy who stold stuff from da Army up ta Knoxville. Lotsa stuff."

Immediately, the thought of military grade weapons started racing through my head. I could have let that idea run away with me because this looked like it might be exciting. Then I took a second to regroup, tell myself it might only be a theft of motor oil and came back to earth.

"What kind of stuff, exactly?" John asked.

"Man's a supply sergeant," Beaver said. "He brag he steal everythin' an' trade fer mo' stolen stuff from udder soldiers an' den sell what's been stold."

"Beaver, the word *everything* takes in a lot. I don't care if he steals pens and paper clips. What exactly do you know he's stolen?"

A little frustration showed on Beaver's face. "Man tell me he get drugs, ammunition, even 'splosives. Dat big enough?"

"Sounds better than paper clips." I looked at John, and he raised his eyebrows. "Have you seen any of this...stuff?"

"I been ta his house an' seen drugs. Don't zactly know what dey wuz, cause I don't mess wiff drugs, 'cept mebbe a li'l reefer now an' ag'in. Ya know what I'm sayin'?"

He didn't wait for an answer.

"I seen Army amminition boxes, too. An' he tol' me he got him some plastic 'splosives too an' sold dem ta some white dude from down Chattanooga way. But I ain't seen no 'splosives."

"You know anything more specific about this?"

Beaver shrugged. "I seen what I seen. Whatch y'all mean more pacific?"

"What's this guy's name?"

"Man's name Solomon Willets. He live up ta Lonsdale, an' woik in one o' dem Army places up ta Knoxville."

"You know what kind of Army unit?"

"Yeah, dat one wit da big fenced lot an' all dem trucks an' bulldozers an' shit."

"Does he work there every day?"

"Naw, once a momf…den mebbe a week o' two in da summer."

"Does the name 844th Engineers sound familiar?" I asked.

"Don' mean nuffin ta me."

"Where's he work full-time?" John asked.

"Some mo-tel on da Interstate. East end o' Knoxville. He do maintenance."

"What's Solomon's address up in Lonsdale?" I asked.

He shrugged again. "I don' know—up off Western, someplace. I kin show ya."

"Okay, you and Detective Gallagher can take a ride and get an address. First, let's get back to the white guy and the explosives. What else did Solomon say about this white man?"

"He say da man's a soldier. Foist he sell him some drugs. Den he come back an' ax Solomon fuh some 'splosives, you know, put in a order. Solomon, he say, 'Easy, I kin git dat,' an' he does. After he sell the 'splosives, Solomon show me da cash. He say da white dude look bad. You know, like a bad-ass, mebbe a little crazy. Solomon tinks he gonna off somebody wiff the 'splosives."

I'm not sure about John, but I get genuinely excited when a stool tells me a story like this. Jeremy Goins looked a little crazy. But Bob Robertson looked more like a soldier.

"When did this explosive stuff happen?" I asked.

"Las' week mebbe. Ax Solomon, he knows."

"And how do you know Solomon? Where do you see him?"

"I go ta dis club on Magnolia. Ya know, a brother's place. Day got dancers once in a while. I have a few drinks, listen ta da music, watch da girls. Solomon be dare all da time."

"Okay, Beaver, if this pans out, I'll tell Officer Puckett to forget about the obstructing charge."

He smiled—a good sign.

"If this is really good, I'll go to the district attorney and ask him to go easy on the assault Tar Baby charged you with, maybe let you skate. I'll give you that little extra—no charge. But remember, this has to be good 4-1-1. Understand?"

Beaver smiled from ear to ear. A gold tooth showed on the top left side of his mouth.

"I'm tellin' y'alls good shit. Got no reason ta lie. I know y'all kin check up on it."

How many times had I heard that? I hoped it was good information. I tried to put a face to the 'white dude' Beaver mentioned and only thought of two possibilities. But, was there someone else?

"John, use your personal car. Then gas it up at the city pump when you get back. Beaver will show you how to get up to the Lonsdale neighborhood in Knoxville," I said. "Beaver, wait outside for a minute, please."

When Beaver left, I took the Beretta I'd confiscated from Bob Robertson out of my jacket pocket and handed it to John. He had already given me back the old Smith & Wesson before he went house hunting with the Collinsons. I didn't want him wandering around the Lonsdale housing project unarmed.

"Until you have your own gun, use this. I doubt you'll need one, but guns are like under drawers—it's very un-cool if you get caught without them." Then I smiled. "If a cop catches you with a concealed weapon, call me. I might be able to get your sentence reduced."

"Why are you so good to me, boss?"

"You were always my favorite, John."

"Frankie used to say you claimed he was your favorite."

"Everyone knew Frank was a liar. Believe me, not him."

"Okay, boss. See ya later."

John and Beaver took off toward northeast Knoxville.

I stepped out of my office, and Bettye said, "Rachel Williamson called just five minutes ago. She wants you to call back. Says she has information you need."

"Ya see, Bettye, sometimes being a cop gets exciting as hell. Young Beaver drops a dime on a mook from Knoxville, and Rachel may have another piece to the puzzle. Am I good or what?"

"Darlin', your talent is only exceeded by your modesty."

"Did you talk to Buck Webbster like that?"

"Buck wasn't my all-time favorite boss." She flashed a smile that could melt the polar ice cap.

"Sounds like you want something, Sergeant."

"Who, me?"

I nodded and tried to look thoughtful "You'd better ask me whatever favor you need soon. Don't let me forget what a big fan you are."

"Go make your phone call, Sammy."

I didn't get the opportunity to pick up the receiver before my phone rang.

Ralph Oliveri said, "Your suspect was an easy one to trace. You know all about his thirty-five years in the Army. Most of that was covered with some impressive security clearances that he got updated at the required intervals. Far as I can tell, he's squeaky clean."

"That's good news and bad news."

"Sorry. I couldn't find any involvement with anyone or anything that would draw attention to him since he separated from active duty. And nothing shown using the AKA of Mitchell either. I ran Jennifer Mitchell for you, too, and got zippo. Two solid citizens. You need to look elsewhere."

"The big question is where?"

"My crystal ball is outta gas." Then he changed the subject. "Hey, I like your man Gallagher. If I ever learn what language he speaks, I'll have a good time working with him. You think Berlitz has a course on tape?"

"It'll take a long time and a superior intellect to understand Gallaghese. Hang in there, bubbee. You're happy with the results so far with his infiltration of the Collinson gang?"

"Well, those two goons didn't exactly plan the gunfight at the OK Corral while John was wired, but it was all interesting stuff from an intelligence standpoint. I can't arrest anyone yet, and it doesn't seem like they have an inclination to off your rock star on Saturday."

"Country and western."

"Huh?"

"She's not a rock star. She sings country and western. And, I'll have you know, after a shaky start we're now the best of friends."

"I've always said people hate you at first sight, and it takes them about a week to either love or despise you."

"My ego suffers each time we speak. But, hey, thanks for the info."

"You're welcome. And you owe me—again."

"Of course I do, Ralphie. I'll just throw out my bill for making your life interesting. See ya."

"Nuts!"

I called Rachel's direct office number and got no answer. The voice mail kicked in, and I left a message. Same results on her cell phone.

It was late afternoon, I wanted answers, and waiting never sets right with me. I called the main station number and spoke with the receptionist. She told me Rachel and her co-anchor just went into a meeting with their producers and station manager—probably a long get-together.

"It's almost time for us to close up shop at five," I said. "I know she'll be getting ready for her news brief during 5 O'clock Magazine and then her show at six. Please, this is important. Put a note on her desk asking her to call me at home or on my cell phone. The cell's the best way to reach me. My office will be closed."

I didn't want the general population of the network to know Rachel and I were buddy-buddy and that she had my home phone number, so I gave both numbers to the young lady. At times like these, I'm hopelessly impatient.

I called John Gallagher's cell phone.

"Where are you?"

"I don't know, boss."

Not the answer I wanted. "How about a guess?"

"It's gettin' dark, and I don't know the roads."

Background noise made it sound like they were driving at fifty miles per hour.

"Beaver still with you?"

"Yeah, he's here."

Grrrr.

"Is he lost, too?"

There was a pause, and John mumbled something I didn't quite hear. "No, he says we're on...Maryville Pike, heading to... Wildwood. Wait a minute. Then we'll turn...somewhere... and...be in Prospect." A long pause. "I'll be there in fifteen minutes."

"Did you get an address for this guy Solomon?"

"Yeah, boss. Beaver saw his car in the driveway. We got the right place."

"Good work, John. Tell Beaver he's a prince."

I called Stan Rose who had already begun work on the road supervising two other cops.

"As soon as Gallagher gets back here with the snitch, the three of us are heading to Lonsdale. Go home, and get into your street-crime clothes."

"What's in Lonsdale?" Stanley asked.

"The informant gave us info on a guy who may have sold our mystery man the atropine."

"How'd you find the snitch?"

"I'll tell you later. This same guy may have taken an order for C-4 from the man who poisoned Johnny."

"C-4? Like explosive C-4?"

"Uh-huh."

Stanley, who usually sounds like a Cal Tech graduate, lapsed into his Ebonics act. "Man, this be da peaceful side o' da Smokies. Whatchew doin' gettin' me mixed up wit ex-plosives fo'?"

"There's nothing ATF can do that you and I can't do just as well. And we'll have John along for moral support. Besides, we're probably not going to arrest this guy, just brace him and get information. Bring your shotgun."

"You want a shotgun? Jeez, you better write a note to my wife if I get into trouble."

"Don't worry, Tonto. I have the silver bullets. Hurry up, and get dressed."

"You think someone's gonna blow up C.J.?"

"Who knows?"

"When are we leaving?"

"As soon as you get here." I tried to sound impatient as I hung up.

Bettye began closing down the PD offices for the night and turned over the radio and dispatch work to the county 911 center. I told her my plan.

"You be careful up there, Sammy. Don't go gettin' mixed up with people who have explosives. Are the Knox County deputies goin' to back you up?"

"A bunch of deputies may scare this guy to death. Too many cops and he may clam up. And I don't want other people to see what I do. I'm more interested in information than locking this guy up right now. I'll leave that to someone else later on."

She put her hands on her hips and feigned an attitude. "And just what are you going to do?"

"Don't ask."

"Sam!"

"Remember, tomorrow night we're all going to the big concert? You can't get mad at me. I have the tickets."

She made a face just as John Gallagher walked in.

I called my wife. "Kats, I'm afraid dinner's going to have to wait for me. John, Stanley and I are going to Knoxville to question a guy who may be involved in the C.J. Profitt business."

"Any idea when you'll be home?"

"Shouldn't be too late. I'll warm up something later."

"Okay, sweetie. Bitsey and I will be here."

"Rachel Williamson may call with information she got from her man in Nashville. I gave her our home number. Please speak with her, and write down what she knows." I didn't think that was much of an imposition.

"You want me to act as liaison with your girlfriends?" Perhaps Katherine didn't agree.

"Not exactly, but I'll be turning off my cell. When I get into an important discussion with a nefarious character I don't want a phone ringing."

"Nefarious character?"

"Just an idiot who steals Army supplies."

"Do I have to mention I want you to be careful?"

"I'm always careful."

"You're asking me to speak with your girlfriend... How careful is that?"

"She's not a girlfriend. Just talk to her."

"Sure. We'll discuss your finer points."

"You'll be on the phone for hours."

"Oh, get lost."

"Thank you, love."

"You're such a creep."

"But I'm your creep, dahlink. Cheerio."

Chapter Sixteen

At ten to six, I took the Western Avenue exit from I-640, drove east a little and then turned north on Texas Avenue. In another five minutes, we were at the corner of Texas and Stonewall. Solomon Willetts' home sat across the street from where I stopped in a neighborhood full of small post war homes. Some looked neat and well cared for, but many appeared to have missed their twenty-year reunion with a paint brush.

We watched the house for twenty minutes. The interior was well-lit, and two cars were parked in the driveway. The night was neither cold nor temperate. Low cloud cover obscured the moon, and the unusually high humidity gave the chilled air an uncomfortable feel.

The dispatcher confirmed both the license plates as registered to Solomon and his wife Etrula Willetts. During those twenty minutes, no one went into or came out of the house.

Prior to leaving Prospect, I downloaded Willett's photo from his driver's license file at the Department of Safety. Solomon was a unique looking person with an elongated cone-shaped head, broad nose over a pencil mustache, and vacant humorless eyes. We'd experience no confusion identifying him.

I thought of two ways to approach our task. We had neither an arrest warrant nor search warrant, so kicking in the door wasn't an option. Judges always liked to see that pesky thing called *probable cause* before issuing warrants, and I didn't have any. But warrants with 'no knock' stipulations are always fun. With one of those, if we ran into resistance, Stanley could butt stroke anyone in his path with the model 37 Ithaca riot gun sitting next to him in the back seat.

Unfortunately, that night we were operating on a wing and a prayer. Or more properly, in the vernacular, we had squat. So, I chose Plan B and the soft approach. We could always get ugly if circumstances demanded.

Stan left his shotgun locked in the car. He and I went to the front door. I sent John around back and hoped to hell he didn't have to use the *borrowed* Beretta tucked into his waistband.

I gave the front door of the Willetts' home a healthy hammering. The porch light came on, and Solomon answered wearing a white T-shirt and forest green work pants. The blast of warm air that met me at the door made me think the Willetts set their thermometer on eighty.

"Solomon Willetts?" I showed him my big oval badge, but didn't say which police department we represented. "We've got serious business to talk over with you, so step outside and avoid getting embarrassed in front of your wife."

His expression dropped. I'd have bet the registration of my restored Austin-Healey that Solomon thought he'd be getting nicked.

"Aw right, but I gotta get me a coat. It's cold out here."

I nodded, and Stan followed Willetts into the house. I stayed outside and waited. In two minutes, they returned. Solomon wore a hip-length jacket that matched his trousers.

I told Stan, "Ring John. Tell him to come up here."

He nodded, stepped a few feet away and used his cell phone.

"Wha's up?" Solomon tried using a strained smile.

I laid a hand on his chest and pushed. "I'm gonna stick a bayonet up your ass, sport, unless you tell me exactly what I want to hear."

He blinked and lost the smile. His jaw dropped again. My *soft* approach seemed to be working.

"Look," I said. "We're not Army CID or the FBI. And I'm not overly concerned how much you've stolen from the Reserves over the years. Understand, Supply Sergeant."

I wanted to bluff my way into cooperation through fear, and Solomon looked scared.

"But, Solomon, old boy, you screw with me, lie to me, even once, and I'll smack the livin' shit outta you and call the Federal cops from Locust Street down here."

Solomon took an involuntary step backwards and hit the shingles. "Whatchew talkin' 'bout, man?" His frightened look began approaching panic.

"Okay, we'll wait here until the Feds bring a search warrant and tear your house apart. And remember, pal, when they find something in that house, not only do you go, but Etrula goes, too. Capiche?"

I didn't think Solomon spoke Italian, but I used the word anyway. Old habits die hard.

Solomon's jaw almost fell to his beltline.

"That happens, and you can pay for your lawyers on the family plan—maybe get a discount."

I paused to let that register. John Gallagher had returned from the back of the house. Now, three surrounded one. But Solomon still remained silent.

"Okay, what's it gonna be?" I asked. "Do we do business now, or do I call the FBI and watch you go for a Federal crime?"

His Adam's apple moved up and down as he swallowed and fought for words. "Whoa, whoa, whoa! Whoa! What da fuck you talkin' 'bout?"

I played another hunch, took out a photo of Bob Robertson and showed it to Solomon. If my ploy didn't work, I was finished and would have to start looking for another person who needed a couple of bricks of C-4. Robertson fit the profile of a bad-ass soldier more than Jeremy Goins. But I still had no idea why Robertson would want to off C.J. Proffitt. When you get desperate for answers, you do drastic things.

"I'm talking about him, genius. You've got his money. He's got your merchandise. What more do you owe him? You want to go to jail to protect him. You want your wife to go to jail *for him*? How far can you carry customer service?"

Solomon choked out a reasonable question. "Who da fuck are you?" His eyes looked like white hockey pucks with dotted centers.

Willetts was beginning to annoy me. I pushed on his chest again, this time a little harder.

"People often call me Speedo, but my real name is Mr. Earl." I thought he might be familiar with music from The Cadillacs.

"Do whot?"

But he wasn't. So, I tried a different approach.

"I'm the guy who walks away from here happy and leaves you alone. Or I'm the guy who turns your life upside down and ruins your next twenty years. Now, isn't this the man with whom you just did business?"

"How'd you know?"

A large marmalade cat walked from behind the house, saw us and turned abruptly, then raced off in the direction from which it came.

"Who gives a shit how I knew?" I said. "Yes or no? Tell the truth, not what you think I want to hear."

"Yes," he said.

"Okay, not that it matters, but why the hell did you swipe atropine from your medics?"

"I jest wanted some pain killers. You know, oxy or some udder shit they got in da farma-cee. I traded for a bunch o' shit, didn't really steal nuffin. Da atra-peen be wit' da udder stuff."

"This guy in the picture," I said. "He ask you for atropine? Specifically?"

"Naw." Solomon shook his head vigorously. "He axed ta see what drugs I got wit me, nuffin pacific. I show him, and he pick out dat. So good fuh me. I figgered where da hell I gonna off dat stuff anyways?"

"Yeah, good for you. How'd this guy find you?"

"We's drillin' one Saturday, an' he walks inta da unit supply wearin' BDUs. He wiff a guy I know, a SFC from one o' da construction companies. My man, da SFC, done ten, eleven year active. He a real soldier-type, airborne an' all dat shit. Nice guy, name o' Wilson Dees. He intra-duce me ta da white guy. Dis white dude, he wearin' t'ree up an' t'ree down on his collars."

Wilson Dees was a Sergeant First Class. Three up and three down in any soldier's language means a Master Sergeant—as in Master Sergeant Bob Robertson.

Solomon kept talking. "He say he from Chattanooga, an' he need somfin he cain't git at his unit down dare. He ax me if we can do some bidness fuh cash money. I looks at him. He looks like a soldier, you know, lifer-type. I says, 'Yeah, we can do bidness, but COD cash only.' He got ta bring cash."

"So he meets you here, he buys the drugs, and then what?"

164

"He go away, simple like. Den a couple days later he call me. He say he want ta see me. He come here again, not at the unit, here at my house, an' say he want some C-fo, an' he pull out mo cash. Only I ain't got no C-fo. I mean, who da fuck keep C-fo in his house? You unnerstan' what I'm sayin'?"

"And?" I tried to look impatient.

"Ya really gonna jus' leave me alone, I tell ya?"

"Yeah, do we look like we give a shit what the Army loses? I want to keep this guy from blowing up a particular civilian. But my business is not your most pressing *problem*. Okay?" I put great emphasis on the last word.

"Yeah, yeah, yeah, don' go gittin' hot on me."

"Hey, Solomon, if you don't quit screwin' around and get to the point, I'm gonna get annoyed and ask my little friend here," I pointed to Stanley who stood six inches taller and eighty pounds larger than Willetts, "to tear you apart and leave your bones for the buzzards. You have an answer for me or what?"

"Yeah, yeah, be cool, be cool. Man, you shore don' sound like a local cop. Where da fuck you from?"

"Middle Earth, asshole. Now, answer the question, or my friend is going to rip off your head."

"Okay, okay, be cool, be cool. I ain't givin' ya no grief. He axed me fuh da C-fo. Only, like I say, I ain't got no C-fo, but I say I kin git him some. He give me fo hunnert dollar down, an' I tell him ta come back wiff another fo hunnert. I call him, and he do, an' I give him two bricks o' C-fo. End o' story. I ain't seen him since—swear ta God."

"When was that," I asked.

"I give him da C-fo Wednesday last. End o' story, okay? Are we cool?"

"Yeah, okay." I patted Solomon's cheek. "You're a good boy, Solomon, a fine American. Now, one more thing," I slammed him against the outside wall of his house, took out my Glock and placed the barrel at the base of his left nostril. "If you get a spark of military camaraderie in you and contact this guy or your friend Wilson Dees and mess with my plans—or I just think you screwed up my plans, I'm coming after you. And I'm going to kill you...slowly. Very slowly, maybe cut off your ears first, then shoot you a couple of times and watch you bleed out. Are we clear on this, Solomon? You understand me?"

Willetts was a soldier, but definitely not a hero. He nodded, his eyes blinking uncontrollably.

I pushed harder. "You believe me?"

Another nod. More blinking. "Yessir. I hear ya. You talkin' da gospel."

I smiled and removed my gun from his nose. "Good, you seem like a nice guy, Solomon. It was a pleasure doing business with you." I gave him a friendly pat on the shoulder. "I hope we don't need to see each other again any time soon."

Before I turned, Solomon Willetts rested his head on the shingles and let out a long breath. Then Stanley, John and I left him standing under the porch light in front of his house.

I switched on the ignition of the Ford, hung a quick U-turn and drove south on Texas Avenue. Two blocks down the road, I turned on the lights and drove faster.

Stan cleared his throat. "Hmm, I guess that went well."

"You may be gettin' old, boss, but this was something like you'd have done thirty years ago," John added.

"I don't know what you're talking about, John. I've never done anything like this before. I don't know what came over me."

"You know, Sarge," John continued, "once I saw him dangle a guy who couldn't swim off a pier until he talked."

"That sounds innovative," Stanley said.

"He never beat anyone," John said, "because he could scare them half to death. They thought he was nuts."

"Maybe they were right," Stan said.

"Hey, guys, I'm right here. Don't talk about me."

"Well," Stan said, "if you figure the end justifies the means, I suppose tonight we got the right results."

"Thanks. I love positive feedback."

"You think Solomon will complain to Knox County about getting hassled by three cops from Prospect PD?" Stan asked.

"You left LAPD too soon," I said. "You think that moron will call 911 and tell them three cops squeezed the truth out of him about his side business of selling misappropriated government property? Did you say, 'Hi, I'm Stan, and the two old honkies are my buddies John and Sam?' Get real. He doesn't know us from the Three Stooges."

"I guess," Stan said. "But you old guys are too radical for me. I can't sleep at night after I work with you."

"Cheer up, Sarge," John said. "I lived with this for years. See how good I'm still doin?"

"Oh, yeah, John," Stan said. "You're in great shape."

"Listen, guys, we have to do something with Robertson. I can't connect all the dots yet, but you don't have to be a rocket scientist to know buying the atropine that most likely poisoned Rutledge and getting the C-4, which is obviously destined for no good purpose, puts him on the top of our hit parade."

"He'll probably wait to do something at the show," John said. "He won't explode anything near his daughter in the motel, so we have time."

"I agree," I said. "I'll call Harley. He can keep Bob and Jenny on ice, and I'll meet him back on our turf."

"Sounds good, boss," John said. "Me and the Sarge can back you up."

"That's the plan, guys, but first, I'm going home to have something for dinner. Let the Robertsons sit in cuffs for a while."

"I need a drink." Stan said.

"Have it before you go back into uniform."

"Is nothing sacred with you?"

I ignored Stan's remark. "I'll think about what we can do while I'm eating. Then I'll see if I can get the last bit of information we need to learn *why* Robertson wants to kill C.J. And I guess his daughter is in on this, too. It would be a help if we knew what was motivating him—or her—or them. Always better to have the answers before you ask the questions."

John said, "Some shit, huh?"

"I'll call you both before I leave home. John, you hang out with Lenny at the motel, and see if anything is shaking there. Toss the room again, and search Bob's room, too. Clay Plemmons will give you a key. Stan, see how the other guys are making out on the road, but stay available to meet us."

When we got back to Prospect, we split up, and I called Harley Flatt in Pigeon Forge. He told me C.J. and company were still rehearsing, and Bob Robertson had taken Jenny out for dinner. He drove his Saab that morning, claiming he wanted to run a few errands. I didn't like the idea of that pair being off on their own, but in police work, you often have to deal with lousy timing.

I filled Harley in on the new information we received from shady Solomon Willetts and requested he and several other cops find and put the arm on my friend the Master Sergeant and provide an armed escort back to Prospect.

Chapter Seventeen

When I arrived home at 8:30, Bitsey seemed excessively happy to see me. After her ritual dance and wiggle, I gave her a quick scratch on the chin before she took off at a gallop through the kitchen, around the living room, into the dining room and back into the kitchen, only to flop over on the floor exactly where she began. It felt good to be missed.

After shaking her head and perhaps blaming me for the dog's hooliganism, Kate said, "Oh, my poor boy, you've had a long day."

She wrapped her arms around my neck, pushed against me and kissed me like we were part of a scene filmed by Franco Zeffirelli.

"Yikes! The women in my life give me a greeting like I'm a returning POW. What's the occasion? Did you wreck the Healey?"

"Of course not. We missed you, and you're home late. Why would your daughter or I have an ulterior motive?"

"Beats me, but being on the receiving end ain't bad from my point of view."

"Good. I made you a nice dinner, have a beautiful bottle of chardonnay chilled to 51 degrees and will trickle some of that whisky from the Glen of the Fiddich over a couple of ice cubes if you say the word."

"Damn, you're affectionate. A Glenfiddich après d'grub would be smashing, but I'm afraid I have a little more po-leece work to do so, the wine will be all for me tonight. I just learned something very disturbing about a guy who's been hanging around C.J. all week."

I told Kate almost everything about our interview with Solomon Willetts and what Bob Robertson had been up to. I've learned to leave out annoying little details like sticking my gun into a subject's nose. She only gets upset and spends days thinking I'll end up in Federal court.

"I don't understand much of this yet, but I can't let this guy stay free and accomplish whatever mischief he has in mind."

Kate snapped at me. "You be careful! You'd better get Ralph and his FBI SWAT people to help you. Don't you think?"

"I think we should eat first and work out all these logistics later. I trust Harley Flatt to bring my suspect to me on a platter."

* * * *

Bob Robertson remained on my mind throughout dinner, and I'm afraid I didn't take the time necessary to savor Kate's scallops mornay over rice with steamed asparagus on the side. I hadn't heard from Harley and was getting impatient.

We finished dinner and remained at the table, drinking the last of the Sonoma chardonnay Kate had chosen.

"I wish I'd thought to show David Chan the photos of this guy Robertson. I should have known he was up to no good after I learned about the false identity thing," I said.

"You can't always think of everything, sweetie."

"His story sounded almost reasonable, and I believed him." I took a last sip of wine. "I tend to cut these ex-GIs too much slack."

"You spent a lot of time in the Army and met some good people. Robertson didn't get his job there by not being a good man."

"Yeah, but maybe I'm getting soft. I should have covered those bases."

"Maybe you're trying to do too much yourself. Give a few jobs to other people."

I let out a long breath and nodded. "Yeah. I used to accuse the old Chief of Detectives of not delegating enough to others. Now I'm guilty of the same."

Kate tilted her head and smiled. It's something she does that means don't worry.

"Did Rachel call?" I asked.

"No one's called. What are you two cooking up? Something I shouldn't know about?" She tried to give her question a light sound, but I sensed a little apprehension.

"I cook, my dear, with no females but you. Are we having a problem?"

"No, no problem. It's just that it seems... You know."

"I don't, but I can guess. You're correct, you have no problem. You may perceive one, but it's unfounded. I need information I can't get through my sources. Rachel knows someone in Nashville. Apparently he's the Hedda Hopper of the hillbilly music world. It sounds like he can give her something that may be helpful to me. She's doing me a favor, that's all."

"It just seems that she does you a lot of favors."

"Yes, she does. And I do favors for her—when I can. Do I like her? Yes. Do I flirt with her? Yes. I flirt with your aunt, too, and she's older than my mother would be if Mom was still alive. I like Bettye, and I tease her and flirt with her, too. I hang out with Ralph occasionally. We go to lunch sometimes. That doesn't make me gay."

Kate rolled her eyes.

"If you made me go through life not dealing with people in a way that comes naturally, I would have eaten the gun a long time ago. Well, maybe not eaten a gun, but you know what I mean."

"I guess." She pouted and looked like a little girl who lost her best friend.

"I took this chief's job because I was here by myself...too often. More often than I liked. I felt neglected. I thought you were the one doing the neglecting. You were busy with volunteer work that took up a lot of your life. All that encroached on my time. Now we're more even. We both have things that occupy us outside the home. My getting re-employed was as much your idea as mine—maybe more."

I reached across the table, picked up her half glass of chardonnay and took a greedy sip. I kept talking, and Kate listened. "It's inevitable that we meet people. These people will affect us either negatively or positively. I just happen to have met two attractive younger women. I'm not having sex with them. I like them. I also like Stanley. Junior acts like my son at times. I kind of like that, too. I like most of the cops. I like the mayor. I guess at this stage of my life, I get attached to people who show that they like me."

As I took a breath, Kate said, "I understand. Are you upset with me? Your ears are turning red."

"I'm not upset. I just want to make my point."

She nodded and sipped her wine.

"You did. Don't get mad," she said.

"I'm not angry. You just seem to be more attached to causes. I spent too many years as a crusader. I don't have the spirit any longer. I suppose I could go on and on, but I won't. You're still my wife and my best girl. My interaction with other people does not diminish how much I love you. You're too smart to be thinking like this. You are not the same to me as anyone else out there. Must I say any more?"

Kate blinked a few times. "Wow, that was some speech. And no, you mustn't." She stood up. "You *must* give me a hug."

"I can do that."

And I did. I also gave her a big kiss and a smack on the backside.

"Ouch!"

"That didn't hurt."

"How do you know?"

"I know what hurts. I'm a cop, I know everything."

"Ha!"

"I have to make a couple phone calls."

"I know."

* * * *

My first call went to Harley Flatt. I caught him in the car with C.J. and Jenny heading to Prospect.

"You have any luck finding Bob Robertson?"

"Hang on a second, boss. Yer breakin' up. I gotta stop the car and git out. Mebbe git better reception."

"I assume the women might hear what we're saying?"

"Yes, sir. Stand by. Lemme git off the road."

I listened to the car stop, the gear shift go into neutral, and the door open and close. I waited a few more seconds.

"Ready to talk?" I asked.

"Yep," he said. "Sorry, boss. We looked around in a bunch o' restaurants and couldn't find nothin'. When we got back ta Dollywood, Jenny was with C.J. She said Bob dropped 'er off and had him a few errands ta run, and he'd meet 'em back at the mo-tel."

"A few errands at this time of night?"

"I'm thinkin' Miss Jenny's got a good face, but a bad heart."

"I guess that's Smoky Mountain language for she's telling us a fib?"

"As my mamaw would say, 'Her mouth ain't no prayer book.'"

"I get your point. Have the Pigeon Forge cops put out an alarm requesting a pick-up on Robertson?"

"Yes, sir, I asked 'em."

"Good. I'll deal with Jenny at the motel. If Robertson should turn up, treat him as a dangerous suspect. You know what to do."

"Yes, sir."

"I know you've had a long day, but I'll probably need you a little longer. Stick around until we get this ironed out, okay?"

"You got it."

Next, I called Rachel's cell phone. The voice mail message told me the subscriber was either unavailable or outside the effective range of reception. I called her home number and left a message with her husband. Being totally unavailable was unlike her, and I needed her information. My impatience was growing like a weed in springtime.

Ralph Oliveri proved easier to find.

"Ralphie, I've got something good for you, something new. But first, we have to talk about what we're going to do in the future with the Collinsons."

If they were connected with Robertson, I wanted Ralph to round up the three Coalition members from Prospect and any of their comrades he thought deserved a little time in an interrogation room.

"I hate to cut you short, buddy," Ralph said, "but this is really not a good time."

"Not a good time? What's up?"

"Ah... I have company. We'll be at my place for a while, and then we're going out."

"You have a girlfriend?" I tried to sound surprised. "Amazing."

"Up yours. Yes, I have a...very nice friend. And I have to go now."

"Whoa, partner, just a quickie. I don't want to break up the romantic mood, but call me Sunday—Monday at the latest, if you want a wrapped-up case involving stolen government property—drugs and explosives being only a drop in the bucket. I'll give you at least two defendants, all your own. A third guy, who I've got my eye on, was the recipient of two bricks of C-4. He'll probably try to use them tomorrow. I don't know why just yet, but I might find out soon. You interested?"

"Okay, okay, I'm interested. I'll cancel tonight. Where can I meet you?"

"Don't cancel your date, dummy. The two subjects can wait. I can act on my own tonight. But think about me working while you're out...having a good time. Where are you going, by the way?"

"I have reservations at The Orangery."

One of the more classy places in Knoxville.

"I'm impressed. You're a typical goombah—pamper a lady with big spending. Well, at least you're not going to Pizza Hut. Okay, sport, I'll talk to you."

"Wait, wait a minute. You sure you don't need me? I'll ask Carl to mobilize a Tac team. You don't want to mess with a guy using explosives by yourself."

"I'll be fine. Don't worry. There's nothing your Tac team can do that Stanley and I can't. Enjoy your dinner. Call me. I'll make you a hero."

"Are you nuts?"

"Some people think so."

"For chrissakes, call Greznik at ATF."

"Maybe later. Enjoy your dinner."

I hung up before Ralph commented.

Then I phoned Len Alcock at the Foothills View Motel. I assumed John Gallagher would have explained everything we learned in Knoxville.

"As you've probably heard, we've got a big problem with Bob Robertson," I said. "Harley can't find him, but Jenny told him Bob would come back to the motel. He took the Saab this morning."

"Mebbe more problem than ya think. He ain't here either," Lenny said.

We spoke for a few more minutes, and Lenny interrupted himself. "Hang on, Harley's pullin' in now."

"Is Jenny right there with C.J.?" I asked.

"Yep, she is."

"Harley's going to stick around and help you."

"Good. He can take his car ta the other side o' the street and give us a warnin' if Robertson drives up."

"Okay, time for you and John to split up. You keep a watch on the outside. If Robertson shows up, call Stanley for more back-up before you confront him. Stan's waiting for a call."

"Will do."

"Consider Bob extremely dangerous and probably armed. If the situation demands, don't hesitate to shoot."

"That bad, huh?"

"Maybe. Have John go to the room. Tell him to keep Jenny in one spot. Cuff her if necessary. Search her handbag or luggage for a weapon. Give C.J. a quick explanation. I'll explain everything to her, or at least as much as I know, when I get there."

"10-4, boss."

"I'll call Stanley now and be sure he stays close to the motel and doesn't get involved in a routine job. And tell Gallagher to be careful."

"Gottcha covered, boss," he said.

I spent the next few minutes on the phone with Stan Rose, who had gone back on patrol, but was still in civilian clothes.

I wanted him to be ready to help out at the motel or make for a quick trip to Dollywood.

It took me twenty minutes to get to the motel. I found Alcock sitting in John's Saturn away from any lights, but still in position to watch the room. Lenny had his marked PD unit parked as a decoy in the lot below C.J.'s suite, and Harley had placed his car somewhere out of sight.

"Lenny, call Stan, and have him meet us now. And tell Harley to get prepared to go back to Pigeon Forge."

Harley knew the music hall better than any of us.

I trudged up the stairs and found John and the two women in the sitting room, C.J. and Jenny on the couch, John on an upholstered chair. No one was speaking when I arrived.

175

C.J. jumped up as I entered the room. Her brightly-colored western shirt and tight blue jeans tucked into a pair of turquoise cowboy boots made her look like a little girl playing dress up. "Sam, what the hell's goin' on here?"

I held up two hands to stop her questions and calm her down.

"Take it easy, C.J. We've got a basic problem with Bob," I said. "And I'm guessing with Jenny, too."

Jenny stood abruptly, and her normally pretty face contorted into a snarl. She looked all business in a forest green pantsuit over a pale yellow T-shirt. "What are you talking about?" She pulled an unbuttoned jacket together and crossed her arms defensively across her breasts.

C.J. interjected, "Good question. How about an explanation?"

"Just what I intend to give you," I said. "Now, both of you, sit down and listen. John, did you check Jenny's purse?"

"Yeah, boss and her overnight bag. No gun, but two cell phones. I made sure she didn't call anyone."

Jenny interrupted again, "Of course I don't have a gun. And what crime is it to have two phones?"

C.J. spoke again, "Sam, I've given you the benefit of the doubt, but this better be good."

"Ladies!" I snapped. "Knock it off. Sit down and listen. This is very good."

C.J. sank back into the sofa cushions and folded *her* arms across her chest. Jenny sat, very properly, on the edge of the couch, her knees together and her hands in her lap.

I looked from one to the other and ended up staring at Ms. Mitchell. "As they say in the old detective movies, Jenny, the jig is up."

Chapter Eighteen

Jenny almost spoke again, but I stopped her.

"Wait," I said. "I'm not guessing here. I know your father is Bob Robertson, not Bob Mitchell. But he's probably already told you about our conversation. I have a statement from a man who sold your father stolen poison and explosives,"

That news visibly moved Jenny. C.J. bolted upright to the edge of the sofa cushion.

"The man identified his photo," I said, looking at C.J. "This is not a guess. I believe this reserve soldier who gave me the information. Two bricks of C-4 will be tough for your dad to explain, Jenny. Would you care to try?"

"He was getting that for someone he used to work with. The man is in construction and lost his license to buy explosives. He needs it for a job."

I chuckled and shook my head. John Gallagher laughed and stuck his hands into the pockets of his khaki windbreaker.

"I'll give you an A for creative thinking. Try again, Jenny. Is your father working for this Coalition for Family Values group?"

"Of course not! That's stupid!" She spat her words at me. "Do I really have to talk to you?"

I hate it when criminals want to take advantage of their constitutional rights.

"No, you don't. You have the right to remain silent, the right to an attorney and all the other rights Ernesto Miranda's lawyer fought so hard to get you. But you don't have the right to not listen. So sit back, and see if what I say makes any impact on you."

It looked like C.J. had gotten a spark of patience. She sat quietly, waiting for me to continue my act.

"The one answer I don't have yet is why your dad, and presumably you, wants to harm C.J. I expect to find that missing link very soon. In the meantime, try this on for size. When we take him into custody, your dad will be charged with something. Right now, we have an attempted murder of C.J. and an assault for poisoning Officer Rutledge. If he plants explosives and they go off, that's arson and either assault or murder if innocent people are involved, and several additional Federal charges are possible because of buying stolen government property—the explosives and drugs."

Jenny waved a hand dismissively. "He has no intention of blowing anything up."

Her eyes reminded me of the last angry pit bull I met.

"Spare me the rhetoric," I said. "There's no time off for good behavior if I let the FBI prosecute first, and he gets time in a federal prison. When he gets out, count on a local prosecutor starting all over again in state court."

She shrugged and shook her head.

"Right now you're good for conspiracy to commit murder. If someone dies in an explosion, you're also going for murder and all the other appropriate charges—you being a prime accessory."

Jenny moved her eyes from me to her employer. "This is ridiculous. C.J., don't believe a word he says."

"Think about some of the prison movies they make," I said. "I don't think a pretty young thing like you would do well if we threw you to the she-wolves inside a penitentiary."

That seemed to have grasped her attention. She stopped making theatrical faces and playing the role of a falsely accused innocent.

"So while you're remaining silent," I said, "think about how much you need a friend on this side of the fence—someone who can add or subtract from the charges piled on your back."

"Do you think you scare me?" Her expression didn't match the brave statement.

"I know you're scared," I said. "You're wringing your hands like Lady Macbeth, and you're turning white."

She looked like she wanted to speak again.

"Shut up and listen," I said. "What happens to your old man gets complicated if you don't help out. His attempt at getting C.J. to eat poisoned food failed, but it's still attempted murder. The cop he poisoned is okay now, he recovered, but that's still a felony assault. Those are the first offenses we'll arrest him for."

Jenny's eyes narrowed as she looked at me. C.J.'s eyes widened in surprise.

"Let's look at what the law says about someone plotting an arson by explosion with intent to seriously injure or kill someone."

Jenny pursed her lips and tried to look annoyed.

"It says that any cop can use deadly force to prevent or terminate your father's actions. In simple English, I can kill him to stop him."

Now, both C.J. and Jenny looked at me with wide eyes.

"I know your father's capabilities. I have no reason to try and sweet-talk him into a pair of handcuffs if I reasonably believe I'm in danger. If I think it's necessary to kill your father to arrest him, the law says, go for it. Still want to remain silent?"

"You're crazy!" she said. "You even said you know of no reason he'd want to hurt C.J."

Then my phone rang. I stood and walked into a bedroom for privacy.

"Oh, Sam, I'm so glad I got you," Rachel said.

"I'm glad you did, too. I was about to run out of ad libs here. What have you dug up?"

"I don't know if this helps, but my contact in Nashville learned something that never made it to the nightly news. Well, the actual suicide did, but the connection between C.J. Profitt and the victim was never publicized. It seems that at the time, the connection wasn't known, but—"

"Rachel, stop. I promise to sit down with you and listen to everything, but right now I'm a little pressed for time. Please get to the bottom line."

The average person may have taken offense at me cutting them short, but Rachel, in her reporter's mode, is far from average.

"Okay, Mr. Impatience, here's the headline. A woman named Michelle Robertson committed suicide five years ago. She took an overdose of prescription pills and alcohol. There was no note. No foul play was suspected. Nashville PD closed the investigation in one night. Much later, Michelle was linked as a romantic interest of C.J. Profitt. When Michelle fell in love with C.J. and C.J. didn't share that emotion, Michelle became depressed. When C.J. broke off the relationship, Michelle ended up taking her own life. Any help?"

The cavalry arrived in a nick of time. "Lady, you've done a great job. I owe you again—big time. I'll call you later. It may be late, but you'll want to take the call."

I stepped into the doorway and raised my voice.

"You're sure the name is Michelle Robertson from Nashville?"

I looked inside to see if my news made an impact on anyone.

Jenny's face dropped. C.J. sat up and looked at me with great interest.

"I assume that was part of your act, so I won't comment," Rachel said. "Call any time, any number."

I said a quick good-bye and hung up. C.J. was about to speak. I held up a hand.

"Your sister, Ms. Mitchell?"

She nodded, but wouldn't look at me.

It always feels good when I call an obvious bluff and win.

"The implication or connection never made it to the papers or TV news, but you knew, didn't you?"

She nodded again and finally looked into my eyes.

"And you told your father?"

Another nod. "Of course."

"The police never found a note, but somehow you knew. Did Michelle speak with you before she took her life?"

"Yes, she did, and there *was* a note. She didn't leave it for just anyone to find. She sent one to me and to her." She pointed to C.J.

C.J. said, "Jenny, I thought you were my friend."

Jenny's face showed an intense hatred. "You killed my sister."

180

"No, I didn't." C.J. looked shocked that someone would think she bore any responsibility.

"This happened five years ago," I said. "Hell of a long time to hold a grudge." Jenny nodded, but said nothing.

"We'll have to talk more about this later, but for right now what's it going to be? Do I send out a general alarm with shoot to kill authorization?" I should have been ashamed of myself for using that corny line. "Or do you help me find your father with my promise to let him come along the easy way?"

"Please don't hurt him. Can't you understand how he felt?"

"I can. I understand a lot about your dad. You may not believe me, but I like him. But this is business, and he and I are both pros. I'll let him dictate how this goes...if you help me."

"All right. What do you want?"

"Where is he?"

Jenny's shoulders dropped, and she slumped back on the sofa. "Dollywood."

"I thought so. Is he there to plant the C-4?"

"Yes."

"Where?"

"In the music hall."

I shook my head in disbelief. The potential damage was staggering.

"When was he going to do this?"

"As soon as everyone left the building."

"Like now?"

"Yes. Everyone began leaving when we walked out," she looked at her watch, "about an hour ago."

"Was he going to hide there until the concert?"

"No. He'd leave when the security guards were changing shifts."

"Smart."

"He is."

I meant cleverly timed move for a criminal. Blowing up a large auditorium and its audience didn't sound very sharp to me.

"Where is he going to plant the explosives? C.J.'s dressing room?"

"No, under the stage."

"Is he using all the explosives he bought?

"Yes."

"Jesus Christ!" The thought shocked me. "Do you know how many people would be taken out with two bricks of C-4?"

She wrinkled her brow and looked as if she didn't understand. "Taken out?"

"Blown up. Killed."

Jenny looked at the floor and shook her head. "No."

"Your dad sure does."

"Oh, my God," C.J. said softly.

Jenny looked at C.J. and then dropped her eyes again.

"What else do you know?" I said. "Is this thing going to be on a timer or command detonated?"

"He was going to trigger the bomb himself."

"Where was he going to be when he did that?"

"In the audience. He'd enter the building just before the concert."

"And you?"

"After the show started I was going to leave, drive away and pick him up later."

C. J. spoke again. "Oh, Jenny."

I shook my head in disbelief. "If he sat in the audience and detonated the bomb, Jenny, there wouldn't be a later. The whole building might come down with that much explosive. Your father would have died with C.J. and a lot of other people."

"Oh, God!"

"Yeah, you think?"

"That's horrible," C.J. said.

Then I understood. "But he *is* smart. A big splash like that would be more appropriate as a statement from that group of right-wing nit-wits than a professional killer. He'd throw suspicion on the Coalition. Jenny would be in the clear."

"What are you going to do?" C.J. asked.

"Get my ass in gear," I said. "I need the local cops to find Bob's car for starters and then seal off the music hall. If we can get there in time and he doesn't leave before the midnight changing of the guard."

"Can I help?"

"You can stay with Jenny. I'll have a cop take her to one of our cells. Meet a Sergeant Bettye Lambert at Prospect PD. Then you have to sit and wait."

"Jenny, what phone would you use to call your father?"

"The one with the dark red case."

"The red one… How appropriate. And if someone called him using the other phone would he know something was wrong?"

"How did you know?"

"As I said before, I've got a pretty good handle on the tricks your dad may use. Are you sure the red phone is the safe one?"

She nodded.

"If you're lying and the red phone number on his caller ID signals a trap or a problem, Mr. Nice Guy is out of business, and your father dies. If he blows up the music hall with me in it, you won't believe how pissed I'll be."

In my peripheral vision, I saw John smile.

"Last chance for the truth," I said. "You want Daddy alive or dead?"

"If you call him, use the red phone. I swear."

"Okay, John, put cuffs on Jenny. I'll get a car to transport her."

I stepped outside and signaled to Lenny Alcock. He walked upstairs. Stan came with him. I gave them a quick explanation.

"Get two cops here to transport the prisoner and C.J. Tell Bettye to open up the office, and stand by. Stan, call Pigeon Forge PD. Have them get all available personnel over to Dollywood. Call Dollywood Security, and have them start looking for Bob Robertson's Saab. Secure the car to limit his escape possibilities, and be sure everyone coordinates with Sevier County to seal off the music hall. Suggest they find Rusty Filmore. He knows the building better than the rest of them. If there's a canine unit and a bomb tech available, have them stand-by, too. I wish to hell we had a chopper, but by the time we got one here, we could almost be at Dollywood. As soon as you make those calls, we roll. Where's Harley?"

"Gettin' a rifle from the trunk of his car," Lenny said. "Figgered you'd want him ta have it."

"Okay, gentlemen, start dialing."

Two Prospect patrolmen arrived within minutes. Bettye started on her way to the municipal building. Jenny was taken into custody, and C.J. went along for the ride. Harley Flatt arrived carrying an AR-15 and jumped into Len Alcock's police car. They started toward Pigeon Forge with lights and siren. John and I rode along with Stan Rose. On the way, I called the Pigeon Forge Chief and the Sevier County Sheriff, personally, telling them this was the real deal, not a drill. I wanted them to make sure their duty officers gave this an ultimate priority.

As soon as I hung up, Gallagher, sitting in the back seat, asked, "Hey, boss, who's Rachel?"

"Just shut up, John, and stop grinning like that. Someone might think you were the village idiot."

Stanley snickered.

All my instincts told me Bob Robertson was a rational man and professional soldier. But if he was willing to die just to cast suspicion from his daughter onto the Coalition, was he capable of some insane plot to keep me from taking him into custody? Maybe he had incurable cancer and took out a million-dollar life insurance policy with Jenny as beneficiary. Who knows what else might have been on his mind?

Chapter Nineteen

Stanley handled the big Ford Police Interceptor through the serpentine curves on 321 North like a NASCAR driver—maybe better, they only go flat-out and to the left. Even at top speed, it took us thirty-five minutes to reach Dollywood. The Sevier County Sheriff sent seven deputies and a lieutenant who arrived before us. One of those men had a police dog. Pigeon Forge sent a sergeant and three patrolmen. PFPD Officer Rusty Filmore was off-duty and responded in civilian clothes, adding another to our ranks. That made eighteen of us plus the Dollywood Security personnel to find Bob Robertson and his car.

Perhaps it was just my hubris, or my mind wandering back more than twenty years, but if I was in Bob Robertson's predicament and only eighteen armed men were after me, I wouldn't have been overly concerned—if all I wanted to do was escape. Guys like Robertson were well trained by Uncle Sam. Thanks to something called S.E.R.E. training—Survival, Evasion, Resistance, Escape—giving a bunch of local cops the slip may have been a piece of cake.

The police dog was our best hope if Robertson took off running. But I was there, too, to see that Bob didn't give us the slip—or detonate the explosive charge he presumably had already planted under the stage of the music hall.

If I'd been driving, I would have focused on getting to the scene as quickly as possible and had little time to think of other things. But sitting there as a passenger my thoughts wandered. During times like these, patience is not one of my strong virtues. I was itching to use the red phone and call Robertson to get the ball rolling. But I knew that would

185

be the wrong thing to do. After mulling the impending scenario over in my mind several times, I realized this wasn't just a case of Sam Jenkins preventing a would-be killer or domestic terrorist from detonating a bomb. It was LTC Sam Jenkins versus MSG Robert Robertson—two former Green Berets engaged in a contest of who's the best soldier. While I would love to live and drink another pint of black and tan or sip another dram of single-malt whisky, I'd be damned if that son-of-a-bitch would be the one who left me looking like a cop who identified the bad guy, but couldn't prevent him from taking down a public building and terminating lives in the process. I'd rather shoot it out with Robertson in the parking lot than let history recognize me as coming in second best. As someone long before me said, 'Damn the torpedoes, full speed ahead.' I wished I was thirty-five again.

* * * *

The other police and security supervisors at Dollywood seemed more than willing to relinquish responsibility for the scene to anyone ready to accept it. I took command and began by asking for information.

I soon learned that a Dollywood security officer found Robertson's Saab 9-5 in the main visitor's parking lot. Other than its presence, the car gave us no additional leads. Two security guards remained in the area, keeping an eye on the Saab. They would contact the Pigeon Forge sergeant by radio if our suspect returned.

The music hall was surrounded and secured, meaning no one left, entered or tried to enter the building since our troops arrived. I told John Gallagher to team up with Len Alcock. Harley Flatt and Rusty Filmore, who had partnered up for most of the week, would again work together. I wanted Stan Rose and his shotgun to stick with me.

An almost full moon acted like a huge celestial spotlight. The clear sky and brilliant moonlight made the surrounding grounds look more like late afternoon than nighttime. We had perfect illumination, but also an abundance of shadows—places a slippery character like Robertson could use to cloak his escape.

We started working our way around the music hall, looking for a break or an open door. We found all six front doors locked and tried two more side doors—also locked. At the rear of the building, I pulled on another door handle. Bingo, the door opened. A piece of duct tape had obstructed the spring-loaded bolt from locking into the doorjamb. Just like Watergate. We entered the building slowly and carefully. Other than a few dim security lights placed high on the walls, there was no other illumination in the building. Two Sevier County deputies, who had helped check the perimeter with us, remained outside the unlocked door in case Bob Robertson made a run for it. They radioed a supervisor to assign additional uniformed cops to check and watch the other doors on all four sides of the building.

I wanted to charge in like Sherman taking Atlanta. I could almost smell Robertson and wanted his head on a pike. But all reason told me to slow down and do it by the numbers. I wondered how many times before we came to a confrontation would I allow reason to override my passion to nail that bastard. I took a breath.

"Before anyone goes off to comb the interior, I guess some negotiations might be prudent. I'll try to contact Robertson. I'm guessing he's still in the building."

Everyone looked at me. Some faces looked impassive, a couple apprehensive. All stood by like paratroopers waiting to jump into a hot drop zone.

I took out Jenny's red cell phone and tapped in Bob's number. It rang, or silently vibrated as was my guess, four times.

"Yeah, baby?" he answered.

One hurdle cleared. One step closer.

"I hate to disappoint you, Bob, but Jenny is presently in an unenviable position, and she let me borrow your red phone."

A moment of silence passed before he spoke. One point for me. "What do you want?"

"Three guesses and if the first one isn't C-4, you're not as sharp as I thought."

He commented immediately. "Where are you?"

"Better question, my friend, where are you? I've got your daughter in custody. It would be a shame to see her take on the attempted murder, conspiracy to commit murder and accessory to theft and possession of drugs and explosives trial all by herself."

"You can't do that. She's innocent of all those things. She didn't know."

I couldn't prevent myself from getting sarcastic. "Oh, of course, old buddy, I'll just let her go because you say so. Get real, Top. I promised her a sweetheart deal for the phone and your location. And I promised not to make killing you my first priority."

Robertson snickered, but made no comment.

"Oh, yeah, she confessed. Not much left to the imagination on her end. If you break my balls here and make me slug it out with you, I just may forget all the slack I agreed to cut her. Understand?"

He got a little sarcastic himself. "If you know where I am, why'd you ask?"

I wanted the sparring to end.

"Can the cat and mouse act, partner, unless you plan on walking back to Virginia and you're going to abandon your kid. We've got your car, and you don't. The music hall is surrounded by forty armed cops plus Dollywood Security. If you decide to tough it out, I can have FBI and ATF SWAT teams from Knoxville here in less than an hour."

"What are you offering?"

"What I promised Jenny—an easy time for her, and you get to walk out of here like a gentleman."

"Give me time to think."

Common sense and training told me to give him time to consider my offer. Let him feel uncomfortable with the silence. Most negotiators say that time is always on the side of the police. But I'm not a professional negotiator, and I've got my own ideas about things. When a barricaded subject like Bob Robertson asks for time to think, he may buy himself the opportunity to get into unwanted mischief. I like things to happen lickety-split. And if nothing else, I felt exceedingly impatient and wanted to get my claws into him.

"While you're pondering your future, Bobby, I'll have the handlers sharpen their dog's fangs. I'll give you five minutes, and then the hounds come in as first wave. Otherwise we iron this out right now."

"You send in dogs, and I'll blow the building."

Not what I wanted to hear, but I couldn't let him know that.

"No, you won't. And thanks for confirming your location. You blow the building, and I charge your little girl with every possible thing a state court will entertain. My goombah at the FBI promises to pick up any thread I leave and take over in the Federal courts. I promise you, Bob, I'll take out my frustration on your daughter. She is your accomplice in everything—including blowing up this building."

Start thinking about Jenny's future, sport.

"That's ridiculous," he said.

Don't let up. "Tough shit. If that's what you decide to do, I'll try my best to see her spend the rest of her useful years in prison. Think about how happy people like Big Bertha and Doris the Dyke will be to see pretty, young Jenny walk in for her first night in lock-down."

"You're a real prick, aren't you?"

You'll only see me in top form if we can't come to a satisfactory agreement.

"I like to get my own way."

"You'll let her go?"

Keep the pressure on. "Don't be ridiculous. She can't walk on this, but a sole charge of conspiracy is a damn sight better than the laundry list of charges I gave you before. Give up now, and I'll even throw in the business card of the best criminal lawyer in Blount County."

"What about me?"

Give him a place to retreat. "You get the best deal your attorney can make. I won't oppose any plea bargains they present to me. You and I walk through this together."

He snorted.

"I won't screw you, Bob. Just another favor between old soldiers."

"You're all heart."

"I know. Oh, yeah, you also have to disarm the bomb and give me a statement about buying the C-4 from that asshole staff sergeant in Knoxville."

"Federal charges?"

"I can live without those, and I've got pull with the agent who'll be going after your supplier. Your statement makes you a friend of the Federal courts."

"Give me a minute."

Like hell. "No!"

"Christ almighty!"

"Welcome to Jenkins' method of negotiation. We talk about things like two friends, and then we do it my way."

"You promise you'll take care of my daughter?"

Another refuge. "I promise."

"Okay."

Success?

"Okay, what?"

"Okay, I'll surrender."

I felt a wave of relief gently splash on me.

"Good. Tell me where the bomb is."

"Under the stage."

"How do we get to it?"

"There are trap doors all over the place."

"Did you booby trap any of them?"

"No, no need to."

Could I believe that?

"Do you have a flashlight with you?"

"Of course."

"Where are you?"

"In the auditorium."

"Here's what you do, I want to see you sitting center stage when I get in there. Turn on your light and hold it between your knees pointing straight up. Put both hands on the top of your head. Do you have a gun?"

"Yes."

"What?"

"A Beretta 92."

"Okay, place the gun ten feet in front of you on the stage. Any other weapons?"

"Just a Leatherman tool. Know what that is?"

"Yeah a little combination tool that makes a Swiss Army knife look uncomplicated."

"Right you are."

"Put it next to the gun."

"Okay."

"You have the detonator with you?"

"Yes."

"That goes in the same spot.

"Okay."

"I'm ready to come in. There'll be a group of us. Shotguns and M-16s, so don't plan on a firefight, we'll kill you."

"Oh, yeah?" He said sarcastically, with self-importance and attitude shining through.

Reapply the pressure. "You may be good, but so are we. If you detonate the bomb while I'm in the building, I will be so pissed that my sergeant back in Prospect will take it out on Jenny. We clear on all this?"

A few seconds passed. "Affirmative. You've got a deal."

Almost too easy.

"Alright, get yourself ready, up on stage."

Robertson agreed to everything that would make me happy. All that remained was to take him into custody and retrieve the bomb, preferably in one unexploded piece. I just hoped he was telling the truth and didn't have a trick up his sleeve.

I looked at half a dozen concerned faces and was reluctant to put anyone else in jeopardy to satisfy my selfish need to nail this man. "Okay, guys, he's ready to go. John, you're not a cop, you don't have to do this."

"I'm an auxiliary cop, right?"

"Yes, but this isn't your job."

"Sure it is. Always has been. Piece of cake, right?"

"I hope so."

"I'm in, boss. Just like always."

I nodded and slapped his shoulder. "Good man, John."

I looked again at the faces waiting for my instructions.

"You others are paid cops, but this is a volunteer assignment. Anyone want to opt out? Help secure the perimeter and no hard feelings."

No one raised his hand. I liked the loyalty.

"Okay," I said. "Should be a piece of cake. Stick with me, guys, and we'll make this happen."

My troops stood close, in a small circle surrounding me. Those who had looked apprehensive before lightened up a bit. I hoped they knew something I didn't.

"Here's how we do it," I said. "When we go through this hallway, we're almost behind the stage. There's another hall beyond all the electronics that leads to the dressing rooms. We split up. Harley, you and Rusty know the building best. Go behind the stage and check the rooms. I doubt he's got an accomplice, but make sure. This is a free-fire zone. If you see anyone, shoot them. Then come back and flank the platform to the extreme left. Wait off-stage, but where you can see what's happening in the middle of the platform. When I ask, I'll need lots of light. You know where the switch panel is?"

"I know exactly where it is," Rusty said.

"Good. We'll give you a few minutes to finish your search. When I'm ready, I'll ask for the lights."

They nodded and moved out.

"John, you and Lenny follow Stan and me. I'll show you where to access the spot just behind the stage curtain. Poke around and find the place where you can get between the big curtain and the wall and wait there. You have an idea where I mean, Lenny?'

"Roger that."

"Okay, I'll let you know when to approach him. Stan and I will walk around to the stage front and come straight at him. He's smart and will assume there are others in the building, but no need to show him how many or where you are."

Everyone nodded and looked determined.

"It'll be dark in there. I don't want to see any of this TV cop shit of holding your flashlights directly in front of you. Robertson's a pro and probably good with a handgun. I hope he told the truth and only has one 9mm with him. But if he decides to do this the hard way and sees a light, he'll shoot directly at it and roll away from his muzzle flash—I would. Questions?"

They had none. We waited another few moments and heard nothing from Harley or Rusty.

"Okay, here we go."

When Stanley and I emerged on the right side of the stage, we crawled and took cover behind the seats of the second row. As promised, Bob Robertson sat cross-legged on the stage floor. His flashlight pointed upward, casting an eerie glow over the stage area.

"Bob, I can see you." After starting the dialogue, I immediately changed my position fifteen feet to my right. Stan followed, but stopped a few feet short of my spot.

Robertson looked like a Hollywood cat burglar, dark pants, windbreaker and a black turtleneck.

I spoke loudly to Robertson. "Take your hands off your head and raise them as high as they go." Then I whispered to Stan, "Move back to your left a few feet. I'm going right."

After I hit my intended position, I extended my left arm as far from my body as possible and shined the beam of my big flashlight at the man sitting on the stage floor. He momentarily closed his eyes and turned his head slightly.

With my right hand, I pointed my Glock at Robertson and lined up the three dots of my luminescent night sights on the center of his chest. The flashlight beam shined bright enough to illuminate him and allow me to clearly see his hands. Illuminated by the small spotlight, he looked like a stage actor prepared to deliver a dramatic line.

"Turn your hands around." I said. "Show me the palms and the backs."

He did. He held no weapon or detonator.

"Turn your head, side to side."

He did.

"Now shake your head—vigorously."

He did, and I was satisfied he had nothing concealed in his hair.

"Okay, hands back on top of your head."

He complied.

I whispered again, "Okay, Stan, you and me now. Stay low. Move around the seats, and approach the stage. It's dark enough and with my light in his eyes, he won't see what's happening. I'll cover you. When you're set, look over the edge of the stage and rack a round into the chamber so he can hear it. Put your flashlight beam on his face and cover him while I jump up and move further to the right. I'll go for the platform edge at about center-stage. I'll tell you before I start moving. Then keep him covered while I vault onto the stage and approach."

"Where are all the shotguns and M-16s you mentioned?"

"I tend to fib under pressure."

"Good to know."

"You ready?"

"No, but you don't care."

"Let's do it."

We accomplished what I described to Stanley in only brief moments. Once on the stage, I faced Bob Robertson directly. He presented me with my largest target that way. Stan moved ten feet to my left and kept him covered with the shotgun. I would not be in a cross-fire.

"Hi, Bob," I said. "We still working on the same deal?"

He shrugged his shoulders, and his arms moved up and down. "Yeah, as long as you look after my daughter."

"You've got my word on that."

"I'm ready."

"Good. Don't move until I tell you."

He nodded, and a second wave of relief sloshed over my ankles.

"Okay, guys." I spoke loudly to the four cops, "Move onto the stage. Everybody shine your lights on the subject."

All four people approached from both sides of the stage. I heard them before I saw them. Then four flashlights found their target and trained on Robertson, who looked like he was ready to take a bow. I moved forward and picked up the detonator, a black plastic object about the size and shape of a pack of cigarettes. A Radio Shack logo decorated the front. It looked simple, only a single switch. Not being much of a technical kind of guy, I wondered what its legitimate purpose might be.

"How do I deactivate the detonator?"

Robertson grinned. I guess he sensed my technophobia. I could have done without his display of smartass.

"Simple, take out the batteries. The compartment door is on the back. Be careful not to touch the switch."

He delivered his line with a full smile, the smug bastard. Then he chuckled. Time to find out if he was really cooperating or just wanted to make one hell of an explosive statement.

I pushed open the sliding plastic lid and pried out two double-A batteries. The next time I saw the Energizer Bunny, I'd blow the little sucker away.

"Is that it?" I asked.

"Yep. Easy, huh?"

"Yeah, I feel so enlightened. Turn over, and lay on your stomach. Spread your legs and put your arms wide to your sides."

He did.

"Stan, come up on the stage. Pick up the pistol and the Leatherman. No booby traps to worry about, are there, Bobbo?"

"Negative on the booby traps." He spoke with another grin. I thought he might be enjoying this.

Stan retrieved the Beretta, dropped the magazine and popped the round from the chamber. He stuck that into his belt and the Leatherman tool went into the pocket of his black leather jacket. I thought the coat made him look like an Afro-American Tony Soprano.

I put the detonator in one pocket and the batteries in another.

"Cover me while I search our guest for weapons," I told Stanley.

I gave Robertson a thorough pat down and found no guns, knives, grenades, anti-tank rocket launcher or... Maybe I gave him too much credit.

"Okay, GI, time to disarm the bomb. You can get up now."

Robertson stood slowly and shook out the kinks his time curled up on the stage floor had created. Five guns pointed at my prisoner, but he didn't show any signs of fear. Robertson was a cool customer.

"Lenny, you and John team up with the guys at the back door and hang out there."

John said, "You don't want us here, boss?"

"Time to clear the building."

He nodded.

"Harley, you and Rusty go to the light switches and turn them all on. I want everything there is. Then go out the open back door and circle around to the front. Tell the supervisors what's happening, and get a security guard to unlock and open all the front doors. We'll exit that way when we're finished. Stay put outside."

"You got it."

"Mention that we'll have the disarmed bomb so the local cops don't get shocked when they see it."

Both men nodded.

"They have their own fire apparatus here in the park," I said. "Get the trucks rolling just in case something goes wrong. I assume the Pigeon Forge chief will let us do our paperwork at his place. Rusty, ask your sergeant for a car to transport Mr. Robertson."

"Yes, sir."

"Okay, guys, get to it and thanks. Stan, take a walk outside."

"Who's going to stay with you?" Stanley asked.

"He is." I pointed to Robertson. "No reason for anyone else to have a problem if this thing goes south."

"I can disarm my own bomb, thanks," Robertson said.

"Alone?"

"Sure," he said.

The man had nerve.

I shook my head. "Get real."

"You have no faith."

"Under the circumstances, Bob, I'm not going to allow you into my system of participatory management. You don't get a vote."

Robertson chuckled.

"Look," Stanley said. "You need someone at your back. That's me. I'm not worried about him disarming the bomb. If he can build it, he can take it apart. I'm here to see that you two old soldiers don't tussle afterward."

"Tussle?" I said.

"Don't you think time is of the essence here?" Stan said.

Just then, all the lights of the auditorium came on in rapid sequence. Harley lit up our world.

"Okay, Stanley, we'll go beneath the stage with flashlights. You hang out up here and relax. Work for you?"

"What are you going to be when you grow up, boss?"

"Who said I have to grow up?"

"Excuse the interruption," Robertson said, "but I'm goin' to need my Leatherman to snip a wire."

Stanley looked at me. "I don't like this. Maybe we should leave the bomb for a technician."

"You see a bomb truck outside?"

Stanley shook his head.

"This is the third world. We don't have one handy."

"Why trust this guy? Leave the building empty and evacuate the area until the Feds get here."

"If we don't trust him, why believe he hasn't rigged the bomb with a command detonator *and* a timer? He's a smart cookie. Maybe he likes to use a fail-safe."

Stan let out a puff of air, shook his head and delivered one of his Uncle Remus lines. "Man, someday you gonna git me kilt."

"But not before I teach you how to speak real English. Go ahead, give him the Leatherman."

Reluctantly, he took the folding tool out of a small leather case and handed it to Robertson. Bob unfolded the handles revealing the pliers end with the wire snips.

"Show time, Top," I said. "Let's go below and get this done."

Chapter Twenty

We found a three-foot square trap door at almost center stage. I tipped the door up. Robertson descended first, and I followed. Wires and cables crisscrossed all over the concrete floor over which we crawled. With less than two feet of headroom above us, moving around put a strain on my knees. Our flashlights were the only illumination. My knees hurt like hell, and the dust made me sneeze.

"Allergies?" he asked.

"Yeah, getting old sucks."

"Tell me about it."

Less than ten feet from the trap door, a black nylon briefcase lay on the floor. As we approached it, my stomach tightened, and I felt a tingle run up my back.

"You don't plan on sending me to the happy hunting ground for spite, do you?"

"Who'd take care of my daughter if I killed you?"

"Hold that thought."

Talking to Robertson was almost like talking to myself.

He unzipped a thick ballistic nylon case. The two bricks of C-4 had been flattened to many times their normal size. Two detonator caps protruded unceremoniously from the plastic-like explosive. Multi-colored wires traveled from the detonator caps to a small receiver device rigged to impulse the explosion.

Like a Claymore mine, the surface of the C-4 was studded with numerous steel ball bearings. I looked at Robertson.

"Ouch, that would hurt."

"It's supposed to."

That was enough to make me stall the disarming for a moment. "We haven't discussed your daughter, Michelle."

"We don't have to," he said.

I didn't agree. "Really think what C.J. did is a hanging offense?"

"She killed my daughter."

"Not directly."

"Close enough," he said.

"A little negligent maybe, but not intentional."

He shook his head. "Not the way I see it."

In my peripheral vision I watched a mouse stop, look at us and then scurry off into the darkness. It had more sense than me.

"I need you to keep your promise," he said. "I trust you because... I don't know why, I just do. You've got to help Jenny get through the trouble I got her into."

"I said I would."

"Okay, I'm ready to do this. Put your light on the device."

He played with the colored wires for a few seconds, sorting them out. I shook my head at how complicated those things always appeared to me. Robertson chose one wire, separated it from the others and placed the jaws of the cutting pliers over it.

I held my breath for a moment before speaking. "I hope you remember how you wired this thing,"

"Sure. Snip the blue one."

"You're holding the red wire."

"Did I mention being color blind?"

A very cool customer.

"I do the jokes. You're the straight man and bomb specialist."

Blithely he said, "Okay."

I resisted an urge to close my eyes. He snipped the red wire, separated the ends and looked up at me.

"All done?" I asked.

"Uh-huh."

"That's it?" I had started to breathe again, but it felt shallow and labored.

"How much more do you want?" he asked.

I took in a large volume of air. My vision sharpened, and I experienced an overall feeling of relaxation. I also felt quite old.

"It's safe to carry?"

"As safe as a couple of bricks of C-4."

"You're sure?"

My shoulders sagged, and I let out another breath.

"Remember? Thirty-five years of experience? Army Engineer Corps trained. Master blaster. Trust me, I know what I'm doing."

"Easy for you to say."

Robertson chuckled. "Yes, it is."

"You know, before you put me in this lousy position, I was ready to take you to lunch."

"How thoughtful."

"I'm like that."

"Well, we still have to eat," he said.

"I'll try to remember and throw a getting-out party for you."

He reached with his left hand and gave my right arm a friendly slap. "That'll be something I can look forward to."

"Before we leave, do I have a second bomb to worry about? Maybe a small one hidden in C.J.'s dressing room? Trip wire activated?"

"No. What you see is what there is."

"And I should believe you because...?"

"Look, you're holding all the cards," he said. "I'm going to jail, but I want that deal for Jenny. You can make it happen. I don't trust anyone else."

"I'm flattered."

"You should be. Search the building. I'm telling the truth."

"Trouble is, I know that trick. Give up a red herring, and then take out a herd of cops with a second device."

"Jesus Christ. Then I'll go with you while you search the building."

"You were ready to die tomorrow to throw suspicion on a bunch of rednecks."

He shrugged. "Well, there was that."

"I didn't have an ulcer before I met you."

He laughed.

"Come on," he said. "I wouldn't double cross you. You're my hero."

I shook my head and realized I needed to make one of the most important decisions of my life.

I shrugged and thought, 'What the hell?'

"Are you finished," I asked, "or did you want to sit here with me and sing a few Barry Sadler tunes?"

"I'm waiting for you."

I pointed to the briefcase.

"You carry it. It's yours," I indicated he should go first.

We made the short crawl back to the trap door. Robertson moved slowly and told Stan he was coming up onto the stage. I followed and closed the trap door.

I spoke to Robertson. "Time to put the handcuffs on."

He set the case on the stage and did a casual about-face, putting his wrists at the small of his back. I cuffed him and picked up the briefcase. Stan looked at it and me dubiously.

"Is that thing safe?" he asked.

"Our demolition expert says it is."

"And we believe him?"

"We've got nobody else to ask."

Stan shook his head. "Oh, great."

I looked at Robertson. He smiled.

"The young feller is a wee bit apprehensive," I said.

"They always are. He been in the military?"

"No, the Air Force."

Robertson laughed. I love that joke.

"Can we finish this tonight?" Stan asked. "Or would you like me to record your comedy routine?"

"Just adding a little humor to an otherwise dull evening, Stanley."

"I've noticed."

"Okay, Bob, now comes the part where we walk out of here like gentlemen."

"I can hardly wait," Robertson said.

"Sure." For a brief moment, I felt sorry for him.

"You know how difficult it's going to be looking dignified in court wearing a prison suit and shackles."

I thought of nothing clever to add and simply said, "Let's go."

I picked up the bomb, and we walked up the theatre aisle past the rows of empty seats, through a set of double doors and into the lobby. Harlan Flatt and Rusty Filmore stood there waiting. Harley held the AR-15 across his chest at port arms, and Rusty's semiautomatic handgun dangled at his side.

"What part of wait outside didn't you two understand?" I asked.

"You said that?" Harley asked. "I must've missed it in all the excitement."

"Sure, that must be it," I shook my head. "Take Mr. Robertson outside. Have someone search him again and take his personal property. No rough stuff, he's cooperating."

Both officers nodded. They understood. I looked at Stan.

"Thanks for the company."

"You're welcome," he said.

"I owe you for this."

"This one's on me. You owe me for sticking around when you *interviewed* Solomon Willetts."

I laughed. "Let's get rid of this bomb."

"I was wondering when you'd get around to that."

Cops milled around the grounds near the music hall entrance like a controlled mob. Police cars were parked at various angles on the blacktop, the grass and sidewalks. Several fire trucks sat close by, their crews watching the festivities. I saw the Pigeon Forge PD sergeant standing next to his marked car and a patrolman opening the back door for Bob Robertson to get in. I walked over.

"Sarge, I've got a disarmed bomb here and nowhere to go with it. Who's the bomb disposal technician?"

"Damn," he said. "Never had ta dispose of a bomb before. When we confiscate farworks or construction explosives, either us or the county takes 'em ta the land-fill, and we git someone ta destroy 'em for us."

My eyes clicked open. Oh, beautiful, I thought. Nothing like experienced assistants.

"Has anyone called BATF yet? They can send an EOD team."

"Nobody asked for one."

Sometimes my job leaves me speechless.

"I don't want to drive around with this in my trunk all weekend," I said. "A bomb tech has to test the C-4 and provide a statement that it is in fact explosive. Can you get it to a safe place while you're waiting on him and detonate it tomorrow or whenever?"

"I suppose. Is it safe?"

"The man who made it disarmed it. He says so. I don't have the expertise to work on it or know any more."

"I guess if the prisoner disarmed it, puttin' it in the car with him's only right."

"Like a form of quality control, isn't it?" I said.

He nodded. "Man better hope he done a good job."

The sergeant turned a key into the lock of his marked unit and raised the trunk lid. I laid the case gently on the carpet.

"I hate to stick you with this, but thanks," I said.

"No problem."

"You'll find that local bomb expert for us? I'll call the Feds."

"Yessir, I'll git'er done."

I opened my cell phone and called John Gallagher, wanting to get the cops at the back door to secure it and join the party up front.

Then I called my wife, told her most of what happened before she heard it on the news—that everyone was safe and not to wait up for me. I planned on being a long time processing this arrest.

As the cop who searched Bob Robertson walked past me I asked, "Have you got a bag with the prisoner's personal property?"

"He jest had some keys, a li'l money, a wallet and a cell phone. I left it all in the side pocket of his jacket."

Immediately things began running through my mind. He had only cut one wire. At the time, I didn't like the looks of that. I remembered he had asked me three times if I'd keep my promise and take care of his daughter and he commented on how difficult it would be for him to maintain his dignity shackled and dressed in prison clothes when he appeared in a court room.

"You left him with a cell phone?" I asked, to be sure.

"Yes sir, uh-huh."

"Son of a bitch!"

I looked at Robertson in the back of the police cruiser, about fifty feet away. He looked back at me, turned a little, sitting forward in the seat. It looked like he was trying to get his hand into the jacket pocket.

"Everybody, take cover!" I screamed, expecting a very big bang.

Cops scattered to crouch and hide behind cars. I pushed Stanley next to the front wheel of his car and joined him. We waited for the big bang.

Nothing happened.

I looked up and over the hood of the cruiser. Robertson stared at me with a confused expression. I stood up slowly and walked cautiously, realizing my speed didn't matter while approaching a car with a bomb in the trunk. At the rear door of the PFPD sergeant's car, I looked at Robertson again. He shrugged his shoulders in an awkward way with his hands cuffed behind his back. He mouthed the word, "What?" I couldn't hear him with the window closed.

The Pigeon Forge PD sergeant joined me.

"Unlock the car," I said.

He gingerly approached the driver's side front door, opened it with the key and touched the command button to unlock all the doors. I snapped open the back door.

"Keep your hands away from the cell phone," I told Robertson.

Robertson smiled. "Now I understand." He nodded. "Pretty sharp. You thought I was going to detonate the bomb with my cell phone." He chuckled. "Don't worry, I've been thinking about an insanity plea, but I'm not crazy enough to blow the car with me in it. I've got no desire to end up a crispy critter."

I laughed at the old Army term for a charred body.

"What were you doing twisting around, trying to get into your pocket?"

"I didn't want anything from my pocket. That cop made me sit on a flashlight, I was moving it."

"You scared the shit out of me."

"You're getting old, my friend. You know, even in jail my pension checks keep coming. I won't be there forever. I don't want to kill myself."

"I need a drink."

"You got two?"

I looked at the Pigeon Forge cop before I spoke. He was standing near his sergeant.

"Get all the shit out of his pockets and put it in a bag for me, please."

The other cops began standing down from my recent alert. Stan walked up next to me.

"That was good thinking," he said. "I never associated a cell phone with a detonator. Not bad for an old guy."

"Are you the only one around here I can trust?"

He smiled. "I guess there's always John."

"He may not speak a recognizable language, but he knows how to search a felon."

"I hear you."

"I've got a couple of calls to make. Contact the duty agent at ATF and arrange for a bomb team to scour the building for additional devices and coordinate with Pigeon Forge PD to deal with the bomb."

"Additional bombs?

"Just a thought I had while we were crawling around under the stage."

"Now you tell me."

I left Stanley to his work and walked away from the Pigeon Forge police car to find a quiet spot where I called Bettye and let her know what we'd been doing all night. She arranged to have an officer drive C.J. back to the motel and keep an eye on her in case the Collinson gang had any ideas of causing trouble at that late hour.

Bettye had lodged Jenny in one of our cells and arranged for the on-call county matron to stand guard overnight. We spoke for a few minutes about the incident at Dollywood, and she promised to see me in the morning.

Thanks to the mayor's famous friend, the Prospect PD overtime fund would be in the red for years.

The rest of the Prospect cops and Rusty Filmore gathered near Stanley's car. The Pigeon Forge sergeant put his cruiser in gear and started Bob Robertson on the first leg of his journey into the Tennessee criminal justice system.

I snapped my cell phone shut. "Hey, guys, meet us at Pigeon Forge PD. Sergeant Rose and I will process the prisoner as quickly as possible. Lenny, take John-Boy, the little fat Irishman somewhere and get coffee, doughnuts and anything else you can think of to help us survive the rest of the night. Gallagher just started a new job. I gave him lots of overtime, free room and board. He's buying."

"You're always so good to me, boss," John said.

As they started walking to Lenny's car, I heard John say, "Hey, Lenny, you know who Rachel is?"

In his own stupid way, John reminded me of another phone call I wanted to make. It was 11:40, and Rachel would have just finished her eleven o'clock newscast. She answered on the second ring and sounded pleased to hear from me.

"You actually answered your phone," I said. "How'd you know it was me?"

"No one else ever calls me at this ungodly hour."

"Well, lucky you. You may want to get right back on the air and interrupt Jay Leno to tell your faithful viewers that *your* information figured significantly in apprehending the man who intended to detonate a bomb at the Imagination Library Benefit Show and kill C.J. Profitt. He was Michelle Robertson's father. We have him and his other daughter, Jenny Mitchell, C.J.'s personal assistant, in custody and one very nasty bomb under wraps."

"Are you okay? Did anyone get hurt?"

"Yes and no respectively. Thanks for asking."

"Did they disarm the bomb?"

"They who?"

"The bomb people, the technicians, you know who."

"We didn't have any bomb technicians."

"Did you disarm the bomb?" Her voice sounded full of apprehension.

"I don't know how to do that."

"How did you make the bomb safe?"

"The prisoner and I crawled under the stage where he planted the bomb, and he did it."

There was a moment of silence.

"You idiot!" Her voice sounded strained.

I tried to sound indignant. "I beg your pardon, madam."

"You heard me. How could you do that?"

"Stanley was there to keep me safe."

"Then the two of you are idiots!"

"Shouldn't you get back on TV? Jay's monologue must be just about finished. Cut in with breaking news."

"Aren't you just so smart?"

"I've always thought so."

"Give me the whole story," she said, "so I can get back on the air. I need more details."

I spent a few minutes relaying my saga of the night Dollywood almost went up in flames. Before hanging up, she agreed to meet me at Prospect PD the next day. I'd be processing Jenny's arrest with Bettye, and there was plenty of time to fill her in on all the small details that would allow her to create a better follow-up story.

Chapter Twenty-One

It took hours for Stan and me to write up Bob Robertson's arrest. When operating in another cop's territory, it's essential to be precise with what you write and how you say it. We crossed all the Ts and dotted all the 'I's, so no prosecutor or defense attorney could complain about our finished product. A job that complicated would have been a long haul under the best conditions, but we were constantly interrupted by high-ranking officers from both the PD and the sheriff's office who had gotten word about the big doin's in Pigeon Forge. A few Sevier County officials and even a couple of executives from Dollywood came out to gawk at us in the police squad room and ask for a quick story.

Robertson categorically denied any involvement with the Coalition for American Family Values. He sounded insulted that I'd consider the possibility he'd associate with a group of rank amateurs. He stood by his original statement that he alone was responsible for the two cases of attempted murder, and Jenny only went along with his plan. I knew some of that was a lie and wondered if I could believe any of it.

John Gallagher added to the confusion by entertaining the two Prospect cops and several local boys, still hanging out near the action, with New York war stories.

I pulled into my driveway at ten-to-five in the morning. In the pre-dawn light, birds quietly flew around the cedars and Leyland cypress trees and onto the feeders hanging around the yard. The air smelled like spring, although the ground hog reportedly saw his shadow, so the weather forecasters expected a few more weeks of winter.

At the moment, weather was immaterial. I felt tired and wanted to sleep, but knew I wouldn't until that afternoon at the earliest. Gasping for a cup of good coffee and a decent breakfast, I trudged into the dark house.

I opened the front door quietly and tiptoed upstairs. Bitsey lay on her bed sound asleep and didn't wake to sound an intruder alarm. I'd remember that the next time she asked to re-negotiate her watchdog contract. Kate heard me and turned over.

"Hey, honey," she said, catching me opening the closet.

"Don't shoot. I'm on the job." I said.

"What time is it?"

"5 o'clock."

"Oh, you poor thing. What a long day."

"But a fruitful one. Like Sergeant Preston of the Yukon, I always get my man. And a woman thrown in for good measure."

I sat on the edge of the mattress, only inches from Kate.

"Are you going to tell me what happened?" she asked.

"I'll tell you my ripping yarn if you get up and make coffee."

"Okay," she said. "Want to kiss me hello?"

"How about a quickie on the forehead? I want to brush the stale taste and lousy doughnuts out of my teeth. My breath must smell like a goat's."

"Mmm," she said, still mostly asleep.

I planted my kiss on her forehead, just below her tousled hair. "Is it too late for a whiskey before breakfast?"

"Samuel, please."

"Okay, you do coffee, and I'll tell my story. I have to go back in at 9:00 and write up the paperwork on the woman. She's in one of our cells."

"Where's John?" Kate asked.

"He went to breakfast with a bunch of cops who wanted to wind down some more. He'll probably entertain them for hours with more war stories."

"Good. We'll have a quiet breakfast."

* * * *

"You idiot!" Kate gasped and practically dropped her cup on the placemat.

Not as quiet as she promised.

"So far no one's mentioned how heroic we were."

"For God's sake, you're not a bomb technician. What happened to clear the area and let the guy with the padded suit do the work?"

"Resources are not so readily available here as they were up in the megalopolis."

"You could have been killed."

"I could have been killed any day I drove the Long Island Expressway, but I survived."

"What am I going to do with you?"

"Be nice. I have a long day ahead of me, and I'm going to take you to that hillbilly concert tonight."

"Grrrrr!"

"Easy for you to say, lady."

"I should have married a man with a normal job."

"You could never love a Casper Milquetoast. And you'd miss all the excitement."

"But I wouldn't have all this gray hair."

* * * *

It took two hours to prepare the arrest report, prosecution worksheet and court information on Jenny Mitchell. With everything finished, I gave her a business card for Joe Costello, the finest criminal attorney in Blount County. Handing her off to a competent lawyer fulfilled my obligation to Jenny and her father.

"Call him," I said. "He's not cheap, but he's the best there is around here."

"Thank you."

"My paperwork is complete on both you and your dad. We've made our deals, and as far as I'm concerned this thing can now play out as it will."

She sat very straight in an armless chair next to the desk I used in the squad room.

"But I've still got a few questions," I said. "Make the answers off the record, or just refuse to say any more—your choice. I'm just being nosey."

A quick tilt of her head and concerned look made it obvious she didn't know if she should trust me. "What do you want to know?"

"Your sister died five years ago. How long have you been planning revenge on C.J.?"

"It's more complicated than that."

"Yeah, it usually is." I must have shown a little attitude.

"It's true, really." She sounded sincere. "I'm not lying to you."

Jenny looked very young, tired, and vulnerable. Getting locked up for conspiracy to commit murder can do that to you.

"I didn't plan on working for C.J. and stalking her," she said. "It just happened."

"Explain that one."

"My father knew I was furious. Michelle was dead, and we both watched C.J. going on, being famous and making money like nothing ever happened. He told me to let it go. He even suggested I see someone—a therapist—and learn how to cope. But I was twenty-six when Michelle died. She was thirty-two. I still thought like a kid and couldn't let it go.

I shifted in my chair to get comfortable. I was tired, and my neck and shoulders were killing me.

"We were living in Fayetteville then," she continued. "I didn't like it there. Too much of an Army town. I was newly divorced, felt sorry for myself, and didn't like my job. So, I took time off, planned a trip to Nashville, determined to find C.J. and... I don't know what. I wanted at least an apology, an explanation, something to account for how she treated Michelle. I wanted C.J. to say she was sorry that Michelle killed herself."

"Doesn't sound unreasonable. Nothing would bring your sister back, but if an apology would give you a little closure, why not?"

Jenny was talking, and I wanted to hear more. A little encouragement sometimes goes a long way.

"I never thought it was too much to ask," she said. "Then things all happened by accident. I tried to see C.J. several times but couldn't. One

211

day, I was waiting in her office to speak with someone and a woman I'd not met before asked me if I was there about the job as C.J.'s personal assistant. That surprised me. So, I just said yes. Two other people interviewed me, and I got to speak with C.J. She offered me the job. I was amazed and thought at an appropriate time I could question her, hoping for a satisfactory answer. What's the worst that could happen? I'd lose a job I never wanted."

I nodded and let her talk.

"As time went on, C.J. got to like me. But I made sure she understood I was interested in men, and nothing ever went in a sexual direction."

I gave her another nod and a smile. She seemed to be at ease and willing to tell her story.

"I never asked about Michelle, but I knew she didn't care. She never spoke of her, even in vague terms. She never looked like she had lost someone important. She was C.J. Profitt, girl with an attitude."

"Michelle died long before you met C.J., and I think an affected image is important to her."

"You've got that right," she said. "Her image is all important. She's the most self-centered person I've ever met. The more time we spent together, the angrier I became. I spoke to Daddy about her. I spoke to..." Jenny took a long pause. "Never mind, he's unimportant. I just began to dislike her more and more. It was unfair that Michelle was dead and C.J. continued along, doing so well. I began to think, maybe I'd feel better if C.J. lost as much as Michelle."

I raised my eyebrows.

"So somewhere along the line you decided C.J. should die," I said. "To even the score, so to speak?"

"Yes. When those notes started arriving, I saw an opportunity where I—we could make her death look like some redneck group was responsible. My father didn't want to have anything to do with my idea at first, but when I kept badgering him, he went along with me, and... Here we are." She paused and shrugged. "I've always been his *little girl,* and he's been pretty easy to manipulate."

"He's not the first tough guy who's caved in to a woman's request."

"I feel bad for getting him into so much trouble."

I shrugged. "It was a bad idea all around, and now you've got to pay the price."

She nodded.

"The timing of those notes sounds like one hell of a coincidence. I'd never trust a jury to believe that you didn't plan the whole thing from the beginning and maybe enlist help from the Coalition. The government can't get operations to work that smoothly. Ask your father about that."

"But it's true." Her voice sounded strained.

"But in the end, you planned for C.J. to die and enlisted your dad's assistance. Was everything your idea?"

She didn't answer.

"I told you, this is off the record. I'm only curious."

"Yes, it was my idea."

"You're lucky I wanted to find your father and prevent that bomb from going off more than I wanted to charge you with the maximum. Under more severe circumstances and without a deal, your goose would have been cooked—big time."

"I know."

"You're lucky. So's your father. He was prepared to die so no one would suspect you"

"I know. He's so brave."

"Yes, he is. Perhaps not thinking as straight as he should, but courageous and loyal to you nonetheless. Who else is involved?"

"This was all my idea."

"That's not an answer. You started to say, 'I spoke to...' and then told me to never mind. Who were you talking about?"

She gave a small, dismissive wave of a hand to end her part of the conversation. "I'm tired. I feel terrible. Is there somewhere I could lie down?"

"Not going to answer?"

"I just want to rest."

"Sure, Sergeant Lambert will show you to one of our guest rooms after you call your lawyer. You can rest for an hour or so before you're taken for arraignment. The lawyer can meet you there. Talk to him about bail. I don't know what an ADA or the judge will agree to."

"Will our deal hold up in court?"

"I'll do what I agreed to. Joe Costello is very good, but the chief assistant DA will give me a hard time."

"What do you mean?"

"She won't like what I offered you. But that's my problem. A deal is a deal. Costello will stick up for you, and the judge will side with me no matter how much the ADA disagrees. The woman's a vampire. She'll cause trouble just to stick it to me, but you'll be okay."

"Are you sure?"

"I'll say preventing an explosion and the probable mass loss of life was more important than getting you a few more years in jail. Keep your fingers crossed."

"Thank you."

"Yeah. Sure you don't want to give me another name. I don't plan on closing this case yet. If I find him or her on my own, I'll never offer them the kind of deal you and your dad are getting."

It looked like she started thinking, but shook her head.

"There's no one else," she said. "No one."

"Forgive me for not believing you."

After her phone call, Bettye put Jenny into a cell. Two of the day shift cops would take her to the Justice Center for arraignment shortly. As I promised, sometime in the near future I would speak up for my defendants during one of the conferences I'd attend with the district attorney generals in two counties.

With Jenny behind bars, Bettye and I adjourned to my office. She poured two cups of the coffee. Saturday is our regular day off, and she had worn civilian clothes, a dark red sweater and a pair of snug-fitting gray slacks. She looked nice. Very sophisticated. No ponytail. Her hair hung down below her shoulders

I repeated my story in more detail than the brief summary I'd given to her over the phone and felt confident Bettye would never call me an idiot. She'd appreciate the snazzy piece of police work I pulled off.

"You are a damned fool, Sam Jenkins!" she said. "I *do not* know what I'm gonna do with you. And that Stanley Rose is no damn better! The pair o' you actin' like super-cops. Lord have mercy! I believe you are nothing but a bad influence on that man."

"I thought you'd be my ally."

"Ally? Sometimes I'd like to send you for a lobotomy, Sam."

So much for being her all-time favorite boss. And never let anyone say that women aren't the main source of inferiority complexes in most men.

Just after Jenny Mitchell left for arraignment, Bettye went home. Shortly after that, Rachel pulled in. We talked for an hour. She never takes notes when she listens to my tales of crime and corruption in the Smokies. I credit her with having a great memory.

We sat facing each other in the guest chairs in front of my desk. When she crossed her legs, three inches of thigh showed. She's got great legs.

"I'm sorry I called you an idiot," she said.

"You should be. I'm a genuine hero."

"Yes, you're very brave, just not too smart."

I smiled at the left-handed compliment. "Thanks."

"What's going to happen to them?" she asked.

"Jenny is going to use Joe Costello as her attorney. He's good, but he won't put anything over on me. Contrary to some of the opinions currently expressed, I'm pretty sharp in a courtroom myself."

"I'll bet."

"Give good odds and you'll win." I winked at her. "As I was saying, I doubt this will get to trial. Costello is great with plea bargains. Jenny Mitchell is nailed. I charged her with conspiracy to commit murder. That's a notch lower than the attempted murder charges against her old man. I let her slide with one guilty plea in satisfaction to all the complicity with the poisoned Chinese food and the bomb."

"Was that a good thing to do?"

"Good for her. Otherwise no matter what lawyer she uses, it'll be hard to make a jury believe she had no knowledge of the poison business. So that was a gift, and Costello will know that. She opened the motel door and received a bag of food from her father who, as far as she and the rest of the world knows, has never been a delivery boy for Wah Lum."

Rachel smiled.

"She knew everything," I said. "But it was more important to take the bomb out of commission. The court system is often a joke, but she'll do plenty of jail time. My deal is nothing unusual."

"She doesn't look like a killer."

"Neither did Baby Face Nelson."

She looked at me through long dark lashes and grinned like a mischievous little girl. "Were you the one who arrested him?"

I made a face. "That was before my time."

"Was it?"

"I could always talk to your competition about these cases."

She fluttered those lashes and blinked a few times. "Keep talking, and I'll be your best friend."

I snorted, but continued. "The Grand Jury could always add other charges surrounding the attempted murder—it's called de novo—and even more stemming from the purchase of stolen Army drugs and explosives, but I doubt they will, if she cops a plea. Costello knows that, too."

"Is that her best option?"

"Sure. When two people conspire to commit a crime, both participants don't necessarily have to be present during all phases of the operation to be equally guilty. Her lawyer will suggest taking the deal and running."

"This gets complicated."

I let Humphrey Bogart answer for me. "That's why I get the big bucks, doll-face."

"You're so modest, I could swoon."

I gave her my shy little boy smile and nodded. "I was generous when I wrote up her case. Without her help locating Robertson at Dollywood and excellent timing, I'd still be wondering where to find him and wouldn't have had such an easy time resolving the bomb situation."

"Easy time? That was a big bomb."

"Little ones hurt almost as much."

She gave me a look mothers reserve for bad boys. "Sure they do."

"Having her in custody gave me good leverage with Robertson when we started the negotiations."

"You actually negotiate terms with people?"

"Well, of a fashion. I have a standard procedure that's worked fine over the years."

"I watch you at news conferences. Reporters may not be a cop's best friends, but you treat us like mortal enemies. I can't imagine you being fair to felons."

"I treat you nicely."

"That's only me."

"Back to your question," I said. "Jenny Mitchell is a hardworking, clean-cut, and good-looking young woman. She felt extreme emotional distress because of her sister's suicide. Misguided in her thoughts by anyone's standard, but Costello should be able to weasel out a lighter sentence that satisfies our DA and the court."

"What do you think she'll get?"

"The amount of time is anyone's guess. But Jenny's not a criminal type. Costello will ask for some minimum security facility—a place where soccer moms go after they kill coaches."

"You're so eloquent."

"That's me, baby."

"Was she really that cooperative when you offered her leniency? I wouldn't think someone who was into a complicated plot to kill a famous person would roll over for you just like that because you told her you'd drop a couple of charges. Are you that persuasive?" She added the last sentence with a smile that could get her into trouble.

I shrugged as part of my modesty act. "She loves her father. Her mother died of cancer at fifty, and Michelle took her own life for all the wrong reasons. I said I wouldn't kill her father if she cooperated."

"You actually said that?"

"Sure."

"And if she didn't cooperate?"

I shrugged again. "It was nothing personal. I kind of liked Bob Robertson. But business is business."

"Sometimes you scare me."

I smiled. "Surely you can't mean that?" Then I fluttered my eyelashes.

"Oh, stop that."

"What?"

"Was Jenny being a pretty young woman any influence on you, Mr. Tough-guy?

"What do you think?"

"I think someone should spank you when you act like this."

"Are you volunteering?" I wiggled my eyebrows.

"Sometimes you're such a... uh..." She shook her head.

"I know. Oink, oink."

She laughed, and at that point, I felt happy.

"How about her father?" she asked.

"He's not in such good shape. There's the attempted murder with the poisoned Chinese food and the assault charge from poisoning Johnny Rutledge by accident. Bettye spoke to the delivery boy last night. He picked Robertson's picture from a group of six headshots. Bob's toast on that charge."

"Robertson must be some cold person. He knew lots of people would be killed."

"He spent a lifetime learning how to combat terrorists. You need to know their methods to fight them. And they are pretty efficient with explosives. He wanted to throw suspicion onto that group of rightwing morons. From a technical standpoint, I think it was a brilliant plan."

Her big brown eyes widened. "That's horrible."

"Of course. That's why he has to go to jail."

"I guess you've sufficiently ruined a couple of lives."

"But I only use my great powers for the universal good."

"My superhero."

Bogie spoke again. "That's me, sweetheart."

One more big smile for Sammy.

"I charged him with a lot. I was tired and cranky that night. It's all big stuff."

"I guess so."

"Joe Costello referred him to a good lawyer in Sevier County, but he's still got major time to do. But I'm sure he'll end up doing the minimum with good behavior factored in and even start off with a bit of a reduced sentence for all his cooperation."

I shifted in the chair and felt like I had jet lag from lack of sleep.

"Robertson's military record will speak loudly to the sentencing judge and the probation officer who prepares the pre-sentence investigation report for the court. There's something to be said for the old adage, punish the offense, not the offender. I won't argue. Bob was one hell of a soldier for thirty-five years."

"That makes a difference to you, doesn't it?" she asked.

"An operations sergeant from a Special Forces A detachment is probably one of the finest soldiers in the world. The country owes him something. He has a debt to pay, but no one should forget his past."

"Did you have a job like that in the Army?"

"No, I would have been his boss."

"Wow."

"Aw shucks, ma'am."

"You're so modest."

"And cute."

She stuck out her tongue. "Says you. What about C.J.? How does she feel now?"

"I think she's happy the whole thing is over. On Monday she'll be back in Nashville." I shrugged. "I didn't ask how she felt about the death of Michelle Robertson—that's none of my business. Let her take that up with her therapist...if she has one."

Rachel reached forward and slapped my knee. "Even if you weren't so brave, you'd be every girl's hero."

"I think you like me."

She wrinkled her nose. "I think you have to take me to lunch."

I suggested Mexican, but she said rice and beans were too fattening. She didn't sound enthused over my favorite Southeast Asian place either. I knew wherever we went, she'd only order a salad with grilled chicken or something equally dietetic, and so I drove to Aubrey's in Maryville. I ordered Cajun pasta with a spicy jambalaya sauce and blackened chicken and shrimp and drank a couple of draught beers. They have a large selection to choose from. Rachel ordered a Caesar salad and a glass of chardonnay.

After I got home, three Killian's Irish Red ales helped me sleep for a couple of hours before heading toward the big concert.

Chapter Twenty-Two

After the number of trips I'd recently made there, I thought I could put my car on automatic pilot and get to Dollywood while I relaxed in the back seat. But it wasn't quite that easy.

As we approached the kiosk at the entrance of the parking lot, Mack and Ma Collinson, Jeremy Goins, and several other Coalition members clogged up the approach road, carrying signs denouncing C.J. Profitt as someone as evil as Stalin and the anti-Christ rolled into one. Mack yelled and pointed at each of the passing cars. Jeremy bounced up and down, raising and lowering his sign, as if listening to an otherwise unheard Rod Stewart song. But Elnora seemed a bit subdued that night. Perhaps Junior Huskey had made an impression on her.

I told the Pigeon Forge police chief about our experiences with my adversaries from The Coalition for American Family Values. Now that the cops from 'action-packed' Pigeon Forge heralded me as the disarmer of bombs and man of the hour in the 'Forbidden City', I knew the chief would consider my enemies his enemies.

Kate wore a sexy little black dress that looked more appropriate for a Manhattan opening night than a charity event in the nation's outlet mall capitol. When we entered the music hall, she got approving stares from a few interested men in the lobby as I showed an usher our passes. He escorted us to a backstage room where we met Ronnie and LaDonna Shields, Stanley, Bettye, Harlan, Leonard, and even John Gallagher. We had all been invited to a cast party in that same big room after the show, but before anything kicked off, Bettye and the other music fans in the group wandered around getting their photos, printed at Prospect PD expense, signed by the assorted mega-stars scheduled to sing that night.

I introduced Kate to C.J. They got along famously from the start. No verbal sniping. No nasty looks. I guessed it was just me with whom C.J. had been destined to have an initial problem. *And I thought I was adorable.*

To my delight, Ms. Profitt figuratively sung my praises. She again apologized to me for our rocky start, hoped we enjoyed the show and promised to find us afterward at the party.

We watched the curtain go up from some of the best seats in the hall. Several entertainers finished their acts before C.J. came on stage. When she made her entrance, the audience went wild. She acted like the personification of a local girl who had made good.

She stood center stage with a microphone in hand, waiting for the applause and hooting to abate. When the room became relatively quiet, she addressed the crowd. Her voice sounded quite a bit more 'country' than it did when I first spoke to her in the mayor's office. C.J. knew what her fans liked to hear.

"Hey, ever'one," she yelled.

The crowd resumed clapping and screaming.

C.J. signaled for quiet and waited for the fans to bring the volume down.

"In case y'all haven't heard," she said, "we've had somethin' of a problem here over the last couple days."

A new buzz made the music hall sound like a giant swarm of honeybees.

"Actually, I was the one with a problem. I won't take up yer time with an explanation 'cause you'll read all about it b'fore too long, but I do wanna thank someone for workin' hard and keepin' me safe and makin' everythin' turn out jest fiiine."

As she stretched out her last word, everyone began clapping again. After a long moment, the applause drifted off, and she spoke again.

"I guess this guy's my favorite man rot now."

A few members of the audience chuckled.

"He's kinda old-fashioned and doesn't know much about country music...'cause he's from New York."

That caused enough laughter in the audience for me to get an elbow in the ribs from Bettye, sitting on my right.

"But I think he'll like this oldie. Sam, this one's fer yew."

She began singing George Harrison's *If Not For You.* I was impressed, and the crowd seemed to love it.

Less than a minute into the song, I noticed the exit door closest to the stage and on my right open. A second later, a stocky dark-haired man stepped into the auditorium and quickly disappeared.

"Did you see that?" I asked Bettye.

"What?"

"I'd swear that was Jeremy Goins who just popped into the room. Get the guys to look over here."

Once I had everyone's attention, I tried to convey my concerns without alerting the patrons surrounding us to a possible problem. I sent Len and Harley to the corners of the stage front to guard against an approach from the audience. They were familiar faces most of the entertainers and production crew would recognize. I wanted Stan and Bettye to handle the backstage area.

"Stan," I said, "call the uniforms outside the building. Get a few men inside to search the area, and look for me. I'm going after Goins."

Stan pulled out his cell phone as my four cops vacated their seats, making only a minor commotion.

"What's wrong?" someone in the row behind me asked of no one in particular.

A muted buzz of people whispering sounded off for a few moments and ended when the rest of the audience began applauding the end of C.J.'s first song.

"What happened?" Kate asked.

I gave her a quick story. John Gallagher, sitting on Kate's left listened in.

"What do you want me to do, boss?" he asked.

"Stay with Kate. If the shit hits the fan, there may be a panic. Make sure she's safe.

"You got it."

I stood and spoke to Kate. "Stick close to John."

She nodded, and I took off.

After stumbling over an aisle full of annoyed music fans, I needed to find the closest set of stairs and head in the direction where I last saw Jeremy Goins. As I hit the ground floor, two state troopers briskly walked toward me. I turned for them to see the badge I hung from my jacket pocket.

"We're looking for a stocky white male," I said, "about fifty, five-nine, wearing a red and black buffalo plaid jacket and dark pants."

One of the troopers, the taller and younger of the pair, spoke into the microphone attached to his left epaulette restating my description of our subject.

"How many officers were sent inside?" I asked.

"Total o' six," the older trooper said. "Two on the opposite side o' the stage, two upstairs movin' around."

"Tell everyone I've got four people in plainclothes around the stage. Look for their badges."

The young trooper made the notification, and we hustled to the back hallway where we split up and began checking every dressing room and utility closet. I ran to C.J.'s first, but found no one, and nothing looked disturbed. The troopers and I crisscrossed in the hallway checking more rooms. When we finished looking everywhere in that wing, the troopers looked to me for direction.

I shook my head, feeling the frustration. "No place else, but the public access areas. Check with the others, and see if they know anything."

The trooper's radio transmission went unanswered.

A few seconds later two deputies on the second floor called stating they had found nothing.

"First floor team one, you on?" The trooper asked.

Still no answer.

"I don't like this," he said.

"Try again," I said.

As he was about to depress the transmit button, a trooper from the other first floor team said, "Have the chief meet us in the men's room, first floor, east hallway."

I looked from one trooper to the other. "Stay here. I'll see what's up."

It took me less than two minutes to jog through the halls and find the public men's room. A trashcan propped the door open, and a uniformed trooper blocked the doorway.

"You found him?" I asked.

He smiled and pointed with his chin. "In here."

I found a Sevier County sergeant standing next to a handcuffed Jeremy Goins who had been pushed face first against the tiled wall.

"What's he got to say for himself?" I asked.

"Found him on the commode. Said he had ta go."

I let out a little air and shook my head. The sergeant took a four-inch Smith & Wesson Combat Magnum from his waist band and showed it to me.

"Had this in a shoulder holster—loaded with three-fifty-sevens."

"Turn him around," I said.

With little ceremony or delicateness, the big sergeant spun Jeremy to face me.

"Who else is with you?" I asked.

"Bunch o' people outside," Goins said.

"My first impulse is to wrap the barrel of that gun around your ears, but I'll ask again. Make it the truth this time. Who else is in the building with you?"

Goins shook his head and made a face. "Like I tol' these two officers, I had ta take me a wicked dump, an' I couldn't hold it. That's why I done snuck in. Ain't nobody with me. I know how to use the commode by myself."

"Why the gun?"

"Second Amendment says I got me the right ta keep and bear arms."

"You have a permit to carry a concealed handgun?"

"That law is unconstitutional. I ain't—"

"Shut up." I said and shifted my eyes to the sergeant. "Tell the others troops to keep looking through the building for other nitwits from the Coalition for American Family Values."

He took a small portable radio from a case on his gun belt and transmitted the message.

"I'll let my people know what's happening," I said. "It's your turf, mind writing up his arrest for trespassing and the unlicensed handgun?"

"Be my pleasure."

We found no one else from the Coalition within the building. When nothing sinister happened and the concert ended, I assumed Jeremy's story of an urgent call of nature had been true.

Goins was written up and taken before an on-call judge for arraignment. He was unable to make bail and spent the night at the PFPD lockup.

Before the night was over, the Pigeon Forge police officers had issued summonses to Mack, Ma, and six other protesters for demonstrating without a license. It didn't surprise me to learn that Hub Welchance and several associates represented the Coalition members when they showed up in court.

Few people, other than the cops on the security detail, knew anything questionable happened during the concert.

Later, at the cast party, C.J. was true to her word and introduced Kate to all the celebrities. I tagged along and renewed our relationships.

The kid with the big black hat told me he was kind of attached to his oversized lid and would keep it a while longer.

Big Toby said he didn't plan on shaving any time soon, and the ratty straw hat was his trade mark and just couldn't part with it. I wrote all this off to not arguing with success.

A couple of the girls giggled when I made a charming fool of myself, and I met a stunning creature named Martina who I thought was one of the prettiest women I've ever seen. She swore she wasn't Russian in spite of her name.

Finally, C.J. introduced us to Dolly herself. Probably happy to meet a couple of people her own age, Dolly and Kate spent a long time talking library issues. I faded into the crowd and sampled more of the champagne that flowed like sweet tea at a Memorial Day picnic.

* * * *

On Monday morning, I called Ralph Oliveri. We made plans to sit down and formulate a strategy to put the arm on Sergeants Solomon Willetts and Wilson Dees. We also admitted that further infiltration of the Coalition for American Family Values by John Gallagher would be a waste of time.

At 10:30, Ronnie Shields brought C.J. Profitt down to the PD before he drove her to the airport for a noon flight to Nashville behind a Prospect PD escort.

Bettye looked pleased. She and C.J. spoke for a few minutes, then Ronnie picked up the conversation with Bettye and C.J., and I wandered into my office.

"I want to thank you for everything," C.J. said.

"It's what I get paid for. You're welcome." I added a self-deprecating smile to top things off.

Sometimes I'm so humble I could faint.

"Your modesty is disgustin'," she said. "And don't think that smile will work on me, mister. Remember who I am."

"Because of this affair, I've been called an idiot and a damn fool by the women in my life. Disgusting doesn't sound all that bad."

She smiled and shook her head.

"But tell me," I said, "what am I going to do if my smile ever fails?"

Her grin turned into a laugh, and she looked very pretty.

"Seriously, Sam, thank you. I don't know what else to say."

"That's enough, but if you could manage a hug, I'll never wash again."

She put her arms around me and squeezed. "Please wash. I can always renew the hug."

It was my turn to laugh.

"That wasn't all that bad," she said. "If another guy saves my life, I might hug him, too."

"He should be as good-looking as me."

"At least."

We looked at each other for a long moment.

"A pleasure to meet you, C.J."

"You, too, Sam. If you ever come to Nashville, just call. I'll have show passes for you and Kate. And, big feller, I'll let you take me to dinner."

"Thanks. That would be nice. But before you go, I have one thing to ask—suggest really."

"What's that?"

"Ronnie showed me your high school yearbook picture. You were a knockout. Let your hair get long. I don't like the spiky thing."

She laughed again.

"Don't push your luck, lawman. I've got an image to uphold."

"You're too pretty to worry about an image," I said.

C.J. actually blushed.

"Well, thank you, sir. You know something? I believe you're the only guy I'd consider fooling around with."

"I think you've made a good choice."

She gave me a not so gentle punch on the arm.

Chapter Twenty-Three

Ten days later, Kate and I sat in the Cherokee Country Club eating lunch with Al and Ruth Steinmetz. The grilled mahi mahi I ordered tasted excellent. What everyone else chose looked equally as good.

At 2 p.m., we put the finishing touches on the second of two horrendously expensive bottles of Colombia River Valley Pinot Gris. Steinmetz certainly didn't care. Like the idiot Kate and Rachel claimed me to be, I offered to pay.

I've never been a fan of socializing with or toadying up to general officers and their wives, but I have to admit these two made good company. Steinmetz acted charming, spoke of interesting things and behaved anything but military during our time together. Ruth was easy to talk with and more than personable. She and Kate seemed to get along quite well. Kate even got her to volunteer some time to entertain the old folks at one of the assisted living facilities where Kate and her helpers provide hours of reading, jokes, poetry, current events, nostalgia and other schtick just short of a Catskill resort comedy routine.

Shortly before leaving, the ladies adjourned to the powder room.

When the girls were out of earshot, the general said, "I understand you went out of your way for Sergeant Robertson and his daughter."

If a woman said that to me, I would have tried to look shy and told her what an old softie I could be. But Steinmetz was a different audience.

"Just business, General. She gave me enough information to find and apprehend her father and prevent any future injury or problems. Robertson rolled over when he saw he was outnumbered. They made life easy for me."

"So you repaid them in kind?"

"I liked both of them. We made two deals in their best interest. I keep my promises as much as circumstances allow. And they were wise to make those choices. They'll have to pay a debt, but not the maximum."

Servers and busboys scurried around throughout the dining room preparing for the start of dinner at 4:30. Only one other table of four guests remained in the room.

"Is that modesty act something you use often?"

"Yeah, but I'm really not that modest."

"I didn't think so."

I offered a gallant shrug and looked out the window. A pair of fishermen in a red and black bass boat overtook and passed a small, tug-like workboat heading south on the river.

"I'm glad I could offer some help in resolving this," he said.

I felt obligated to say, "It was considerable."

"Yes, it was."

"Now who's being modest...sir?"

He laughed. "Not long ago we spoke of debts."

"Are you ready to collect?"

"Not just yet."

"Uh-oh."

"You've been in this position before. We all have."

"Yeah, but I'm getting too old for this shit."

"You're in good shape for an old man."

A busboy removed the ice bucket and empty wine bottle. Our waiter walked over and asked, "Is there anything else I can get you folks?"

I shook my head, fearing the bottom line of the check.

"No, thanks, Jake," Steinmetz said.

The waiter left, and the general looked back at me. "Where were we?"

"Your last comment sounded like encouragement, not a compliment."

"Right. Perhaps both. I may be calling you for a little help some day. Mind if I leave our pending business on account?"

"I'll wait with bated breath."

229

He laughed again and drank the remainder of his wine.

The waiter returned and placed an embossed leather folder on the table between us. Steinmetz didn't make a move. I picked it up and looked. The check was astronomical. The tip I calculated looked like the national debt of a small banana republic. I stuck a credit card in between the two halves of the folder and sighed inwardly.

When Kate returned from the ladies room, I wanted to leave and do something to sooth my aching checkbook.

Part one of the C.J. Profitt saga had been a true pain in the ass. Part two would begin shortly.

* * * *

Ralph Oliveri and I sat in my Ford F-150 in the parking lot of the Sears' parts and repair shop just a few hundred yards down the road from the 844th Engineer Battalion compound. No one would have made us as two cops on surveillance.

"Why in hell do you need a pick-up truck anyway?" Ralph asked.

"Anyone with a big piece of property in the woods can always use a truck," I said.

"How many times a year do you use it?"

"You mean use it as a truck and not take it to the store or to pick up the mail?"

"Yeah, how often does it have truck value?"

"I don't know, eight, ten times a year."

Cars and pickups began trickling out from the soldier's parking area. I assumed the weekend drill had officially ended.

"With the car the city gives you to use, you have four vehicles." Ralph was acting parental. He shook his head. "Two people, four vehicles. That's stupid. I'm not your accountant, but you could save a lot on car insurance if you got rid of two vehicles."

"I need the truck—sometimes—as a truck. And I sure as hell won't sell my Healey to save a couple of hundred bucks a year. Do you have any idea how many '67 BJ-8s are left in this country? Especially one in like-new condition?"

"Not a clue."

"Very few. That car is better than an investment in the market."

Our debate ended when a dark blue Chrysler 300 with flashy twenty-inch chrome wheels left the compound and drove past going south on Weisgarber Road.

At 5:15 on a Sunday night, Sergeant First Class Wilson Dees had just finished his weekend obligation with the 844th Engineers and started heading home. I spoke into one of the small radio transmitters Ralph issued to the four of us. John Gallagher and Ralph's partner, Special Agent Bonnie Rowatt, sat in John's electric blue Saturn a half mile south of us off Weisgarber at the corner of Lonas Drive.

"John, the subject is southbound, coming at you," I said. "You can't miss the car, a navy blue Chrysler 300 with a set of big hip-hop wheels."

"10-4, boss."

John acknowledged my transmission, and I pulled my truck out of the parking lot, rolled down the hill and waited for the stop light at Middlebrook Pike. Two cars separated us from Dees. Less than a half mile down the road, our subject stopped for a second traffic light and then signaled a left turn onto Lonas. The light changed, and he accelerated.

"Pull out now, John. He's making the turn," I said.

Gallagher moved his car into the traffic lane and drove slowly. As Dees came close to the Saturn's rear bumper, John switched off the ignition, slowed to a stop and turned on the four way flashers. Dees sat less than half a car length behind the Saturn when I pulled my truck to within two feet of the rear of the Chrysler and boxed him in.

Four of us left our two vehicles. I walked to the driver's door of the Chrysler to confront Wilson Dees. Ralph and Bonnie stood on the passenger's side with their guns pointed at Dees. I held my gun next to my right leg and my badge in my left hand. John approached the driver's door and stood to my left looking straight at the subject. Dees' head swiveled back and forth looking at us and the handguns pointed at him.

I tapped the muzzle of my Glock on the car window. He rolled it down and strained to turn and look behind his left shoulder and focus on me.

"Sergeant Dees," I said, "we're with the police and the FBI."

"What?" He sounded like I said we planned on abducting him to an alien planet.

231

"I'm a police officer. Switch off the ignition, and put your hands on the wheel."

He hesitated, still looking up at me.

"Do it!" I spoke much louder for emphasis.

He complied.

"Listen to me carefully," I said.

He nodded.

"Do you have a weapon with you?"

"A folding knife on my belt."

"A gun? Either on your person or in the car?"

"Negative."

"Step out of the car, turn and put both hands on the roof. Do it slowly."

He did.

"Lean on your palms and walk away from the car."

He did, and I kicked his feet further apart

"What's this about?" he asked, still acting cool.

"You'll know in a minute. Don't move while I search you. Is there anything sharp on your person I need to know about?"

"The knife's in a case on my right side."

"Nothing else to get me pissed off?"

"No."

I removed a sturdy and expensive-looking switchblade from a black nylon pouch, but found no other weapons.

"I'm arresting you for criminal facilitation of an attempted murder. You know what that means?"

Dees added a touch of cool to his voice. "Why don't you tell me?"

"Why don't you lose the attitude, Sarge, or I'll leave your snazzy wheels sitting on this dark street for a few hours while we go somewhere to chat."

"Aw right, what do you want?"

"You up for a discussion about Bob Robertson and Solomon Willetts?"

He swiveled his head ninety degrees to the right to catch a look at me in his peripheral vision. "I got a choice?"

Dees was a light-skinned black man a couple inches shy of six-foot-tall. He had large and intelligent eyes and a look of annoyance on his face.

"Doesn't look like it."

He shrugged the best he could while leaning against the car.

I cuffed Dees and took him to the back seat of John's sedan. Ralph slid into the rear next to the prisoner. John drove, and Bonnie followed in Dees' Chrysler, while I picked up the tail end in my truck. Fifteen minutes later, we all parked at the Federal building and took Wilson Dees up to the FBI offices.

By any cop's standards, the Knoxville FBI field office is posh—a snazzy reception area, quality carpet, nice furniture—real comfort for our G-men...and women.

Ralph guided us into an immaculate interview room down the hall from the resort they call the agent's squad room.

He pointed to a padded office chair behind a three-by-five utility table. Wilson Dees sat. I picked up the conversation.

"You're here because I can do my arrest paperwork in an hour and then hand you off to these agents if that becomes necessary."

Dees wrinkled his forehead and looked confused and concerned.

"No one is going to ask you any incriminating questions," I said. "We don't have to. And I won't insult you with lame threats or silly scams. If you want a lawyer, call one."

I picked up a Knoxville Yellow Pages from a shelf behind me and tossed it on the table next to a phone.

"If you decide to retain counsel, you and he can speak before I complete your arrest package. Then I'll turn you over to someone from the FBI, and you won't be afforded an opportunity for a deal from my agency or theirs."

Dees was a good-looking man in his mid-to-late-thirties and well-built as you'd expect a former Special Forces soldier would be. He shot quick glances from me to Ralph and ended up back with me.

"Now, listen closely," I said. "If you're willing to hear what we have to say and engage in a short conversation, these agents may ignore the pending Federal offenses and concentrate on someone they're more

233

interested in—someone you have information about. What's your pleasure…phone a lawyer or have a talk?"

He looked at me for a long moment and turned his eyes back to Ralph who leaned against the doorjamb with both hands pushed down into his jeans pockets. Then, for a brief moment, he stared at Bonnie, a pretty redhead who scowled at Dees like she would like to cut him up and feed the pieces to her pet alligator. She stood against a wall in the interrogation room with her arms folded over her breasts. He moved on to John who sat impassively across the table from him and finally back to where I stood.

He nodded. "I'll listen to what you have to say."

"Remember what I told you. I'll do the talking. Speak only if you want to."

He nodded, sat back in his chair, and folded his arms across his chest. His sage green and tan camouflage fatigues were a little wrinkled after the weekend drill. His eyes looked tired.

"Number one, my intention is to charge you for assisting Bob Robertson in obtaining lethal drugs and explosives with the intent to kill C.J. Profitt. You know all about that."

Our subject did well at displaying a poker face. He said and did nothing and remained expressionless.

I stuck my hands in my pockets, took a couple of steps to his left and continued. "Robertson is in custody in Sevier County. His daughter is locked up in Blount County. Neither one has named you as an accomplice. Guess who that leaves as my informant?"

Still no reaction.

"Okay, I'll try to impress you a little more. Number two, the FBI is interested in charging you with complicity for misappropriating government property and violations of various laws governing drugs and explosives. Based on the quantity of atropine and amount of C-4, you're talking major time—if they get involved."

His eyes widened, and he shifted in the chair.

I wanted to show him there might be some light at the end of his tunnel, if he cooperated. "However, perhaps your part in those crimes was one of accessorial conduct, not as the actual individual with the intent to buy and use the drugs or explosives as a means of premeditated murder."

After I said *murder*, he squinted and dropped his arms to his sides.

"Bob Robertson and Jennifer Mitchell are already in custody—dead meat, so to speak. Solomon Willetts is another story. For all we know, the assistance you offered your old friend, Robertson, was your first indiscretion in the legal system."

His face softened with a little hope.

"You were on active duty in the Army for nine years and in the reserves now for almost four. Your record is better than clean...it's impressive. Willetts, on the other hand, is a sleaze bag. See where I'm going with this?"

He nodded.

"You give these agents a statement upon which they can base an application for a search warrant for Willetts' home, and they may be inclined to overlook the Federal charges against you stemming from Robertson's crimes."

"What happens to me in state court?"

"You're going to be charged, but I can bring up your military record, document the cooperation you've given me and the Feds, and request that the district attorney agree to a favorable sentence recommendation... if you plead guilty and let your lawyer arrange a good deal. If you opt for going to trial, you take your chances with me and then later with the FBI."

"I have to rat out Willetts?"

"Put rather crudely, but yes."

"I still have to do jail time?"

"You'll be charged with a felony criminal facilitation of an attempted murder and a couple of additional charges. I don't know what the sentence will be. It depends on how motivated I am to work my magic with the DA and how cool your lawyer can be at the same time."

"I've got thirteen years into the system...what happens to my Army time?"

"It's just my opinion from being in the same system for twenty-one years, but I'd say your days of playing soldier are over. The best you can do now is look for some favors to keep you from getting a dishonorable."

"A dishonorable discharge for taking a friend to meet Willetts?"

The strain in his voice betrayed the look of bravado he tried to affect. "All I did was introduce Robertson to that wheeler-dealer."

"Oh, really? Want to explain how you knew Robertson?"

"We were stationed at Fort Devens, Massachusetts together, 2nd Battalion, 10th Special Forces."

"I know that much."

"When I met him, he was my team's senior engineer NCO. I was the junior sergeant. Later on, he got promoted to E-8, and I got his spot in the detachment. That meant a promotion for me. He pushed for me, too. I owe him for that. When the battalion moved to Colorado, I moved with it. Robertson was reassigned to the Special Warfare Center at Fort Bragg. That's all."

"I knew that, too. Now, let's mention how you accompanied a retired master sergeant, wearing a uniform and claiming to be from a reserve unit in Chattanooga to meet Willets. You knew that to be a lie."

Dees dropped his eyes and started picking at a cuticle.

"You thought Robertson's need for a massive amount of atropine and two bricks of C-4 was a legitimate one?"

Dees looked into my eyes, but said and did nothing.

"Let's treat each other with a proper amount of respect, shall we? I've been straight up with you so far. And I won't tolerate any bullshit in return. Understand?"

"I hear you."

"I hear you, what?" I snapped.

He hesitated, but only for a moment. "I hear you, sir."

"Are you forgetting anything else that tied you and Robertson together?"

"Like what?"

"Wilson, let's stop sparring here. I'd love to get you to cooperate with my two friends from the FBI, but I don't need you to say another word, and I'll still look like a hero to my bosses. Let's talk about your involvement with Robertson's daughter, Michelle."

His poker face turned into a tragedy mask.

"After I arrested Robertson, I didn't sit back in Prospect twiddling my thumbs. I made a phone call and learned about you, because a sharp young lady who works for me expended a lot of effort tracking your telephone activity for a very long time. For instance, you weren't just innocently living in Knoxville working at your civilian construction job and attending reserve drills when Bob Robertson looked you up. You made the first in a series of phone calls timed around C.J. Profitt's publicized trip to East Tennessee. My sergeant tracked your calls to and from Bob Robertson in Virginia and Jenny Mitchell in Nashville."

"You did all that?"

"Ain't technology grand?"

Dees closed his eyes and shook his head. I felt like I just jumped a fence with a foot to spare.

"I wouldn't have to stretch a hungry District Attorney's imagination much to get you charged with at least conspiracy and most likely as an active accomplice to two attempted murders and poisoning a cop who should have known better than to taste some tainted Chinese food."

"I didn't know a cop would get poisoned."

"Who cares? Your problem, Sarge. Not mine. If the cop had died, you'd be charged with felony murder. Your intent doesn't mean diddly."

"What happened to the cop was a mistake."

"Yeah, tell that to him. For all I know, you three planned this murder for five years. Circumstantial evidence sends guys like you to the slammer all the time."

Dees rubbed his right hand over his face, and his eyes blinked like a camera on motor drive. Good signs for the astute interrogator.

"Remember the intended victim is a famous singer whom almost all Tennessee loves—judges and juries, too."

Dees decided to stop looking me in the eye and spend more time checking the condition of his fingernails.

"I had a long conversation with a Command Sergeant Major who's got almost forty years of service." I bent over slightly and got close to Dees' face. "Sure, he wanted to protect one of his former boys, but when I started talking about being an accomplice to attempted murder, he began thinking about the pension he could lose if he perpetuated a cover-up. He got the idea that I'd love to collaborate with Army CID and drag more people into your mess."

Dees looked up again and sighed. He was definitely wearing down.

"Tibor Szabo cares more about his future than your well-being." I moved again and put my nose six inches from Dees' face. "With all those unpleasant issues aside, the Sergeant Major and I spoke of our very high ranking mutual acquaintances in the Army, and then we got to the details about your personal life. He remembered a good-looking, young black sergeant with a very pretty white girlfriend—the daughter of this young sergeant's mentor and supervisor."

Dees closed his eyes and shook his head. I stood up to give him a little breathing room.

"Bob Robertson looked at you almost like a son. And as I mentioned before, he never gave you up. He cooperated with me to get his daughter a sweetheart deal."

Dees sniffed loudly and refolded his arms protectively across his chest. His body language told me we didn't have far to go.

"Hey, look, Wilson, we're not asking for you to turn on Bob. Bob's one of the boys. Like you and me, he's been in the racket. But Willetts—now he's just a dishonest, straight-leg supply sergeant who didn't mind dropping a dime to jam you up. Hell, it didn't take Willetts five minutes under pressure to name you and ID Robertson, just to save his ass."

"Is Willetts all you want?"

"Willetts, yes, and I want you to sign a confession. I owe these agents for something totally unrelated. I'll let you slide on the greater charge if you give them a case against Willetts. Have your lawyer look for a deal with a plea. You do that for me and I'll forget about my conversation with Sergeant Major Szabo."

He began shaking his head. I wasn't sure what he meant or what he was about to say. I soon found out.

"You know how lucky I felt when Michelle said she'd go out with me?"

I shrugged and let him continue.

"Then imagine what I felt when she sat next to me in my car and told me how she liked women more than men?"

A single tear rolled down his right cheek. He pushed it away with the back of his hand. I shot a glance at my two Federal colleagues. Ralph looked empathetic, and even Bonnie had softened up.

"I'm sorry," I sat on the edge of the table and leaned forward.

Dees sniffed and continued. "At first, I thought she was lying. I thought it was just me. Either me being black or me not being good enough for her, or I didn't know what."

A couple more tears followed the first one. He ignored them. I had no doubt Wilson Dees could have taken a beating easier than explaining his past.

"I owe Bob Robertson for sticking with me in those days, too. He convinced me it wasn't about me. He was okay with her decision—about her lifestyle. He didn't hate her for being what she was, like some fathers would have done."

It was difficult for me not to feel sorry for all the players in this affair—all but the Collinsons and Jeremy Goins.

"Bob knew I still loved Michelle just like he did. We talked after Michelle started working in Nashville and tied up with the big time entertainer Miss C.J. Profitt." He almost spat out the last half-dozen words. "I tried to joke about it, but then C.J. dumped her, and Michelle got depressed. Michelle always talked to Jenny. And Jenny told Bob and me."

I began my Dutch uncle act. "I can't imagine how difficult it was for you."

He nodded and fought back the tears. "Bob covered for me at the unit when I went to Nashville to see Michelle. I guess I had some stupid idea she'd come back to me. But after we spoke, I knew that wouldn't happen. I left her less than a week before she killed herself. Jenny called me when she heard—after she got the suicide note in the mail." He almost choked on the word *suicide* and took a long moment to compose himself before saying, "I've stayed in touch with Bob."

"I'm sorry for your loss—I truly am. And I think by cooperating you'll end up with the best deal you can hope for. What do you say? I won't leave you hanging out to dry."

Dees shrugged and let his shoulders drop a couple inches. I'm not sure he cared what happened at that point.

"I'll do what you ask. Just give me your word you'll hold up your end of the deal?"

"You've got it."

We all spent a couple of hours completing our relative paperwork. Wilson Dees picked an attorney from the Yellow Pages after he signed a confession for me and a statement for Ralph. The lawyer showed up quickly and wasn't happy that his client made an important decision prior to consulting with him. However, after a long talk with me, he seemed to think that Wilson hadn't fared too badly. I filed my paperwork with the Knox County DA, and John and I took Dees to the sheriff's detention facility at the City-County Building to be held for arraignment the next morning.

At 6 a.m. on Monday, Ralph, Bonnie and six other agents executed a search warrant at Solomon Willetts' home on Texas Avenue. Two agents from Army CID were on hand to record the details and bring the bad news to Willetts' reserve commander.

Ralph's team filled a stretch van with enough stolen government property to put Solomon away for a long time. Bonnie told me that Willetts kept telling them he had been given immunity for helping three local cops. Unfortunately, Solomon didn't know who they were or from where they came.

Epilogue

John Gallagher finally closed on his new home. He borrowed our Aero-Bed and a few other necessities and moved in while he waited for his wife and a Mayflower moving van to arrive from Florida.

John loved his new house and East Tennessee in general and spent his off-duty hours wandering around the area, learning the roads, and seeing the sights. And he seemed happy to be working at Prospect PD.

I found a gun dealer who gave the classes required to obtain a concealed-carry handgun permit to expedite John's application. And Ronnie Shields promised to call in a political favor and have someone at the Tennessee Bureau of Investigation rubber stamp their approval on the final phase of the permit's journey. In no time 'Detective' John Gallagher would again be armed and dangerous, this time serving the city of Prospect.

I went to Old Town Police Supply in Knoxville and ordered a Prospect PD badge for him, the only one with detective engraved on it.

Dallas Finchum passed his medical and psychological exams, as I expected he would. One afternoon Stan Rose and I took him to the high school athletic field, watched him run a timed quarter mile, do a few simple job-related exercises, and put the physical agility phase of his testing out of the way.

John Gallagher interviewed Dallas twice. The kid wrote notarized statements about every time he stepped out of line during his life, about a couple of traffic tickets, a parking summons, a suspension from high school for having a fist fight, and the date rape charge at UT Chattanooga.

John found very little of interest except the date-rape incident that Dallas claimed to be unfounded. We waited for the polygraph examiner's report to see if the *box* detected any inconsistencies in young Finchum's story.

At one o'clock on a Wednesday afternoon, Bettye went to lunch, and John sat at her desk answering the phone and dispatching our cars. In time, I suppose, the entire department might get to understand Gallaghese.

My intercom buzzed.

"Hey, boss, the mail just came in. Dallas Finchum's poly report's here.

"How does it look?" I asked.

"The report says no problems, but beyond that, it doesn't say much at all."

"Wait a minute, John. I'll come out."

I walked to the desk and took the report John handed me. It consisted of three quarters of a typewritten page. The letterhead and subject information took up one third of the text. To say the report was brief would have been an understatement.

"He never mentioned the rape charge, boss."

"I see that." I shook my head. "I wish he did, so we had something in writing telling us he covered it in detail."

"Hard to do the follow-up interview with no confirmed details, huh, boss?"

"Could be this guy's not much of a writer. Give him a call. See what he tells you."

An hour later John walked into my office.

"I used to complain about a couple of the polygraph examiners back on the job, but this sheriff's guy sounded like an *imburamous*."

"Is that a cross between an imbecile and an ignoramus?"

John shrugged. "Yeah, boss. Anyways, he sounded like he's annoyed 'cause I called. Like I questioned his ability and the test. He got all defensive, said the charge against the kid was bullshit. Says the girl lied and faded away 'cause the cops in Chattanooga caught her in the lie. Said he didn't want to be the one to drag up dirt the kid wasn't responsible for."

"Not his call."

"It's a cop thing. He figures Dallas will be on the job soon."

"You buy the kid's story?"

"I listened to him and believed what he said was *possible*. Dallas didn't know what happened between the cops and the complainant. I read this report and think the examiner should have mentioned the rape. I asked him specifically to cover the incident in detail. He could have cleared the kid." John shrugged. "Ah, who knows? I guess it's true."

"Did you get anything back from the university police or the county dicks that caught the case?"

"Yeah, the college cops only documented the complaint and, 'cause it was a felony, kicked it to the sheriff's guys. The county says the charge got dropped. The complainant decided not to prosecute."

"Any mention of a hospital, a doctor, or a rape kit?

"Nope."

"That's strange."

"You bet."

"Did she refuse treatment?"

"No mention."

"Get in touch with the girl?"

"Called her home number twice. She didn't return my calls. Caught up with her at work, and she didn't want to talk about it."

"Life would be easier if this never happened and the kid was squeaky clean."

"Not this time," John said.

"I wish the polygraph examiner could double for Hemingway with his reports, but if we have nothing more... Sometimes a cigar is just a cigar."

"Cigar?" John looked confused.

"If there's no other derogatory information, I guess we can hire the guy."

"I guess, boss. Hey, you haven't started to smoke cigars, have you?"

"No, John, never."

* * * *

243

We hired Dallas Finchum. He attended an associated agencies' class at the state-run police academy in Nashville and passed with flying colors

Getting a political hack's relative pushed upon me didn't please me, but it also didn't do much to drain my stress battery. I'd spent years living with politically motivated things dropped in my lap and usually did my best to set aside my ego and move forward.

Actually, I liked the kid, and I knew Bettye did, too.

But I didn't like the dangling polygraph report. Only time would tell if choosing Dallas Finchum as our new police officer was a good or bad thing.

THE END

Author's Disclaimer

You've read and heard the disclaimers people make when they pull off a dangerous stunt. "Don't try this at home."

I draw your attention to the method of handling an explosive device utilized by Chief Jenkins and supported by Stanley Rose and the Pigeon Forge police sergeant.

No competent police officer would ever attempt to disarm a bomb, or if one were found in supposedly safe condition, to transport the device somewhere for destruction unless they were thoroughly trained to do so and drove a vehicle designed for such a task.

Kate, Bettye and Rachel were all correct in their assessments of Sam's actions; he behaved like an idiot.

Sam did, in opposition to my objections, violate a few more basic principles of good police work and dragged his faithful companion, Stan Rose, into the scene with him so he could weave his story and show you a suspenseful episode at the Dollywood music hall.

For years, the rule of thumb when encountering a suspected explosive device has been to evacuate an area around the device at least three hundred feet and contact an explosive ordnance expert.

Those untrained persons who take it upon themselves to deal with bombs should be left in books or films—works of fiction.

WZ

About the Author

Wayne Zurl grew up on Long Island and retired after twenty years with the Suffolk County Police Department, one of the largest municipal law enforcement agencies in New York and the nation. For thirteen of those years he served as a section commander supervising investigators. He is a graduate of SUNY, Empire State College and served on active duty in the US Army during the Vietnam War and later in the reserves. Zurl left New York to live in the foothills of the Great Smoky Mountains of Tennessee with his wife, Barbara.

Zurl has won Eric Hoffer and Indie Book Awards, and was named a finalist for a Montaigne Medal and First Horizon Book Award. He has written four novels and more than twenty novelettes in the Sam Jenkins mystery series.

Author Links:

Author website: http://www.waynezurlbooks.net
Twitter: http://www.twitter.com/#!/waynezurl
Facebook: http://www.facebook.com/waynezurl

Other books by the author at Melange
From New York to the Smokies
A Leprechaun's Lament
Heroes and Lovers